Outlaw!

Continuing the saga of 'HUSCARL'
Olaf Slagbjørn - now the most wanted man in England
by Norman Kings obsessed with vengeance.

GRAHAM DALBY

Contents

Chapter One
Caldbec Hill – Aftermath

Duke William awoke around half past five, an hour before the dawn. A cold sea mist had surrounded the lower ground of the battlefield which was now illumined from the steep apex of Caldbec Hill by a beacon, created and lit by the Norman knights, partly for the safety of their horses picking their way through the corpses, and partly to deter any further resistance from Anglo-Saxon reinforcements. Many units had arrived but, seeing that the Normans had taken the summit, assumed rightly, that the battle was lost and so slipped away into the night. William was in a foul mood as his throat was parched from breathing through his mouth whilst asleep, his nose being blocked with dry blood. It pained him greatly too when his valet attempted to set the broken bridge of his nose and only caused it to bleed once more. Outside, some of his surviving knights huddled around a fire waiting for William to appear. These included the young Hugh d'Avranche, Guillaume de Malet, Hubert du Mont-Cannisy, William fitz Osbern and Bishop Odo of Bayeux. As the sunrise gradually began to break, the full extent of the horror on that hill began to unfurl.

William stumbled out of his tent nearly tripping over several bodies. "Who are these people," he roared "and why are they here?"

"They are the last of the sons of Godwin: Gyrth, who you yourself killed, Leofwine and what is left of King Harold," explained Guillaume.

"Mon Dieu! Such carnage like I have never seen before," said William, squinting up the steep slope into the sunrise.

"'Ow many did we lose?"

Odo proffered a rough estimate: "I have done an approximate count but it's hard to see which are ours and which are theirs in this light. It looks as though we have lost about 2,500 dead, severely wounded or maimed. One third of our entire army. Their losses I would put at about 4,000 but it includes the flower of their nobility and now England has no king but you, my brother."

At this, William almost managed to smile.

William fitz-Osbern coughed: "We would have around two hundred more knights alive this morning if we hadn't charged into the woods and hit that disastrous ancient rampart concealed by long grass. The great ditch is impossible to see in the gloom and what's more they had very good archers who accounted for the deaths of so many knights and caused the others to try to charge them down. They rode straight into the trap. It was terrible to hear the screaming of the men and horses."

Duke William's face turned dark with rage: "Archers? Harold had no archers to talk about, just a handful."

"A handful that never missed," added fitz-Osbern.

"That cursed Norwegian, Olaf! Guillaume, tell me you got him. Tell me he is dead!"

Guillaume replied: "I will look around the pit of death which our people have named *Malfosse* and see if his body is there, but I suspect he must have slipped away under cover of night."

"As I told you last night, I want him caught. Take twenty knights and follow the London Road out of Hastings. He is bound to be heading back to the safety of the capital. I will take half the army to reconnoiter the route from here to Dover. I shall meet you back here on the16th by when I want all Norman bodies buried in that great ditch. Make camp at Senlac Hill just out of range of the stench of the Anglo-Saxon bodies who will lie out here to be pecked at by crows and dogs. Bury the Godwins at the top of Caldbec Hill, the site of their destruction. Guillaume, bring me the head of this Olaf."

"Yes sire."

As Guillaume strode off to pick twenty utterly exhausted knights, Bishop Odo wondered at the mental state of his stepbrother who could, on the field of some six and a half thousand warriors slain, still have time to concentrate his mind on a solitary archer.

Chapter Two
The Flight of Olaf and Rhys

Olaf felt the powerful grip of Rhys' hand on his arm.

"Come on boyo it's really time to be somewhere else."

Olaf looked back to see Hugh of Ponthieu hacking away maniacally at Harold's mortally wounded body and aided by Eustace of Boulogne, both of whom Olaf knew from their Normandy excursion. Reaching Oakwood, they realised that a total flight was taking place as the shield wall had come apart and warriors were desperately scrambling through the undergrowth. Olaf was surprised to feel some sort of brickwork under his feet and stopped short, grabbing at Rhys to stop also. This ancient parapet was some sort of fortification heavily overgrown and concealing a twenty-foot drop. Circumnavigating this lethal trap, Rhys called out to the handful of Welsh archers who were following them.

"Mind that drop!" he shouted in English. They veered round the hazard and found themselves staring straight at a line of English soldiers who were clearly set to do battle rather than flee. Their captain called out to them:

"We've just arrived from Gloucestershire to re-enforce King Harold. Why are you running?"

"The King is dead, and the line is broken," gasped a breathless Olaf. "But if we form up here and they follow us on horseback we can wreak havoc using that lethal ditch that we nearly fell into."

The men of Gloucestershire, though thoroughly shocked by the news, were well up for some revenge.

Sure enough, the screams of fleeing stragglers being cut down by cavalry were soon audible and the seven archers all with full quivers retrieved from the Norman volleys, stood ready by the ancient rampart with a shield wall of West Country farmers behind them. In the gloom, the knights slowed as they looked for new victims to ride down. This would only work if the horses were moving at the gallop. Olaf suggested to the captain that they attract the Normans by beating their shields. This indeed attracted great shouts from the Norman cavalry who rushed forward on their exhausted mounts. Five riders immediately fell from their saddles as only two of the archers missed their targets. It had the desired effect, and a host of cavalry charged the infantry line straight across the parapet and down to their deaths some twenty feet below. Some survived the initial fall by falling on a horse, only to be crushed to death by another horse from above. And still they came charging and crashing until the ditch was a terrible mêlée of thrashing horses and screaming men. As darkness fell, the other riders withdrew, leaving their comrades-in-arms to be finished off by the Gloucestershire Fyrd.

Olaf turned to Rhys: "Come on, it really is time to go now. Let's see if we can find that London Road and see if that spotty lad, Edgar the so-called 'Ætheling' is anywhere near up to leading England against a very professional and well-equipped Norman army."

They left behind the shouts and screams as nightfall effectively prevented any further conflict and made their way Northeast in the hope of picking up the road. From the high ground they could just make out the lights of Hastings and there, sure enough, was the road to London. They were utterly exhausted but knew that they needed the cover of darkness to travel. Olaf's shoes were worn through, and he wished desperately to find a horse that might have escaped from the battle.

As if by providence, Olaf's eyes closed to a squint to try and make out the silhouette of a horse feeding in a nearby field. It was clearly a Norman horse given the jutting pommel and cantel which served to hold the knights in the saddle when charging with couched lance. Olaf asked Rhys to cover him with his bow less there should be a resting knight nearby. The horse threw up his head with a snort and then resumed his grazing. Olaf approached with gentle words and was able to take the reins and kneel down next to the horse's head whilst scouring the countryside for any signs of movement. All seemed quiet. The owner must have been very tall as Olaf adjusted the stirrups to better fit his shorter legs and swung himself up into the uncomfortable leather saddle so very different from soft Viking fur 'armchair' saddles he had enjoyed on his long ride to Nidaros. His new mount was tall but compliant and Olaf trotted back to the gathering of archers and a number of the Gloucestershire Fyrd.

"Well, that's you sorted proper-like," said Rhys, his longbow armed and pointing to the ground. "Do you think we can find some more for us fellows?"

Then Olaf remembered: "I left my horse back at the crossroads where we all met at the Old Hoar Apple Tree. If the Normans haven't yet come down from Caldbec Hill, there may still be some horses as we left more than a hundred mounts."

The Hoar Apple Tree at Caldbec

"That means heading back to the battlefield. But I suppose if it means not walking all the way back to London we should give it a try," said Rhys with a shrug.

In the dark, it wasn't difficult to find their way back. For a start, Caldbec is the highest point in the area being some 2100 feet above sea-level, and it now benefitted from a lit beacon and the moans of the wounded and dying could be heard from a distance in the still night air. The great Hoar Apple Tree marked the crossroads and there on the northern slope of the ridge were a section of exhausted Norman soldiers guarding the Saxon ponies near the ancient tree. The fire they had lit made them perfect targets for the archers, but Rhys argued against it saying that if they cried out it would bring a large force down on them from the ridge above. There were but a dozen Normans and about half of them were sleeping. The men of the Gloucestershire fyrd moved with stealth, quickly and silently dispatching the soldiers whilst the half dozen archers covered the ridge should they be spotted by the dismounted Norman knights. There were more than enough mounts for everyone, and they walked their horses quietly up the London Road. After several miles they felt it safe to mount up. It was at this point that the men of Gloucestershire announced that they would be heading home to protect their families and so filtered off towards Tunbridge Wells and the Weald of Kent. Olaf and the Welshmen headed towards Bodiam and thence Northeast to Rochester to share the tragic news across the country and on to London. They arrived at Rochester two hours after sunrise and were treated to a cooked breakfast from the shocked monks of the Cathedral.

Rochester Cathedral

Chapter Three
The Road to London

Olaf and the six Welsh archers had made the journey to Rochester in the dark in an incredible twelve hours and, apart from a few desperate stragglers from Harold's army who had fled the battle before the final slaughter, they met no-one on their journey.

William had left the scene of his great victory to march along the coast to ensure he could not be surrounded by any secondary Saxon force from Dover or Canterbury. But there was to be a shock and more bloodletting along the way. They reached the small fishing village of Rye where the 3,500-strong force took everything that was edible from the villagers at sword-point. When they reached Romney however, the sight that greeted William was of many hundreds of Norman soldiers lying slaughtered on the shingle without their chain-mail armour and their ships blackened and smoldering at their moorings. This had been the missing part of his army which had landed some twenty miles East of the appointed landing site at Bulverhythe in the Manor of Pevensey.

Soon the air was filled with smoke and screams as the Norman soldiers set about inflicting a total act of vengeance until the area was reduced to corpses and the charred remains of what had been a pretty Kent fishing village.

In Rochester, Olaf and the Welshmen managed to snatch some much-needed sleep. Olaf was reminded of Astrid as the gentle sound of the monks 'Terce' plainsong echoed around the cathedral and cloisters, lulling them into an exhausted sleep. This indicated it was nine o'clock or the third hour of the monks' day. At midday a brother came and shook Olaf out of his deep reverie.

"You must wake up now and prepare to leave. We have received a pigeon-note that William has already arrived at Dover and the garrison are of a mind to surrender the castle to him without a fight. We have packed some food for you and your horses are fed and watered. It seems the Normans are pillaging the town in search of food which means they are going to have to live off the land. If London can hold we may yet starve the army through the Winter."

Olaf's head was still half asleep, but he was awake enough to admire this monk with a general's mind.

With some difficulty and much cursing, the Welsh archers were aroused and told of the Norman movements. Rhys was pragmatic, as ever, and pointed out that, having just fought a nine-hour battle then a forced march of some forty miles to Dover, they would be in no condition to move North anytime soon and, when they did, they would converge on Canterbury first. Nevertheless, the monks hurried them onto their mounts and sent them in the direction of London.

London was about six hours ride on horseback and, as the sun set on the river Thames, Olaf and the archers made camp on the South side of the river where they found a barn furbished with clean hay.

They had seen and smelt the smoking fires of London some distance back but agreed that, as there seemed no imminent danger from Normans, it would be safer to cross the river in daylight and catch up with some more rest.

They would have rested far less peacefully had they known the whereabouts of Guillaume de Malet and his twenty mounted knights. Having reached the ancient iron foundry of Tunbridge Wells they found tracks of foot soldiers and horses heading West. They then had the good fortune to come upon a straggler who had sprained his ankle and was hobbling with the aid of a branch he had hewn as a crutch. Hearing the hooves behind him he had no option but to let himself be taken. Helmeted and with a Saxon shield and axe the Norman knights were in no doubt that he was one of the group who had inflicted such terrible carnage on their fellow knights the previous evening. The unfortunate could expect no mercy and got none. The Normans inflicted terrible tortures upon him to discover the whereabouts of Olaf and the archers. All he could tell them through his screams was that they had parted company and headed North-East. It was enough. Guillaume now knew that they were heading to London. The body of the Gloucester warrior was left dead and horribly mutilated as the riders pushed their tired horses North through Sevenoaks until finally, out of necessity, stopping to rest in the old Anglo-Saxon town of Otford where they forced the local inhabitants to bring them food. They did not know it but Olaf's journey from Rochester to London and Guillaume's journey from Tunbridge Wells formed a perfect triangle so the two parties had every chance of converging at the apex, which was London Bridge.

Welsh longbowman

Chapter Four
The Saving of Ansgar the Staller

Olaf and his party were awakened quite early the following morning by a burly lady who owned the farm and wanted to know why they

thought they could stable themselves on her property. Rhys calmed her with his lilting Welsh accent:

"Well, it's like this see, I'm a Welshman who's been fighting for King Harold with my friends. This little blond lad here is from Norway but still has been working for the late English King."

At this, her eyes widened:

"The late King! You mean the King is dead? Did our people lose the battle against them foreigners?"

"Well, I'd like to call it a draw, but our people were on foot and they had cavalry and archers and armour and apart from about twenty longbows, no archers to talk about. And we had all these farmers who kept breaking out of the shield wall and running down the hill every time they feigned that they were retreating. It was chaos."

The burly lady began to cry:

"My 'usband went with the fyrd to foight with King 'Arold. He's a big man but no soldier, that's for sure. He was brave though; he wouldn't run away or nuffin' loike that. D'you suppose he's dead then?"

"I'm sad to say, lady, that if he didn't run away then it is very likely he is lying on that slope with most of the other fyrd. The housecarls stood and fought around the dead King's standard until the very last of them were slain. The fyrd, with no armour, rusty axes and no training stood no chance against mercenary knights wearing chain mail."

"You can stay here awhile. I'll fetch you all something to eat."

With tears streaming down her face the farmer's wife went off back to her cottage. Olaf spoke quietly:

"There will be no shortage of widows in Southern England this Winter but a great shortage of husbands, I fear."

Just an hour and a half's ride behind Olaf's troupe, Guillaume was having difficulty rousing his horsemen from their exhausted sleep after a good supper in Otford. They felt that trying to find a few archers in this sprawling countryside was akin to searching for a needle in a haystack. But Guillaume was adamant as he was sure Olaf would try to cross at the closest bridge to get into the relative safety of London and that meant going via Southwark. Guillaume had reconnoitered

London whilst spying for Duke William and knew all the bridges along the river Thames. In this he was absolutely correct.

Thanking the farmer's wife profusely for a delicious breakfast of bacon, eggs, milk and freshly baked bread, Olaf and the Welshmen set off towards the smoking cottages of the village of Southwark on the South bank of the Thames. Olaf thought once more of Astrid and her squeals of delight when the monks at Lindisfarne had served them such a breakfast. He had made up his mind about his future. He would promote his friendship with the young King Edgar the Ætheling and then head North to hook up with Edwin and Morcar should the Normans succeed in taking London. But Olaf had seen London and knew what a formidable and easily defended city it was. Only if the English capitulated would William succeed, otherwise, he was in for a long cold winter laying siege to the city's defenses. Edwin and Morcar must be heading to London if they had yet heard that their sister Ealdgyth was now a widow and Queen Dowager.

By two o'clock Olaf and the archers had reached the partially fortified gates of Southwark where they were challenged by armed men on sentry duty. Olaf explained that they had just come from the battlefield near Hastings.

"We know," said one of the guards. "A rider has got here ahead of you telling us to expect Ansgar the Staller" (Royal standard bearer).

Rhys interjected: "I saw him near the King, he was cut down by a knight, but I killed the Norman before he could administer the coup de grace. I got 'im with an arrow to the throat to be sure... so, he survived then?"

"So it would seem. Apparently, his brave London boys dragged him, badly wounded, to safety and are trying to reach London. The scout says there was a column of about twenty riders, almost certainly Norman knights, about five miles behind but they stopped to rest at Otford."

"Otford is it?" says Rhys. "Well, they could be here anytime now with a posse of Normans ready to ride them down. Olaf, lads, I think I feel another scrap coming on. I say we head back a short distance and if we can reach Ansgar and his Londoners before the Normans do, I might be able to save his life for a second time."

Olaf had already turned his horse about and had placed his bow across the saddle in readiness; the other archers did likewise.

"Ansgar must survive," said Olaf. "I met him here at court during Harold's coronation. Edward the Confessor had appointed him "Staller" – a senior household position. We need him to hold London together and support Edgar the Ætheling as king. I'm not sure I trust either Edwin or Morcar who will only be worried about their estates in the North."

The guards looked at Olaf with respect and astonishment that this diminutive Anglo-Viking, still in his early twenties, should have such a wise and informed head on his shoulders.

The archers spurred their mounts and headed back the way they had come.

"Send some shield men to follow us as we might need to set up a fighting retreat," Olaf shouted over his shoulder. The sentries were already on the case.

They had not gone as far as two miles along the famous Roman road to Canterbury known as Wæclingastræt (Watling Street) and were approaching Blackheath when they saw what they were looking for. Four men were carrying a stretcher constructed of shields on which lay the blood-soaked body of Ansgar, propped up on one elbow and roaring instructions to his men who were retreating in a crescent-shaped shield wall. Behind them the twenty knights were walking their horses in line formation with lances raised preparatory to a charge.

Guillaume did not give the order. His eyes squinted in the Autumnal sunshine, but he was able to make out that this group of some thirty warriors seemed prepared to make a stand around their wounded lord. These were not his prey as there were no archers. A movement some distance behind the foot soldiers distracted his attention. A small party of mounted men were heading towards the infantry shield-crescent, one of whom seemed smaller than the rest. Guillaume felt a rush of adrenalin as a glint from the lacquered varnish on Olaf's bow confirmed them to be the men he was looking for. The six archers spurred on their horses and reached the shield wall crescent just as Guillaume screamed:

"En avant chargez!" and the Norman line moved up the paces from trot to canter and full gallop. At one hundred yards it was easy pickings for the Welsh who dropped four riders followed by a fifth who had come into range of Olaf's bow.

"Arrêté!" Shouted Guillaume, and ten of the horsemen heeded the order to stop. The remainder, whose blood was up and continued forward, crashed into the spears and axes and arrows of the Londoners and were hacked to pieces.

From the comparative safety of a copse some two hundred yards away, Guillaume hissed under his breath: "Merde!" Not only had he not killed Olaf but he had to tell Duke William that he had lost a further ten knights. He was starting to hate this little Viking almost as much as Duke William did. There was nothing for it now but to wait for William to send re-enforcements. It would take a considerable force from here on and his orders to kill Olaf would have to be put to one side.

In the distance a cohort of some fifty axemen came jogging down the road, blowing hard, to re-inforce Ansgar's men.

"Good of you to join us but I don't think those boyos over there will be looking for a fight until the rest of their army gets here," shouted Rhys. Having just run two and a half miles carrying heavy wooden shields and axes, the London group were relieved not to have had to fight off a mounted attack.

"Well done everybody! Now get me back to London where I can get cleaned up and have the doctor see to my wounds." Ansgar was clearly feeling better and it was not long before they crossed London Bridge. Rhys wasted no time in explaining how he had saved Ansgar's life, not once but twice. Ansgar had asked Olaf: "Don't I know you?"

"Yes, my lord. I served the late King Harold in Normandy, at Stamford Bridge and finally on that hill near Hastings. You may have seen me at his coronation or at his wedding?"

"Ah yes, you're that randy little Viking who was ploughing Ealdgyth just before Harold Godwinson married her. Good job Harold didn't hear of it although everyone else at court seemed to know, even Harold's sister Queen Edith."

"Harold only had one love and that was Edith Swanneck. Ealdgyth was just a marriage of politics to keep Edwin and Morcar on side. Ealdgyth told me herself that their wedding night was impossibly awkward".

"Well, it can't have been that awkward as Ealdgyth is with child right now."

"Ah yes?" Olaf spurred his horse to bring this difficult conversation to a close. He heard Ansgar roaring with laughter behind him and then cursing the pain that this brought to his wounds.

The force of eighty men withdrew cautiously watched by the ten surviving mounted Norman knights which included an incandescent with rage, Guillaume de Malet. What neither side knew though was that Duke William had dispatched a force of some five hundred mounted knights from Dover up Watling Street to ask for the surrender of London. They might just have got it had it not been for the arrival of Ansgar the Staller which was greeted by the citizens of London with great cheering and ringing of church bells.

Guillaume de Malet

✬

Chapter Five
The Battle of London Bridge

The city of London was found to be much changed since Olaf had passed through just over a week ago. The streets were swollen with people who had made their way there for protection. Two small armies were on their way headed by Edwin and Morcar and stragglers from Hastings were in a mood to defend London against the invading Normans. Rhys and his compatriots headed straight for the nearest inn which by chance was the very place that Olaf and Rhys had dispatched Gospatrick and his gang on the London Embankment. Ansgar headed to his large house near Westminster and Olaf headed for the palace of Westminster in search of Ealdgyth. Although Edgar the Ætheling had been proclaimed King by Archbishop Ealdred, Ealdgyth was still the dowager Queen Consort and would therefore still be housed in the palace. Olaf was recognised by the guards and a lady-in-waiting was sent for to usher him into the Queen's presence. Her room was attended by several nuns and a mid-wife. The lady-in-waiting explained that Ealdgyth, who was now aged thirty-two, had experienced a long and difficult labour but the skill of the midwife had prevailed, and she had given birth to a healthy boy whom she had named Harold, after his father. Olaf twitched slightly at this but otherwise kept his composure as he was announced into the chamber at a whisper.

Ealdgyth lay in her bed propped up by pillows and managed a faint smile as she saw Olaf appear with his bow and quiver. Her face was drawn and ashen but her eyes still sparkled. Her dark hair fell in great curls across her shoulders. Beside her lay a tiny bundle sleeping peacefully.

"Olaf! How wonderful to see you. So, they didn't manage to get you then? Did you run away?" Her eyes sparkled with mischief.

"Only after the King had fallen, and even then, I nearly managed to get Duke William. I hit his helmet and gave him quite a bloody nose. He saw that it was me, so I made a tactical withdrawal into the woods where we set up a deadly ambush for the knights who were chasing us. We killed a great many and then slipped away under cover of night. How is the baby?"

"Oh, he's doing fine now that he's finally out but, as you might expect, he does resemble his father somewhat closely." Again, the mischievous twinkle. "Forgive me but I must rest now. Fionne, would you ask Esla to show Olaf to Edgar's empty room. He has moved into Harold's apartment now that he has been declared king."

Fionne, the lady-in-waiting, made a short curtsy and left the room only to return a few minutes later with a very attractive maid who announced herself as Esla. Olaf followed her to a smaller room in the palace where Esla lit a fire and made up the bed. All the time she prattled away rather in the style of Astrid, asking a hundred questions about the battle, how Olaf knew the Queen and what was to become of Londoners once the Norman army arrived. Olaf was very weary and asked Esla if she might find a bathtub. Esla giggled:

"Well, I didn't like to say sir, but you do smell as if you'd slept in a barn."

"That's probably because I have, now go and see if you can find that tub." Esla scurried out and returned with another maid struggling with the weight of a large brass tub.

Olaf watched them patiently as they emptied kettles of steaming water from the fire into the tub. When finally, it was almost full the two maids turned their backs to Olaf to allow him the privacy of undressing and stepping into the bath. Esla used some wooden tongs to pick up Olaf's clothes and the other maid giggled as she held her nose against the stench.

"We'll just go and wash these for you sir, there's a robe for you on the bed," and with that they left Olaf with some soap and a towel to reflect on how much easier it would be if there was a sauna.

As the water began to cool, Olaf reluctantly left off his ablutions and put on the very regal-looking robe which, he guessed, must have belonged to the young Edgar the Ætheling as it fitted him perfectly even though the boy was just thirteen. His admiration for the garment was curtailed by a commotion outside. From his window vantagepoint, Olaf could see armed men scuttling about, shouting and encouraging others to head towards the South Gate facing Southwark. Olaf found his boots and, while stretching down to lace them up, noticed a leather scabbard protruding from under the bed. On pulling it out he found it to contain a beautifully made sword more suited to ceremonial than warlike duties. The studded belt was perfect for holding his robe in place as he had no other clothes and, buckling it around his hips, he looked more like a prince of the realm than a common archer. Leaving his bow behind in the room, Olaf rushed down the stairs and into the courtyard.

Across the river, Guillaume de Malet's fury had been appeased by the unexpected appearance of Duke William's seneschal, William fitz Osbern and five hundred mounted knights, sent as a vanguard to reconnoitre the defences of London. Fitz Osbern had been ordered to harry the hamlet of Southwark putting it to fire and sword in order to instill fear into the defenders of London. This they set about doing with gusto but, instead of intimidating the Londoners, the sight of Southwark burning only succeeded in filling them with fury.

Furthermore, the sight of their young king with flowing golden locks running fearlessly to the gate without armour or shield acted as a rallying cry to do battle with the Norman invaders.

Outside the palace of Westminster, a huge throng were looking for some sort of leadership as Angar's wounds were being attended to and he was unable to leave his house. Olaf's regal-looking robe was starting to get noticed. It was certainly noticed by Rhys who had come rushing out of the inn and was now by the South gate.

"Olaf boyo! Get yourself over here quickly, there's a fight brewing, so there is, and me and the boys wouldn't want you to miss it."

The other archers shouted and gestured over the commotion. Like a warhorse at the sound of a horn, Olaf drew his sword and charged towards them. A huge roar went up behind him:

"It's the King! It's the Ætheling! Protect the King."

The expression of astonishment on the face of Rhys was shared by his colleagues as they saw Olaf charge straight towards them pursued by about a thousand armed men roaring "Protect the King!"

The great gates were swung open to reveal the eighty-yard dash across London Bridge into the burning Norman-occupied Southwark. Olaf had a rush of blood and was leading the beer-fuelled Welsh archers, followed by a huge mob of cheering Anglo-Saxons armed with spears, axes, swords and shields. Because of the smoke and crackling of wood, the screams of the inhabitants of Southwark and the shouting of the Normans, Olaf's boisterous counterattack went largely unnoticed by the mounted knights. A dismounted knight with a flaming torch in one hand and a screaming woman's hair in the other was the first to register astonishment as Olaf's elegant sword slid through his mail shirt and into his chest. Olaf had seen enough fighting to know to twist the blade as he pulled it away leaving the wide-eyed knight to slide to the floor still clutching the poor woman's hair. Two mounted knights appeared from behind a burning house and charged towards Olaf, one with a mace and the other with couched lance. With no shield Olaf on foot stood no chance. But the throng of armed Londoners pushed past Olaf and formed a defensive circle of shields and spears giving Rhys and the archers a clear shot at the rider with the lance whilst an elated axeman brought down the mace-waving knight with a huge blow that almost cut him in half.

Word had passed around the Norman force to pull back to regroup as William fitz Osbern managed to instill some order into the pillaging knights. Olaf had no such luck with his bloodthirsty rabble who were still pouring over the bridge and rushing into the smoke-filled streets in search of Normans. There could be no possibility of a shield wall in such confined spaces and as the Norman cavalry, now in orderly groups, charged into the streets of Southwark it was an uneven struggle with many of the Londoners being struck down. The fighters around Olaf had formed a protective ring but still a number were killed by enemy horsemen and their long-reaching lances. Olaf himself received a nasty slash to his arm as more and more Norman knights guessed incorrectly that here was the next king of England who needed killing. The danger to Olaf was now acute and Rhys screamed at him to pull back, a course of action with which his newly acquired housecarls fully concurred. They retreated back to the bridge where the six archers were able to cover him with accurate archery whilst the London warriors prevented any Normans from reaching the bridge. Just as at Hastings though, so many of the English foot-soldiers had gone too far forward and were being hacked to pieces in the streets by the Norman cavalry whilst the remainder fell back to safety over London Bridge.

Once the survivors had all bundled in, they made their way to Westminster, shouting and cheering as if they had won a great victory. Standing in their path was the glowering figure of Ansgar the Staller, his wounds bandaged and now in full battle regalia, leaning heavily on his great war axe.

Anglo-Saxon Housecarl 1066

"What the bloody hell is going on? Who the Hades gave orders to charge out there?

"We followed the King!" came the shouted reply from the assembled Londoners with Rhys and the Welshmen roaring with laughter.

"What king? Surely you aren't going to tell me that you followed a half-pint, pretty-boy Norwegian in a bath robe? Edgar! Or should I say, Your Majesty? show yourself sir!"

A downy-faced youth with pimples appeared on the steps of the palace trying to balance a simple golden crown on his head which did not fit. He managed a feeble smile and a nervous wave. Olaf made a small bow of acknowledgement to Edgar the Ætheling who had been pronounced King of England by Archbishops Stigand and Ealdred. In a voice that had only just broken from a boyish treble he spoke not to the crowd but to Olaf.

"Sir, I believe you have my sword? My wobe you may keep, as it now has blood stains on it, but my sword if you please."

"Your sword also has blood stains on it, my Lord, but it is from a Norman knight who was trying to defile an English maid. He now lies dead in Southwark". As Olaf unbuckled his sword-belt a great cheer went up which said only one thing....that they wished it was Olaf who was the Ætheling rather than this timid youth.

In the room above the two maids had returned with Olaf's clean clothes which they hung in front of the fire to dry. They then filled two buckets of the bathwater to throw out of the window when they heard a great cheer from outside below. Instinctively, they both rushed to the window in time to see Olaf move towards the steps holding out the King's sword, scabbard, and belt. At this moment a gust of wind caught the now unsecured robe, blowing it apart and allowing the two maids a perfect view of Olaf's muscular, hairless torso and his unusual blond manhood. The girls shrieked with laughter as Olaf blushed and pulled the robe together once more. After handing Edgar the belt and sword he managed to catch the rope belt that was thrown from the bedroom window above by the chuckling maids.

"Oooh, I could!" said one clearly beguiled maid.

"Oooh, *I would*!" replied Esla with a wicked twinkle that betrayed she had already made plans.

"Who said you could use my woom, Olaf?" asked Edgar.

"Well, Ealdgyth, Queen Dowager, invited me as you had moved into the late King Harold's apartments."

"Oh, well I suppose that's all wight then. What is this power you hold over Queen Ealdgyth? It seems she'll do anything for you."

"Yes, so it would seem", replied Olaf, who then tried to keep a straight face at the snort from behind. Olaf couldn't work out whether it came from Rhys or Ansgar, but he suspected Ansgar.

An awkward moment was averted by the arrival of the delicately formed Esla who bowed politely to Edgar and pretended not to notice the admiring looks from the heaving mass of testosterone assembled in the square. After seeing Olaf's wounded arm and the blood dripping out of the sleeve, she announced:

"I think we had better have this seen to sir. We have your clothes drying in the room upstairs."

Ansgar laughed, "Yes, yes, make sure this Pretender to the throne is seen to properly young lady. He was one of Harold's Housecarls and fought bravely for the King on many occasions."

"Oh yes sir" said Esla with a curtsey, "I'll make quite sure he is seen to properly."

Rhys exploded with laughter followed by all those who could hear. Edgar looked confused as the couple went into the palace.

"Such ribaldry before a King of England!"

Ansgar was distracted by a posse of clergy including the two Archbishops, Stigand and Ealdred who were pushing their way towards him through the crowd of armed men.

"Make way for the Archbishops!" a clergyman shouted, "we wish to speak with Edgar the King and Ansgar, the senior nobleman."

Ansgar turned painfully using his long axe as support for his wounded leg:

"I am Ansgar the Staller, and here is Edgar the Ætheling, proclaimed, but not yet crowned, rightful heir to the throne of England."

Stigand spoke first, wearing his archbishop's long robes, his mitre and holding his crook of office.

"We need to debate the matter of the accession. Can we move into the Great Hall to start the proceedings. I have had a pigeon messenger from St Albans that both Earls Edwin and Morcar are on their way here with their forces and could be here at any time now."

"Well, that's a bit of good news at least," said Ansgar. "perhaps they can explain why they didn't come down with Harold to fight at Hastings? If they had been there, it might just have made the difference. They're as slippery as eels those two. Do we know if they have declared for Edgar or are they just waiting to see the outcome with William the Bastard?"

"Oh, I think they have declared for Edgar, but we do need to discuss the viability of supporting a thirteen-year-old boy against one of the fiercest warriors in Europe. They will be outside our walls shortly with three and a half thousand professional soldiers who have, just recently, destroyed most of our nobility and our entire army." Stigand's eyes were shifty in trying to avoid any eye-contact with Ansgar and Edgar.

"W-will they try to kill me?" Stuttered the Ætheling.

"Probably," grunted Ansgar.

"Unless" interjected Stigand, "unless that is, you agree to William's claim to the throne of England and, as there have been no coronation oaths taken, you would be quite free to stand aside in favour of Duke William."

"William the Bastard" corrected Ansgar.

"Illegitimate or not, if we fight him and lose, he will burn London to the ground and slaughter all its defenders", said Stigand with a touch of panic in his voice.

"My Lord Archbishop," Ansgar turned to Ealdred, Archbishop of York, "what are your thoughts on this?"

Ealdred spoke for the first time:

"I suggest we go into the Great Hall right away to get out of this cold. Then we can wait for the earls of Mercia and Northumbria to arrive and then come to a decision. There is no doubt however that Edgar is the Ætheling of the House of Wessex, descended from Alfred, but had he been made king as was his right, he would be lying on that hill beside Harold right now. When Edwin and Morcar arrive, we will convene as a *Witan* given that all the other senior nobles are dead, and that we are the senior clergy in the land."

And with that, the party made their way into the Great Hall of Westminster where a great fire had been lit against the cold. Above them an impressive array of carved angels looked down from the huge hammer beams overhead.

Graham Dalby

The Beams of Westminster Great Hall

Chapter Six
Submission

Olaf climbed the wooden stairs with the aid of Esla who proved quite sturdy in supporting his weight with his good arm until they reached the bedroom. The other maid was there to greet them with a wet cloth she had dampened from Olaf's dirty bathwater. Olaf knew things about cleaning wounds which he had originally picked up from Freya and Ålfgerd the Lech and one thing he was certain about was using freshly boiled clean water and herbs before stitching the wound. Olaf called out to her:

"No, that's not the way!" and she drew back in surprise. At that moment the door was opened and Fionne strode in imperiously:

"Girls, what are you doing here? You are needed in the Queen's chamber right away. What on earth do think you know about surgery. Off with you now!" Esla and the other maid looked at her in disbelief and disappointment. This was their patient and they had been denied the opportunity of nursing him. Desperately trying to hide their resentment at this Lady in Waiting, they bobbed and left the room seething with feelings of injustice.

The latch fell back down to secure the door and Fionne moved towards it to slide the bolt across, thus preventing any intruders.

"Right young Olaf, having saved you from certain infection from those amateur poisoners perhaps you would like me to look at your wound?"

"You are very kind my lady. I learnt much about surgery in Norway so I was alarmed that two lovely young maids would have given me blood poisoning or gangrene in a very short space of time."

"Do not worry young warrior. I have served the Royal Household since I was a young maiden at the court of Cnut the Great and then Edward the Confessor and now the Dowager Queen Ealdgyth. You are in safe hands."

She gently slid the robe over his shoulders to reveal a nasty slash through the bicep just above the elbow, still oozing blood. With speed Fionne brought the water to boil and let it cool for a short while. Then she took a clean cloth and pressed it firmly against the bleeding arm. What happened next was a shock as she had left a knife by the fire and now, before he had anytime to realise what was in store for him, pressed the red-hot blade against the wound with a hiss and smell of burning flesh. He had seen something similar with his brother Magnus but had little idea of the pain inflicted. Olaf screamed as Fionne applied another cloth with snow from outside the window. The relief was instantaneous. Olaf fell backwards onto the bed as Fionne wrapped his arm in a tight bandage. Lying naked on the bed, Fionne produced a bottle of soothing oil and rubbed it into his exhausted body.

"All right pretty boy, let's get you wrapped up and asleep to recover your strength. You might well need it!"

Fionne was pleased that she did not need to put in any stitches in the short term and was content to let Olaf sleep.

Returning to the Queen Dowager's bed chamber, Fionne, Lady in Waiting, found the two maids changing the bed linen as Ealdgyth sat in a chair, breast feeding young Harold.

"My two brothers Edwin and Morcar are on their way here so I should like to freshen the place up to greet them. How is my handsome boy? The girls have told me he has been fighting the Normans half naked! I know this because they were washing his clothes at the time. Is he badly wounded?"

"It's a nasty gash from a sword that wasn't too sharp as the thick velvet robe prevented the cut from going to the bone and losing an arm. I have quarterized the flesh, so it probably won't need stitching. Are you getting all this Esla?"

Both maids had stopped work and were listening intently. They both jumped at this rebuke:

"Oh yes, m'lady" they chorused, and resumed making up the bed.

Down the hallway, Olaf had fallen into a deep sleep. After an hour the shock to his body had caused a fever to set in and when Fionne left Ealdgyth to check on her patient that is how she found him. His forehead was covered with perspiration which she dabbed with a cool cloth. Then the second stage of shock set in when Olaf began to shiver and convulse. Fionne ran back down the corridor and asked Ealdgyth if she might borrow Esla and they both swiftly returned to the room to find Olaf shivering and speaking Norwegian in his delirium.

"Esla, take off your clothes quickly now!"

"My lady?"

"Remove your clothes, quickly and get into bed. We must keep him warm and mind that wounded arm."

Esla did not hesitate a second time. Slipping out of her clothes, the shadows from the fire flickered over her well-honed and shapely body.

"Now into bed with you and use your body warmth to break that fever and thank the Lord for blessing you with such a fine bosom."

"Yes m'lady. Ooh! He's absolutely boiling!"

"Yes, and he needs to sweat out that fever so get in there nice and close."

Esla did as she was bidden but thought to herself that this was not quite what she had in mind. Still, it was better than emptying chamber pots and she snuggled in close.

Outside, a light snow was falling which partly muffled the sound of a large party of riders who had come down via Hatfield to Lincoln's Inn Field and thence to Westminster. They were led by the two brothers, the Earls of Mercia and Northumbria, Edwin and Morcar. Their forces had been very badly mauled at the Battle of Fulford Gate and again during the fierce defeat of Harald Hardråda's army at Stamford Bridge after the timely arrival of Harold Godwinson and his army. When word arrived of the Norman landing in the South the two Earls told Harold that they needed a few days to recover but would follow with their forces within a week. Thus, they both survived the great slaughter on Caldbeck Hill and were now come to take their sister Ealdgyth and her baby son Harold, to safety in York. That was assuming they weren't expected to stay and defend the boy-king against the Norman army.

The air was acrid with the smell of smouldering dwellings in Southwark where the snow had dampened the fires. Under cover of darkness, the Norman knights, led by fitz Osbern, moved out and headed West along the South bank of the River Thames. William had sent orders to meet the riders at a place called Wallingford and told them to harry and burn everything along the way through Hampshire and Oxford. Meanwhile, Edwin and Morcar arrived at the Great Hall, bringing with them a posse of senior clergy; Wulfstan, Bishop of Worcester, Walter, Bishop of Hereford and the monks of Peterborough's choice of replacement abbot for the one who had died of his wounds at Hastings.

Whilst Olaf shivered and sweated in blissful ignorance, the fate of England was being decided by *Witengemot* late into the night. The consensus was that to resist William any further would be folly, especially when it became patently obvious that Edgar the Ætheling was quaking in his boots for his own safety and showed no signs of leadership or courage whatsoever. Stigand stormed out saying he was going to his bed to sleep on the matter but by the morning it was discovered that he and his retinue had left London to ride West to Wallingford and swear fealty to William.

The Ætheling party was beginning to come apart as the main players began to think more of their own wealth and future prosperity, given the seemingly inevitable fact that William was the last man standing and held all the cards unless England could find an alternative leader very quickly. Even Ansgar, disabled by his wounds and the most protagonist of the Witan, realised that, without a strong leader, they stood no chance against the well-equipped, well-led and disciplined Norman force. With a heavy heart he declared, along with Edwin,

Morcar and Archbishop Ealdred, that they would have to take Edgar to William's camp and swear fealty. Edgar submitted to this with barely a murmur.

The following day was cold and bright when Esla awoke to find the body of Olaf beside her was no longer feverish and shaking. Olaf's matted yellow hair was strewn across the pillow, but Fionne was relieved to feel the temperature of his forehead had returned to normal.

"Esla, you have done a great service to the young man this night. I think without your help he would not have made it. Now go and get washed and changed and return with your colleague and fresh warm water to get him bathed from this putrid fever."

"Oh, m'lady, did you stay up all night with us?" said the still sleepy Esla.

"I did", replied Fionne. "It was the wish and command of the Dowager Queen Ealdgyth, and she was adamant that this young Viking warrior who served the late King Harold so loyally should be given every medical assistance to get well, and, in that Esla, you excelled."

"Oh, thank you m'lady. We don't often see beauty in our menfolk. They tend to be hard and rugged and hairy. But this one m'lady is beautiful and brave as a lion. D'you know, he led the charge against the Normans wearing just a dressing gown?"

Several weeks passed and Olaf's strength began to return as news of the calamity into which the English Witan was plunging itself was becoming painfully clear. Apart from the London citizens themselves, anyone who had a vested interest in keeping their property, their lands, their position and their money had decided that the only course of action was to welcome William and his conquering, mercenary army into London to crown William king.

The party of dignitaries who went to the new camp at Berkhamsted included Edgar the Ætheling to swear fealty to William. The nail in the coffin for the defenders of London was that both Edwin and Morcar sent letters of fealty but headed North, taking with them their sister, the Queen Dowager, Ealdgyth, and her new-born son, Harold, a fair and blue-eyed babe of just four weeks.

Rhys and his 'boyos' had been employed to go along with Ansgar to bodyguard the Ætheling and had been in William's tent to witness the swearing of fealty. Guillaume de Malet was there and immediately bridled at the presence of the archers. There was urgent talk in French as to the identity of the archers until it was confirmed that Olaf was not a part of the group. At this point William issued a loud and angry decree which the monks, acting as scribes, took down as fast as they could scribble by candlelight. On the journey back to London, Ansgar who, being a nobleman, spoke French, related to Rhys the substance of the angry decree issued by William Duke of Normandy. He had decreed that one of King Harold's archer-housecarls who went by the name of Olaf, son of Slagbjørn, had attempted to murder Duke William, the rightful heir to the throne of England. He decreed that Olaf was hereafter to be regarded as '*Caput Lupinim*' (let his head be a wolf's head) and denied all protection of the law. Let him be hunted like an animal throughout the land and let anyone who kills him be rewarded with gold.

"Oh my God!" gasped Rhys. "He's declared Olaf an Outlaw! We need to get back fast to let him know that he is in great danger. We must get him out of London before William gets there.

Back in London Fionne and the maids had packed as much of Ealdgyth's belongings as would fit onto a small cart. Fionne sat in the carriage with Ealdgyth, the baby Harold and a plump nurse. The two maids were paid off and discharged. As the palace was now all but empty, Esla made her way to Olaf's room where she found him sleeping by the warmth of the fire which had been recently made up. Olaf awoke as he felt something warm and soft next to him.

"Lady Fionne said that you should thank me for saving your life."

Esla's eyes twinkled in the firelight's glow.

Olaf thought that, considering the whole of England seemed to be in a state of submission, what a churlish thing it would be not to submit to this very pretty young lady's gentle request.

Chapter Seven
Christmas Coronation

Rhys and the archers rode hard from Berkhamstead and galloped across the wooden bridge at Cripplegate on the Northwest of the London Wall. The sentries didn't even challenge them. Clattering into Westminster, Rhys dismounted and bounded up the stone stairs to Olaf's apartment.

"Come on Olaf boyo, we've got to leave right now....oh! hello beautiful, what have you done with Olaf?"

Esla was sat up in bed with her hair down and the covers pulled up to her chin. Her eyes flickered involuntarily towards the bay window. Stepping out of the shadows, Olaf lowered the bow which had been aimed at the door.

"Oh, it's you Rhys. You did give us a fright. We thought you were Normans."

"Well, they won't be far behind now. They've all surrendered you see, all the Earls, the bishops and, of course, the Ætheling. William will march here with his whole army at first light. So put some clothes on and I'll give you the really bad news. And say goodbye to this nice lady."

"No! Olaf, take me with you. I'm not staying here!"

"I don't suppose you ride do you?" asked Rhys. The swishing of her long hair indicated the negative. "I'm sorry then as I have to tell Olaf he has been officially declared an outlaw with a price on his head and a posse of Norman knights detailed to kill him at the earliest possible opportunity - and they know he's here."

"Outlaw! Oy herregud!" gasped Olaf, "Odin's sacred trousers, I only broke his nose!"

Olaf kissed the sobbing Esla: "Thank you for everything sweet Esla, I owe you my life but if I don't go right now, I won't have a life. Those Norman knights will stick me like a pig if they catch up with me."

Esla nodded, understanding, but deeply unhappy to lose someone who she was only just getting to know and love.

Olaf gathered a few belongings including the Ætheling's robe and, of course, his hunting bow. Although there was a risk they might run into the Norman advance guard, Cripplegate was still the fastest route to head North and it was unlikely they could be here so quickly. Imagine then their astonishment to hear the sound of a large, mounted party clattering across the bridge of Cripplegate just as they approached. Olaf and the archers instinctively dismounted and drew their bows ready to sell their lives as dearly as possible. As their targets drew closer, Olaf's sharp young eyes discerned by the gates flickering torches that the shields were of the Saxon and Danish design, not the long kite-shape shields favoured by the Norman knights.

"Who goes there?" shouted Rhys and the horses pulled up sharply with much snorting and tossing of heads for they were both hungry and thirsty and looking forward to losing their riders in favour of a warm stable and some fresh straw.

A clergyman came forward in a long cloak:

"Let us pass, sir! I am Stigand, Archbishop of Canterbury and we have just sealed a peace with William of Normandy. His advance guard will be here in an hour or so and then we will make plans to acknowledge William of Normandy as the rightful King of England."

"Odin's trousers! Did we not stand and fight for nine bloody hours at Hastings so the Church can just hand over England to the invader?" screamed Olaf into the darkness. "Where is your loyalty to the rightful King?"

A small horse with a diminutive rider trotted forward: "Olaf, you are wight. The clergy and the earls, they have betwayed me and England. They have sold us all for their miserwable skins. Here is my sword you used so valiantly against the Normans; I am not worthy of it, it is yours. Go North and join with Edwin and Morcar. As soon as I am able to escape from William's gwasp I will join you and we will thwow this Bastard King back into the sea."

Edgar the Ætheling was for the first time sounding like he was gaining some courage in the knowledge that his council were giving away his rightful throne.

Olaf and the archers stood aside as the considerable entourage walked their horses into London. A stocky, armoured man rode past and called out:

"Olaf! I can barely look at ye for the great shame I harbour. But there was nothing to be done against so powerful a force. We've been ruled by the Danes in the past and now we must accept to be ruled by the Normans. It won't be pleasant that's for sure, but as nothing to what he'll do to you if he catches you. You cannot take this road, the Normans are just a short ride behind. Go to Ludgate and get a boat from Blackfriars. It's your only chance."

It was the wounded figure of Ansgar the Staller who had, that very day, sworn an oath of fealty to William in the hope of retaining his lands.

Olaf strapped the decorated sword around his waist and marvelled at the torchlight flickering off the bejewelled scabbard:

"Rhys, what's to be done? Shall we make a run for it?"

Olaf was out of good ideas and there was a feeling of panic coming over him which he didn't like.

"Well, you see, it's like this. I noticed the knight who has been doing all the chasing seems to know you and seems to be on some special mission to bring you before William dead or alive. Do you know who I mean?"

"Yes, I know him. He's a spy for William as he's half English and called himself William Mallett to ingratiate himself with Harold whilst we were in Normandy. His real name is Guillaume de Malet and he has clearly been ordered by William to take revenge for my failing to kill him at Hastings."

"Right boyo! My plan then is to hide up here as they will expect us to flee North out of London. We need to take him out as he is the only one who can actually recognise you. It'll be much easier with him out of the picture. Then we can take a boat to York as Ansgar advises and you can mix with all those other Vikings and not be noticed."

The six archers dispersed into an Inn down some backstreet. Olaf hurried back to Westminster and was just in time to catch Esla leaving with her clothes in a bag. She was delighted to see him, and he helped her up onto his horse. By great fortune for Olaf, Esla's parents had both died very young leaving a small dwelling for their daughter and two boys in Moorgate by the boathouses. But when they arrived, the place was completely locked up and empty. Upon enquiring from the neighbours, it seemed that the boys had immediately taken the offer of a war axe and shield and had followed Harold down to Hastings. They had yet to return.

As Esla lit the fire and warmed some broth she had brought from Westminster, away, over on the London Wall, a large body of mounted knights were making their way into the centre of London to secure the city for William's great arrival in the capital after sunrise the following day. Esla found some ale and even some mead which reminded Olaf of home and the neighbours brought round a little salt beef and some bread, making a passable feast. They sat around the fire as Esla told the astonished neighbours of Olaf's heroic deeds. After enjoying the mead and the warm fire, Olaf's eyelids began to close and the neighbours carried him onto a straw bed where he slept soundly, oblivious of the chatter or even of the thick falling snow which muffled the hooves of the Norman knights, busy securing the darkened streets of London from any possible uprising.

As the sun arose the following morning and a full-throated cockerel gave vent to his morning call, he noted that there was no echo to reverberate his cry. This was because of the fact that the heavy snowfall was muting not just his cry but also the arrival of William and the main part of his invasion force. Warily, they made their way through the streets with the horses chewing their bits and throwing their heads in anticipation of the tension which was palpable. The Norman soldiers were expecting trouble as they approached Westminster. But there was nothing to see here. There was just a timid assembly which included archbishops Ealdred and Stigand, a bevy of churchmen, civic dignitaries bearing casks of gold and silver, a few ealdormen and finally the somewhat pathetic figure of Edgar the Ætheling, rightful King of England, with Ansgar the Staller at his side.

Olaf, now fully awake, became aware that there were a number of armed men in the house as he could see through the curtain that had partitioned off his sleeping quarters. His sword and scabbard were on the floor beside him, and he quietly reached for the blade and slid it out, glinting from its sheath. A lilting voice had noticed the sunlight on the blade and called out:

"We're all friends here Olaf so you can put down the fruit-knife!"

Olaf pulled back the curtain:

"Rhys, how did you manage to find me here and who are these people?"

"They're English so they are and all with peculiar names that start with Æthel – something or other. All except this fellow called Wigmund who has a right to be here. This is his house."

A tall man in his mid-twenties, with a terrible recent scar on his face, nodded to Olaf.

"Hello Olaf, I am indeed Wigmund and brother to Esla who told me all about you last night. Most of my friends, including my younger brother now lay dead on that blood-soaked slope. The Normans are calling it Senlac, meaning 'lake of blood.' I was lucky to get away after the line collapsed and a Norman knight gave me this badge of honour. It was the last thing he ever did. Ældgorn here cut him in half with his axe." A large, bearded man smiled and nodded, leaning on a fearsome double-handed war axe.

Wigmund continued: "We met Rhys and the Welshmen in a tavern by the river and got talking, when they mentioned they were looking for this Norwegian archer who was staying with one of the Queen's maids called Esla. It was a happy coincidence. We also heard talk of the Normans offering a reward in gold for the head of this same archer and there seemed many in that tavern who might be willing to take on the job. The Normans have got the whole of London cut off with guards on every gate. The Coronation is tomorrow, Christmas Day, and there are a lot of twitchy soldiers in every street. We have about twenty men we can count on to cause a diversion so that you can sneak out at Ludgate and take the boat, Esla has arranged, out of the Thames Estuary and up to East Anglia or even further North. You must take Esla and keep her safe. She has rather fallen for you it seems. Rhys and the five archers will accompany you for protection."

Olaf had a point to make:

"There are only two Normans who know what I look like; one is William of Normandy, and the other is Guillaume de Malet, who has been charged with my capture and execution. I must kill him before we depart. We can set up an ambush outside Westminster Abbey where he and his men will be on guard, assuming he is not in the Abbey itself."

"We could make a fire outside the Abbey," growled the hitherto silent Ældgorn. "They've evacuated all the houses around the Abbey so no archers could hide in them. They're all empty. We could burn them during the Coronation and all the smoke would blow into the Abbey causing panic."

"Well now, not just a pretty face boyo!" laughed Rhys.

Ældgorn rumbled a laugh revealing his two remaining teeth.

William Duke of Normandy entering London

The morning of December 25th was lit with bright sunshine which sparkled prettily on the crisp snow that had continued to fall on the faithful leaving midnight mass. But today the sky was azure-blue and the air was filled with the pealing of bells across the city.

Duke William of Normandy rode into London from a hunting lodge in Barking which was both comfortable and safer than staying in London with a large population of citizens who might wish to avenge Harold's death and defeat. Soldiers flanked him and looked nervously around for any potential assassins. As he entered the great Abbey of Westminster, he was greeted by Ealdred, Archbishop of York who was conducting the ceremony ahead of Stigand, Archbishop of Canterbury. The Abbey was packed out by Norman nobility and Englishmen keen to protect their lands and titles by swearing fealty.

Outside was a large crowd being carefully watched by twitchy and nervous Norman foot soldiers with their commanders mounted. Wigmund had assembled a company of thirty men plus Olaf, Rhys, Esla and the five Welsh bowmen. With the falling snow and the hive of activity of people coming out of churches after midnight mass, they had been able to store all their weapons in one of the unoccupied houses close to the entrance of the Abbey. Only Normans were permitted to carry swords and lances on this day.

To prevent anyone entering this store, Ældgorn had set up a large brazier from which he was selling hot chestnuts and warm cider to the grateful onlookers.

Inside the Abbey, with everyone standing, the choir sang anthems as William made his way slowly up the great fan-vaulted nave towards the throne of England, placed at the top of the steps into the quire. All down the length of the nave foot-soldiers were positioned with their backs to the procession to keep a keen eye on the congregation. Either side of the wooden throne, painted in gold, were lecterns for the two bishops to read out the service, Ealdred in English and Geoffrey, Bishop of Coutances, in French.

William sat between the two and, like the kings before him, promised to rule wisely and justly. At this point there was a deviation from the accustomed Coronation rite as, although William could claim kinship with Edward the Confessor, he had seized power through battle and the killing of the last king. It was, therefore deemed expedient to ask the assembled people whether they accepted him as their Lord and King. This was put first in English and then in French in answer to which the crowd shouted loudly in Latin: "Vivat Rex! vivat Rex!" which reverberated around the great Abbey.

The noise of this was not understood by the Norman guards standing outside and they began pushing at the crowd with their shields and drawn swords. Some of the ladies began to scream and their men to push back. This was just the confusion needed and, at a shout from Wigmund, Ælgorn kicked over the brazier in the direction of the house behind him. There was a pile of fresh straw by the doorway which quickly caught alight. From the crowd men began to rush into the doorway, emerging from a side door armed with weapons. These included Olaf and the six archers who had fire arrows already prepared. Individual Norman soldiers caught in the rioting crowd were quickly dispatched as Olaf and the archers set the surrounding buildings ablaze, increasing the screaming and panic of the throng. The noise was clearly audible to the congregation and, as smoke began to pour in through the, as yet, unglazed windows, the panic swiftly spread into the Abbey. The people inside suspected it was being burnt down by those opposed to the crowning of William. There was a stampede to the great West door which was thrown open by the guards who were the first ones out into the rioting square. The thirty or so armed Englishmen were being helped by men in the crowd who were attacking the Normans with their fists or any sticks or staves they could lay their hands on. The problem for the Normans was to know who the enemy were as nearly a thousand members of the congregation comprising Norman nobility and Englishmen who had sworn fealty to William had now poured out of the Abbey into the square.

Guillaume de Malet remained mounted and was slashing at anyone unfortunate enough to be in his path. He had seen the fire arrows and his concentration was now solely in that direction. A path opened before him as people were keen not to get trampled by his horse or slashed by his flailing sword. There, dead ahead of him he spotted Olaf, bow in hand surrounded by other bowmen. Spurring his horse forward he clattered the forty yards over to where they were. Olaf had heard the neigh of the horse and drew his sword, shouting to Rhys to cover him. In an instant Guillaume leant to his left in the saddle, his sword ready to decapitate the small Viking. An arrow whistled and caught Guillaume in the left shoulder seconds before the left-handed rider swung the killer blow. His sword fell from his grasp behind him giving Olaf a split second to swing his sword deep into the thigh of his would-be slayer. With blood spurting from his wound and clutching the arrow in his shoulder, Guillaume slid from the saddle and crashed onto snow covered cobble stones, thereby saving him from a broken neck. Some Normans tried to reach him but were caught in the throng.

Olaf grabbed Esla, who had just been hugging her brother in a sibling farewell: "Come on Esla, this is where we leave."

Drying her eyes, her face hardened to the task:

"Follow me, I know the way!"

Expertly, she led them through familiar narrow backstreets, now devoid of any Normans and, before long, they reached the City Wall and the practically unguarded exit at Ludgate. Two English guards were sat on the floor, leaning against the tower stones, drinking ale and laughing. They had seen the smoke from Westminster, and it didn't seem to concern them too much.

"Bit of trouble over Westminster way!" Rhys called out to the guards.

"Well, I hope they've set fire to that Norman bastard! Pass friends!"

And with that the group walked under the portcullis, over the bridge and were on their way along Farrington Street and down to the River Thames at Blackfriars. Soon they could hear the water lapping up against the wharf and they filed down a narrow passage known as Puddle Dock. And there it was, bobbing about on the high tide, its mooring ropes creaking against the timber jetty.

Ludgate

It wasn't a longboat as Olaf was used to but more a square, flat-bottomed Cog suited for trade. It reminded him of the boat that Harold had taken to cross the Channel to rescue the two hostages – and that didn't end well. It had a small tower at the rear which would be useful for archers, but it wasn't built for speed, that was certain.

The boat came with four sailors for the price and had been paid for by money given by Ansgar. A sailor stood up in the fo'c'sal trying to get a better view of the fire around Westminster Abbey. The smoke spiralled high into the Christmas Day sky. He called out across the muddy water: "Happy Christmas, bastard invader of England!

And God help us now!"

Chapter Eight
Sea Voyage to York – The Fury of William I of England

Olaf and Esla boarded the vessel up the swaying gangplank followed by the six archers. The sailors were good loyal men desperately unhappy about the seizure of their native land. They had stocked the cog with meats, ale, wine and vitals and had a plentiful supply of furs against the North Sea winds. Esla sat next to Olaf and shivered. She was leaving London for the first time in her life and was nervous and distraught at leaving her last surviving family member behind to face the Norman tyranny that was about to unfold. The archers were happy enough finding plenty to eat and drink and felt much safer on the cog.

The ropes were untied and the remaining sailors jumped aboard as the large square sail unfurled in the midday breeze and they drifted gracefully Eastwards up the estuary, past the snow-capped church roofs and smoking dwellings celebrating Christmas Day. On the other side of the river, they passed the charred remains of what was once the thriving community of Southwark and paused to lower the mast when they reached London Bridge. Olaf's thoughts became a flashback to a screaming woman being dragged by the hair through the burning village and the expression on the face of the Norman would-be rapist when he realised he had been run-through by Olaf's sword.

The smoking buildings of Westminster were fading from view as they rounded the river bend but the pandemonium around the Abbey was still at full chaotic fever-pitch. In the square stood a large body of Normans which included some of the very senior nobles such as William fitz-Osbern, Hubert du Mont-Cannisy, Hugh d'Avranche and Odo, Bishop of Bayeux. Of the English there were far less but included Stigand, Archbishop of Canterbury, Wulfstan, Bishop of Worcester, Walter, Bishop of Hereford and Ansgar the Staller, who was enjoying it. Inside, despite the smoke and shouting, Ealdred, Archbishop of York proceeded with the Coronation Rite in a practically empty Abbey. Quaking, the Bishop Goeffrey of Coutances stood his ground and faithfully translated as Ealdred administered the Holy Oil in making William the anointed king and presented him with the Orb and Sceptre and Crown of England. It was done. William was now officially King William I of England and Duke of Normandy. The moment for which he had been waiting all his life had finally arrived and here he was sat on a throne in an empty Abbey with smoke and mayhem all around. How could this be? Who was responsible for this catastrophe?

"Where is Guillaume de Malet?" Screamed the newly crowned King of England. "Where is my brother, Bishop Odo? Bring them to me now!!"

A soldier returned shortly with the portly and bejewelled Bishop of Bayeux and Hugh d'Avranche.

Bowing to his brother, Odo explained that Guillaume had been badly wounded in the riot outside.

"He was in charge of my security during the service. The people were unarmed, we saw to that. How can this be? Bring him to me now, wounded or not!"

Hugh d'Avranche waved at four soldiers to follow him out of the Abbey to collect the wounded Guillaume.

Outside, the fighting had all but stopped as the armed men had melted away into the backstreets, leaving fifteen dead foot soldiers, five wounded civilians and a badly wounded, unhorsed knight, who was now being carried into the Abbey. Unable to stand, Guillaume was still clutching the arrow stump in his shoulder and wincing with pain.

"Quickly Guillaume, before you die, tell me who was responsible for this. Tell me quickly and I will have you taken to the surgeon."

Through clenched teeth Guillaume recounted how the plan had been cleverly executed by experienced warriors and that the fire had been started by non-other than Olaf, 'the Outlaw' and his fellow brigands.

"He is a dead man!" screamed William. Take me to my lodge and we will celebrate my Coronation, tomorrow, we will find the perpetrators and they will feel my wrath. But now it is Christmas, so we feast. Take Guillaume to the surgeon with all speed. With this he picked up his helmet, handed the Crown, Orb and Sceptre to Odo and stormed out of the Abbey his face red with rage.

The light was fading fast as the cog-boat hove into the small fishing village of Southend that had been founded by the Saxons in the 7th century. There was a priory there and the party were offered warmth, shelter and food to see out an eventful Christmas Day, 1066. They had not realised that they had sailed right past the hunting lodge at Barking where William was feasting and celebrating his Coronation. The monks of St Mary's, Prittlewell numbered just eighteen and were joined by Swein of Essex who was the local Lord of the Manor having joined them for the Christmas feasting. When they heard that Esla had been one of the Queen's maids and that Olaf had been Harold's archer-housecarl and that Rhys and his men had inflicted great damage on the Normans both in Sussex and in London, Swein asked the Prior to reward these men from the treasure they knew was hidden in a 7th century burial mound in Prittlewell. The Prior nodded and left into the night with a few of the monks. The travellers feasted on wild boar, capers, roast guinea fowl and wine from the monks' vineyards. Olaf told of his great journey from Lindisfarne to York, his meeting with Rhys in Wales, his time with Harold in Normandy and his two last great battles near York against Harald Hardråda and near Hastings against William 'the Bastard'. There was much cheering as Esla continued the story of Olaf's 'dressing gown' charge against the Normans on London Bridge and how this very day they had ruined William's Coronation. The wine flowed and the monks sang wassail drinking songs to the crackling of the great Yule-log. Olaf thought how like a Viking Christmas this was and his thoughts wandered to remembrances of his father dressed up as 'Old Man Winter' handing out carved wooden gifts to the children.

Olaf was brought back to the present by Esla squeezing his hand as the wooden door of the Priory Hall was thrown open to admit a Prior, two monks and an icy wind. The Prior was carrying a wooden chest which he placed on the table in front of Swein who stood up holding his wine goblet and proposing a toast to the assembled guests:

"As it is the Feast of Christemas, let us present our gallant visitors with gifts just as the three Magi did to our Saviour on the day of his birth. Let us see what the Prior has chosen for you. Esla, for service to the Queen, this Saxon broach, fashioned in gold and set with precious stones is yours to treasure. Olaf, as you are pure Viking, I hope you will treasure this amulet wrought and fashioned in both yellow and white gold. Brave archers, there are six leather pouches here containing silver coins and one extra gold coin for Rhys for taking good care of Olaf in battle. These are not only a gift from the Prittlewell Priory but from the Anglo-Saxon King Sæberht who died four hundred years ago. His tomb is well hidden and we shall make sure the Normans never find it." Olaf's party thanked the Prior and Swein for their generous kindness and then drank until they fell asleep by the warming Yule-log.

(Editor's note: The actual tomb was finally uncovered by Sir Tony Robinson and his Time Team in 2003, over 900 years later.)

The day dawned late with a heavy fog which had come off the sea to engulf the ship and the priory as the sun tried hard to break through. The prior was taking a service in the chapel with the monks but a cauldron of hot porridge or grøt, as Olaf called it, was being kept warm by the fire. They breakfasted quickly while Esla scribbled a note of thanks on some parchment and the team returned to the jetty where the sailors were brewing some soup. Within minutes the sail was up and the cog was being pulled out to deeper water by the brisk but biting West Wind that the Greeks named and personified as Zephyrus. Esla cuddled up tightly to Olaf for warmth and pulled her fur hood around her ears. Rhys called out from the sterncastle "Put him down Esla, you'll wear him out!"

Olaf laughed but was happy for the extra warmth, not to mention the affection being given so freely.

Fortuitously, the gentle zephyr from the West soon became a powerful Sou'wester as the sailors put it and, with the wind now at their backs, they headed around the East coast of England at a goodly rate of knots. By sunset, they had passed East Anglia and were approaching the mouth of the Wash when the sailors turned the ship into the wind and began tacking in a zig-zag fashion to manoeuvre the vessel Westward along the Norfolk coast to a small hunting lodge and fort grandly entitled Wisbech Castle. Built of wood, it wasn't much of a castle, but Rhys had said the owner was someone of whom he had heard and who was fiercely opposed to William's invasion. He may well be a good man to get on side as he was reputed to have killed a bear with his bare hands. Olaf thought again of Eric and smiled to himself.

Mooring the boat, they disembarked and made their way along a small road that led to the lodge which was lit and emitted the pleasing aroma of a log fire. Banging on the heavy door, it finally swung open and revealed a housekeeper who peered suspiciously into the darkness at the travellers.

"We are looking for Hereward, the one they call The Wake," asked Rhys.

"Some call him Hereward the Exile as he was outlawed by Edward the Confessor and is now staying in Flanders with Count Baldwin V. I am Leofric the Deacon and I am ensuring that his property is safe. Do you have news from London? If you have you may come inside and warm yourselves. I have not enough food for eight of you but I do have a warm fire with plenty of ale and mead which I am prepared to share with you for any news about the invasions."

They all shuffled into the spacious hunting lodge and Leofric produced flagons and drinking horns along with two large jugs of ale and mead.

"I get precious little news stuck out here although I did hear that the Bishop of Peterborough died of his wounds on that bloody battlefield they are calling Senlac and our monks sent a replacement down to London who was installed by a thirteen-year-old boy who is now the King. Am I right in saying he was Edgar the Ætheling?"

"You were right Father Leofric," said Rhys, "only now the Normans are in London. Edgar and most of the remaining nobles and clergy have sworn fealty to William and yesterday the Archbishop of

York placed the Crown of England on that Norman's head and anointed him with Holy Oil in Westminster Abbey. But sit you down and we will tell you of the fun we had on his Coronation Day."

There was laughter from the party and they pulled up benches and filled their flagons as Leofric listened wide-eyed.

At the hunting lodge in Barking, William awoke with an aching head and was not in a mind to go back to London whilst the locals were still in such a dangerous mood. But he did order his men back in to demand that locals be forced to help in the building of a central wooden castle inside the London Wall to prevent any further uprisings in the city. As he peered into the mirror while shaving, his broken nose reminded him that Olaf still lived, and he pondered the vengeance he must wreak upon this upstart. His Coronation had been ruined, he had been publicly humiliated and one of his closest officers had been seriously wounded. His fury knew no bounds and he sent inquisitors into the city to try and extract any information they could about the riot and the fire. He had so much to do as the country was far from being conquered. He called in Hugh d'Avranche and ordered him to ride North into Mercia and Northumbria and demand that the brothers Edwin and Morcar ride back with him to Barking to swear fealty to the new king. He sent Odo to hold Dover and rewarded him with the lands of Kent. William fitz Osbern was given the Isle of Wight and all lands adjacent including the Wessex capital of Winchester where he commanded a castle should be built.

Thus, ended that fateful year of 1066 with England a conquered land. Castles were springing up everywhere to subjugate the English. Edwin and Morcar, the two most powerful of the surviving English nobility, returned with Hugh d'Avranche and arrived at Barking early in 1067 to swear fealty to William, seeking pardon for any hostility they had shown him and surrendering all their property and themselves to his mercy. William kept them with him as hostages and arranged a trip home in March from Pevensey, taking with him Archbishop Stigand, Edgar Ætheling and the earls Edwin and Morcar to limit the chance of revolt in his absence. He was greeted as the conquering hero in Normandy but the English came with him as part of his retinue rather than as captives and were treated honourably. He was reunited with his wife Matilda who was now declared Queen and who accompanied him on his victory procession across his Dukedom. The festivities continued from Easter through to late Summer with William endowing various churches with great riches, purloined from his conquest. It was all too good to be true for William until, in late Autumn, ominous news began to filter across the channel from England that an insurrection, encouraged by what was left of the Godwin family, was in the offing.

Chapter Nine
Olaf in York

Father Leofric had listened intently to the stories of the assembled guests when there was a bang upon the door. It was the captain of the boat who bore a worried look:

"Forgive my interruption but we have a small crisis looming. That Sou'wester is whipping up into what could be quite a storm."

"Do you have food on board?" asked Leofric.

"We do indeed, sir," replied the captain.

"Well, then I suggest you return with Rhys and his men and collect all you can carry and return here with your crew. Olaf, you should stay here and look after the young lady."

Rhys shook his head ruefully: "Every time, isn't it?"

Olaf grinned. The six archers and one sailor battled out into the icy wind with flecks of snow swirling about their faces and returned half an hour later with the other three members of the crew and all the victuals that the boat had in its stores. Leofric was delighted as his own stores were depleted:

"Well, that's more like it! We have enough here to see us through till Twelfth Night!"

The storm raged for a couple of days and the sailors were reluctant to leave the relative safety of the Wash for the very angry open waters until things had calmed down enough for them to head out and up North to the Humber Estuary and thence up the River Ouse towards York - just as Hardråda had done last September. The delay in their sailing meant that whilst they were hunkering down in the warmth of the cabin, Hugh d'Avranche and his body of knights were battling on horseback through the wintry conditions over terrible roads to reach Morcar in Mercia and Edwin in Northumbria. As it transpired, they were both in York having rescued their sister, the Dowager Queen, now deposed, Ealdgyth and a young baby named Harold. Incredibly, d'Avranche reached York in just five days and delivered to the earls the good tidings of their summons to London by the newly crowned King William I of England. This was received by them both with no surprise, but with a fatalistic resignation of something that was unavoidable and inevitable. Edwin and Morcar decided it was probably for the best to protect their interests if they did travel back down to London, or Barking as it turned out, in order to make peace with the new power and authority in the land. They could not have guessed that they would be taken to Normandy and paraded around the Dukedom as part of William's eight-month victory celebrations.

When Tostig was Earl of Northumbria in 1064, authority North of the Tyne was held by Gospatric of Bamburgh who had unwisely headed to Westminster to threaten Tostig that Christmas. On the orders of Queen Edith (Tostig's sister), Olaf and Rhys had killed him and his six guards. After the great Northern rebellion of 1065, Tostig was ousted and Morcar was declared Earl of Northumbria. His first act was to cede Gospatric's authority North of the Tyne to his nephew, Oswulf, to keep the peace. Imagine Morcar's horror, therefore, after arriving in Barking to swear fealty in January 1067 to discover that King William had appointed Copsig, Tostig's thegne and claimant to Bamburgh, as the new governor of the northern part of Northumbria.

On the last day of 1066, Olaf and his party, having landed at Ricall on the River Ouse, paid and thanked the sailors, and made their way up to York on foot. Olaf, with the adoring Esla, realised he might be in an awkward situation seeing that he was, in all certainty, going to meet up with two previous lovers.

They reached the Southern gate of York at sunset and Olaf had another flashback, this time of the slopes of Fulford Gate and the English warriors slipping down the bank into the river to be surrounded and massacred even as he managed to get Edwin and Morcar through the gates to safety with less than half his force. The gates were now shut and guarded. Olaf called out to the sentry:

"We ask that you let us in. I am Olaf and have served the late King Harold and am friends with the Earls Edwin and Morcar."

The guard called back from a watch tower:

"You are too late. The Normans have been here ahead of you and have left, taking the two earls with them to swear fealty to William."

Olaf was shocked to hear this news as he was counting on them to organise some resistance from the North.

"That is most unfortunate. Will you not let us in? I own a house within these walls, this lady here is a maid of the Queen and these men have fought for the late King. Is the Queen still here?"

The sentry replied: "If you mean the earls' sister Ealdgyth, then, yes, she is here and staying at Earl Morcar's apartments. I'll send word to her, but I have orders that no-one is to enter or leave York at this time."

After an eternity of about twenty minutes, the bolts were slid back and the gates creaked open. The party crossed under the gateway into York. The guard had said that the Queen would wish to see them in the Great Hall. Using the massive Minster of York to guide them, they soon made their way to the stairway of the Hall that was so familiar to Olaf. Looking across the grass close, Olaf could see a light and a smoking chimney coming from his cottage and he hoped that Astrid was still there. Olaf led Esla up the stairs and the Welshmen followed. Olaf used his bow to knock on the heavy door which was immediately opened by two guards who recognised Olaf.

"Ah, it's you, Little Norseman. Come in, you are expected. Wait here and I'll inform the Queen."

The group shuffled in out of the cold. A heavy tapestry hung between them and the hall, so they had no view of who was there.

"It is Olaf and a party of archers come to call upon you m'lady."

"Well show them in for goodness sake!" shouted an imperious voice. Esla recognised it at once.

"Lady Fionne!" And she rushed past the tapestry dragging Olaf with her. The hall was warm with a roaring fire and two sleepy wolfhounds were hogging the best place in front of the hearth.

In a large high-backed chair to one side of the fire was the widowed Dowager Queen, Ealdgyth.

"Olaf and Esla! I am so happy to see you both safe. And who are these brave men who have escorted you? I recognise you do I not?" she said pointing.

"Rhys of Prestatyn at your service ma'am. And these are my lovely boyos, but their English is a bit limited mind as they all come from North Wales. I'll introduce them to you. This is Arwen, then Osian and Griffith who we call Griff, then Gethin and, finally, the youngest, Rodri. They all served your husband the King at Caldbeck Hill that they call Senlac. It was a terrible fight and I'm sorry we couldn't save him."

Each of the tall longbowmen had come forward and bowed to the Queen in an act of fealty and the Queen nodded and smiled into the faces of each. Fionne stood tall and imperious behind her.

"Well, my two brothers Edwin and Morcar have left with the Normans and taken some of their men with them, so we have plenty of spare beds for you all. Olaf, I expect you would like to go and see Astrid. Esla, come and sit by me and tell me of your great adventure." Esla looked astonished as she had never heard Astrid's name mentioned before but did as she was bidden, giving Olaf a long, hard steely look.

Olaf made his way across the grass close to the cosy cottage he remembered so well. He found the door on the latch and pushed it open. As always, a cauldron of venison was cooking gently by the fire watched by a toddler standing in a protective wooden cage filled with cushions. Nearby was a crib containing a sleeping baby and there was Astrid with her back to him, peeling vegetables.

"Is that Olaf the Heartbreaker?" She spun round and threw her arms around him with her characteristic squeal.

"How did you know I was coming to see you?" asked Olaf.

Queen Ealdgyth sent this little bundle over for me to look after with a message to expect you sometime soon."

"So, whose baby is that?"

"Ah, this is baby Harold, the Queen's son who will never see his father. Or will he? He does seem to have his father's look's and I don't mean King Harold!" Astrid threw back her head and laughed before hugging Olaf in a muscular embrace.

"Come here you naughtiest of Vikings!"

Olaf noticed that Astrid was no longer a bubbly, slight young girl but had filled out considerably into a strong woman.

"And who is this young man? Don't tell me it is Anders? How he has grown and, yes, he does have quite a lot of Renweard about him."

Astrid's smile dropped and her face became saddened:

"I will always have Anders to remind me of my poor darling Renweard."

"So, you have not remarried then?"

"No, I have had the attentions of Earl Morcar to keep me busy. He doesn't think I'm properly born for him to marry but I don't think he'll ever marry. He just showers me with gifts and trinkets and makes sure I want for nothing. Certainly, I comfort him on a cold winter's night but I am a widow and he is still young and has his looks. I know the Church disapproves but that's because they never get any!" Again, Astrid threw back her head and laughed and little Anders rattled the wooden bars of his playpen. Olaf joined in the laughter.

"Are you staying for supper my darling boy?"

"No, but thank you. I am balancing a difficult situation with the affection of the Queen's maid, the possible desire of the Queen's Lady in waiting and the fully established affection of the Queen herself. If I were to stay the night with you there would be an earthquake."

Astrid sighed and smiled:

"Then I suggest you may only safely sleep with the Benedictine monks, but from what gossip I have heard you wouldn't be that safe there either."

Olaf laughed, kissed Astrid warmly and inspected the sleeping baby:

"He's a good-looking boy, there's no doubting it, and he doesn't have the Saxon nose!"

"Off to your Royal dinner and fine ladies now and say goodnight to Anders or you'll upset him."

Olaf did his duty as uncle and left with a warm heart for Astrid, a girl who never failed to amuse him.

He returned to find that the servants had been hard at work and the hall was now laid and set for a feast. Queen Ealdgyth sat at the head of the table with Fionne on her right and Esla on her left. Next to Fionne she had seated Olaf and next to Esla she had seated Rhys, much to the annoyance of the maid who was still fuming regarding Olaf's visit to an ex-mistress - or so she believed. The archers were all interspersed with pretty, noble ladies from York who were variously appalled at having to dine with common soldiery and equally intrigued at their youth and good looks, coupled with an atrocious command of the English language. After a few flagons of wine though the language barriers were overcome amidst much laughter, fluttering of eyelids and flirting on both sides. Esla was not happy but made polite conversation. Olaf sat, wide-eyed in terror, as Fionne massaged his upper thigh and gave him that terrifying 'I choose you' look that he knew only too well. As the wine began to take hold of the diners and the hour grew late, the Queen made an astonishing announcement:

"My ladies and you brave soldiers, I must retire to my chamber. Ladies, I invited you because your menfolk were slain either here at Fulford, Stamford Bridge, or down at Hastings. These brave boys fought at the King's side and are the few survivors. Should you wish to comfort them or wish them to comfort you then I see this as nothing the Church could object to. I shall convene a war council tomorrow for which I need to prepare tonight. The rest of you, I bid a good night." Esla squealed in anger and frustration and dragged an uncooperative Rhys away to her sleeping quarters. The others drifted away kissing and caressing each other.

Esla was more than a little drunk as she had been drinking hard to drown her anger at her lover being taken from her in this way. She had hoped to make Olaf jealous by going off with Rhys in such an obvious way but he had not stirred. Pulling Rhys into her allocated chamber she tried to kiss him but got no response. She pulled his hand onto her breast, but he just froze.

"Do I not please you, Master Rhys?"

Rhys was awkward and embarrassed and not at all his usual assured self.

"My lady Esla, if I tell you the most difficult secret that I hold in my heart will you swear by all that is holy never to divulge it to a single soul?"

"Well, I am more than a little drunk, so I probably won't remember it by the morning. But I am intrigued so yes, tell me."

"Well, it is very difficult for me to confess to this, but may I ask you, did you fall in love with Olaf when you first saw him or later?"

"Well, he was wounded, and I was desperate to help him so yes, almost immediately."

"He saved my life in Wales and was so kind to my boys and I took to him in such a way I have never felt for anybody. I followed him and looked after him in many battles across the land. There was nothing I wouldn't do for him. I love him, you see. There now, I've said it. The Church would burn me for that but was it not the Church that teaches *'the greatest of these is Love*?"

Esla listened, shocked but then understanding.

"Well, I wasn't prepared for that one. Olaf has no idea I suppose?"

Rhys shook his head.

"Well, Rhys, I think you have sobered me up quite a lot. We must spend the night together if just for appearances, but I swear to you that your secret is safe with me."

Rhys and Esla were now bound by a sacred bond of secrecy and they both slept in separate beds as brother and sister.

Back in the hall Olaf was left with the two sleeping dogs, the Queen and her lady in waiting. Ealdgyth stood up and spoke:

"I will take the dogs out and check on baby Harold. Fionne, would you kindly show Olaf to his room and see that he has everything he needs."

"Of course, ma'am."

And there was peace in the Great Hall at York.

Chapter Ten
The fate of Copsig

Queen Ealdgyth had once been Queen of Wales and her mind was full of ways to plot uprisings against the Norman invasion using forces from different parts of the country. She had many good contacts in Wales and Hereford, including the aptly named Eadric the Wild. She did not know Hereward but was delighted with Olaf and Rhys' contact with Father Leofric who was Hereward the Wake's Deacon and bondsman and could raise Caine in and around Peterborough and Ely. She had been good friends with her sister-in-law Edith, another Dowager Queen, and a Godwin, who was based in Winchester. Her two brothers could summon insurrection in the North and she had Olaf to send to either Norway or Denmark for help. And finally, there was Edith Swanneck who had no less than five boys fathered by Harold Godwin, and then Harold's mother Gytha. Gytha was seething for revenge having lost four sons (Harold, Tostig, Leofwine and Gyrth) and her youngest, Wulfnoth, was still held in captivity in

Normandy. With all this in mind, she summoned what she chose to call a Council of War.

Ealdgyth opened the proceedings in an unexpected way:

"Good morning, gentlemen, I trust you all slept well?" There was embarrassed murmuring and Rhys thought that, judging by the bags under their collective eyes, they most probably didn't get much sleep at all.

"We have a problem here in Northumbria," she continued, "and it concerns problems left over by Tostig. He was hated whilst he was Earl here, so much so that his brother Harold had him deposed and banished by order of King Edward the Confessor. In his place he put my brother Morcar who was made Earl, and the peace was sealed by Harold marrying me. The first thing that Morcar did was to appoint Oswulf, nephew of the murdered Gospatrick of Bamburgh, to have control of land above the River Tyne. But that idiot William has now appointed Copsig, Tostig's equally hated lieutenant to an earldom of Oswulf's part of Northumbria and he is demanding back Bamburgh as his ancient family home. We will have civil war here if this is not sorted and we need to be united against the Normans. Olaf and Rhys, take ten of Morcar's warriors and your five archers and head towards Bamburgh and see if you can stop Copsig before he gets there."

Olaf rolled his eyes; he knew he should have got some sleep last night. The Welsh bowmen were probably thinking the same, but in Welsh.

"Esla will stay with me and she may return to my employ. Now set off and you have my blessing to use any force necessary to stop Copsig or even Oswulf for that matter. Oh yes, be careful of Oswulf, he has considerable support up North and if he even gets a sniff that you two killed his uncle Cospatric then withdraw to York."

Rhys' face lit up in recognition:

"Ah, now I know who you mean. That would be the big boyo we skewered outside the tavern down by the Embankment, wasn't it?"

Olaf remembered it clearly as it was his arrow.

"All right, enough chatter, go and see the farrier and the armourer. There will be horses and weapons for you to collect and the kitchen has prepared food for your saddlebags."

It was clear that Queen Ealdgyth hadn't slept much either to have so much prepared and ready for their journey.

Within an hour, the small group of seventeen riders were setting off out of York and heading North to Bamburgh, a good two-day journey. To reach Bamburgh they followed the road to Newburn on Tyne. There, had they known it, was Copsig himself and his entourage, enjoying a good rest after a very long journey. Copsig had brought a considerable sum of money with him and was generously treating his men to a lavish banquet. Oswulf had fled from Bamburgh when he had word that Copsig was coming with a force of armed men. He took refuge in the forest but put word around that the invading King's tax-collector and Tostig's number two were on their way and that he needed men to fight them. There was no shortage of volunteers and, by the evening of the banquet, Oswulf felt strong enough to swoop down to Newburn on Tyne and catch Copsig stuffing his face with a capon and downing a copious quantity of ale. Oswulf's men burst into the hall, scattering the diners from their benches, and laying about them with swords and axes. Copsig managed to crawl under a table before making a dash for the door, slamming it behind him just seconds before an axe embedded itself in the wood. Desperately, he ran to the only place of comparative safety, a small wooden church across the courtyard. As he turned to close and bolt the door, he saw Oswulf and his followers pour from the banqueting hall with shouts of:

"There he is! Surround the church!"

Copsig slid the solid metal bolt across and leant back against the door, his eyes desperately seeking another door in the darkness before it was too late. There in the corner was a heavy curtain and behind this was the vestry door. But it was too late as there were axes already hammering at this one last exit which fortunately was already locked. He would have to wait until dawn and then perhaps surrender. Oswulf had other ideas. Soon, fire arrows were thudding into the wooden-thatched roof and the lit torches the raiders had carried were now being tossed through the window slits. Copsig was literally being smoked out. It wasn't long before Copsig, his eyes and nose streaming and his lungs gasping for air through the thick smoke, came staggering out of the main door of the church. He fell to his knees, coughing violently. Oswulf shouted: "Hold him!" and two burly men pined his arms behind his back. There was no negotiating. Oswulf swung and his axe slammed into Copsig's neck, severing his head with a single blow and causing all who were near to be showered with warm blood. There was a quiet, dull thud as the head hit the grass. There had been no time to scream. Copsig was dead in an instant. Now, all was still, save for the crackling of timbers in the old Saxon church and the sweaty panting of Oswulf the executioner.

Olaf and his small fighting force reached Newburn on Tyne the following morning and were immediately aware that a fight had taken place in the town centre. There were bodies laid out on the grass outside the banqueting hall built in the Viking style. Although it was raining, the remains of the small Saxon church of St Michael and All Angels were still smouldering and a body of clergymen were chanting some funeral rites. An altar boy was swinging a small silver thurible, filling the air with the aroma of incense. Quite a crowd had gathered around a body of a wealthily dressed corpse whose severed head had been placed at his feet. Overhead, a number of crows had assembled, scenting business, and they cawed to their colleagues who were forming an orderly line on the roof of the hall. The circle of villagers opened at the site of armed men approaching, enabling Olaf and Rhys to inspect the bodies and listen to what people had to say. It appeared that William had sent a new Earl to collect taxes who had been one of Tostig's men. They referred to him as Copsig but when Olaf picked up the head, he recognised the face of Cospatric of the line of Uhtred of Bamburgh. Rhys spoke up to clarify:

"Not to be the same as his uncle Gospatrick who we skewered by the Thames....confusing isn't it?"

"I remember this lad when we had to ride to Bamburgh to set Tostig's dinner trap for him. Well, he won't be getting his inheritance now, that's for sure. Who has done this?"

The villagers seemed more relaxed when they heard Olaf's Viking accent. It was the Southerners they couldn't abide.

"It was Oswulf and some local men," said a villager. "I was working in the kitchen and saw it all. If you have coin, I have enough left-over food to feed your little army here."

"Sounds good to me," said Rhys, "I think we've seen enough dead bodies for one day."

Olaf and his entourage of sixteen men filed into the hall, pleased to get out of the rain, and the cook was happy to receive a second payment for his culinary skills. These were so much enjoyed that they decided to postpone their advance until the following day or, at least, until the rain stopped.

Olaf and his men slept in the warmth of the hall, having been well fed and watered and, in the morning, they decided to continue North

Bamburgh

to try and catch up with Oswulf and his men. What they did not realise was, as they slept off the hospitality Copsig had organised for his now deceased party, two of Oswulf's supporters had ridden out to warn him of the arrival of Olaf and his band. Oswulf had reached the small fort at Alnwick when the news arrived and decided to stay put rather than attempt to reach the castle at Bamburgh and risk being caught on the march.

Olaf's men reached Alnwick mid-afternoon following very easy to follow tracks on the muddy path. Stopping just out of arrow distance,

Olaf and Rhys rode forward to parlay. The gate of the fort opened and out rode Oswulf with two burly locals.

"What is it you want and why are you following us?" Oswulf was full of suspicion and carried a spear at a threatening angle.

"We have been sent to keep the peace by Queen Ealdgyth, sister of Earl Morcar, who gave you your title. By what we have seen at Newburn, it seems we arrived too late. Did you know that you have decapitated an appointee of the new Norman King?"

Oswulf growled: "I am the Earl up here and Copsig had a claim to Bamburgh. Wait! I remember you now.....at Bamburgh, you were with Copsig when Tostig sent that peace invitation to dine and slaughtered our people!"

Olaf had already tensed up and was ready for Oswulf's clumsy stab at him with his spear. Grabbing the spear with both hands and deflecting it from his stomach, Olaf pulled Oswulf from the saddle and snatched the weapon from him. Oswulf, though unhorsed was able to keep hold of the saddle and was attempting to stop his horse from turning away so that he could reach his axe which was attached to the saddle bag. It was just the seconds Olaf needed to spin the spear around, spur his horse forward, and plunge the lance into Oswulf's chest. He gasped in surprise at the speed of the attack and fell back into the mud leaving his horse free to gallop away. The two large local men had drawn their newly acquired swords, purloined from Copsig's men, but never got the chance to use them. A whistling of arrows from the longbows behind struck their targets with deadly accuracy and both riders cried out as the missiles thudded into their padded leather jerkins.

"That's my lovely boyos for you. That one has collected three arrows in him and the other, two. None of them missed, you see?" Rhys turned his horse to re-join his men. Olaf sat looking at Oswulf struggling for his last few breaths. There was no sign of anyone in the fort coming out to continue the hostilities and he was out of range of any English arrow. He too rode to join the company. Killing at close quarters was never easy.

"Well, that appears to be our job done. We now have no need to carry on to Bamburgh, I suggest we head back to York."

Everyone was in agreement. They had kept the peace.....in a way.

Chapter Eleven
Uprisings across the Conquered lands

William had left Odo, Bishop of Bayeux, in Kent and William fitz Osberne in Winchester to guard the South of England whilst he was on his progress through Normandy. Their policy was to build castles using English labour and, from the comparative safety of motte and bailey constructions, maintain a policy of utmost subjugation. Not surprisingly, the English did not like it and plotted ceaselessly for a way to throw off the Norman yoke.

The first insurrection was somewhat bizarre, and it occurred at Dover. The castle's commander, Hugh de Montford and William's brother Odo, Bishop of Bayeux and the new Earl of Kent, had ventured North of the Thames to oversee a castle being built at Berkhamsted. They had taken a good many of their soldiers with them. For reasons best known to themselves, the men of Kent had decided that they didn't want Odo as their Earl but preferred Eustace II, Count of Boulogne and had sent messages asking for his help in taking Dover

Castle. This was odd because this same Count had attacked Dover in 1051. But he had joined a failed attempt to oust William in 1053 which resulted in his son being taken hostage and was, therefore, obliged to join William's army of invasion in 1066. Indeed, it was said that he was one of the four knights who had hacked Harold to pieces at Senlac. But he hated William and, therefore, might be helpful in supporting the men of Kent in their fight against the Normans. Furthermore, Eustace had previously been married to an English princess, Godgifu, daughter of Æthelred the Unready and sister to Edward the Confessor. Edward had tried to invest Eustace as castellan of Dover Castle, but a riot broke out resulting in over forty deaths. Nevertheless, the final big plus in his favour was that he wasn't a Norman.

Eustace received the news with enthusiasm and set about raising a small invasion force. He then sailed into Dover by night, hoping to hook up with a larger Kentish force at dawn and climb the cliffs to attack the castle. The Norman garrison, realising that the army arrayed against them was not large but was due to be reinforced by many more English warriors, decided to take the fight to Eustace and his Anglo-French army. The garrison threw open the gates and launched a frontal assault before they had even had a chance to form up. Unfortunately, Eustace's men had the clifftop at their backs and the Norman garrison succeeded in forcing many over the white cliffs and to their deaths on the rocks below. It was a total rout with the reinforcing army dispersing at the sight. Eustace managed to slip away leaving his men to their fate and took a ship back to Boulogne in the knowledge that all his lands given to him by William would now be forfeit.

Meanwhile in the Southwest, where the Godwin survivors had fled, things were starting to heat up. Harold's mother, Gytha had set up camp inside the walled city of Exeter. She was joined by Edith

Swanneck and her three boys, Harold's sons, Godwin, Edward and Magnus, all in their late teens and eager for revenge for the death of their father. Gytha had them sent to Ireland with money to raise a mercenary army. To the North on the Welsh borders, Eadric the Wild was already causing the Normans considerable grief around Hereford. Eadric was one of the wealthiest thegns in Shropshire and could maintain a considerable force in terms of weapons, horses and provisions. Gytha had sent a message to Ealdgyth in York to send a messenger to her nephew King Sweyn of Denmark to land in the North. Olaf was the obvious choice and was dispatched in the late Summer of 1067 to sail firstly to Norway and thence down to Denmark to plot another Viking invasion. To the East, after the death of Count Baldwin V of Flanders, Hereward the Wake returned to his estates around Ely and Peterborough to find they had been given to Norman knights and his uncle had been removed from his position as Bishop of Peterborough to be replaced by a Norman priest. The date for the combined uprising was set for early the following year. Ash Wednesday fell on February 6th in 1068 and this was the date that was passed on to William via his spies as the day of the great planned uprising of his newly conquered land. Although it was early December William decided he would brave the Channel and hasten back to England and nip this thing in the bud. He did not know where this conspiracy was emanating from but he was determined to find out. And so it was that William spent Christmas and the first anniversary of his coronation in London trying to gain intelligence of the forewarned insurrection.

Early in 1068, Gytha had sent out messages to other cities to rise up and join the general rebellion on February 6th. Unfortunately, several of these were intercepted and passed up to the King. William may well have had his suspicions but now he had rock-solid proof of where, and particularly, who was the guiding force behind this plot. Despite it being the depths of winter, William summoned the fyrd to supplement his cavalry and began the long march down to Devon to snuff out this Godwinson rebellion. For the very first time Normans and English were fighting on the same side.

On arriving at the gates of Exeter, it seemed there would be no fight as a delegation of citizens rode out to say that they would obey William and throw open the gates of the city if he would agree to tax them at the pre-conquest rate. Hostages were handed over in a show of good faith. William had yet to arrive. When he did, he found that, whoever was trying to sue for peace, had been replaced and the townsfolk were busy preparing the walls for a siege. Gytha and her supporters had persuaded the townsfolk to fight. William noted that the ramparts were all manned by fighting men. He ordered one of the unfortunate hostages be brought to the city's wall and blinded in full view of the defenders. This horrific spectacle only hardened the resolve of the men of Devon and their contempt for the new Norman King was articulated by a large Devon man showing his bare backside to the Normans and letting forth 'en farte lyk eek en thunderclappe' to the ribald cheering of the defenders, which drowned out the wails of the poor, blinded hostage.

The next eighteen days were filled with violence as the King's army attempted, without success, to storm the city and mine the fortifications. It seems that the sappers may have had some success as part of the wall collapsed. The defenders seemed well disposed to have continued to hold but for the desertion of Gytha and many of the Godwin faction who slipped away under cover of darkness to the comparative safety of Bristol, where they hoped that they might meet the Godwin boys, returned from Ireland with an army. Exeter sued for peace and were treated with surprising mercy by William who built a castle inside the city walls. After a short visit further West to Cornwall to put down a few small uprisings and disturbances, William decided to head back to Winchester to celebrate Easter there and sent for his wife Matilda to come and join him. He clearly believed that England was now safe enough for his queen and his daughters.

∽

Chapter Twelve
Return to Orknøye (Orkney) Olaf's Saga

Meanwhile, back in York, Olaf had spent a somewhat awkward time after returning from the scrap at Alnwick to bear the news that both protagonists were now safely dead. As Copsig, an appointee of the King, was beheaded it meant that William had no one to represent him in the North, particularly as he held both Earls Edwin and Morcar as hostages. It was only a matter of time before a sizeable force of Normans headed towards York. Before he left England, William had reinforced his decree that Olaf must be caught and brought to trial as a matter of the utmost urgency. This was vehemently bolstered by an incandescent Guillaume de Malet who radiated pure hatred and was still suffering greatly from the wounds and dishonour he had suffered at the hands of a mere archer.

The reason for Olaf's awkwardness was not from any Norman threat, it was that Queen Ealdgyth had been his lover and he was almost certainly the father of the baby Harold. Add to that the presence of Astrid, Esla and Fionne and that the indiscreet Esla had told Astrid about the predilection of Rhys towards him, then yes, awkward would seem to sum up the situation. Imagine then, Olaf's relief, when Ealdgyth told him of the message from Gytha Godwin asking her to send an emissary to the courts of Norway and Denmark with all possible haste.

By chance, a Norwegian trader in York had let it be known that he had a ship in Whitby returning empty to Bergen via the Orkney Islands and was inviting any paying travellers to help fill the boat. Olaf visited Astrid to ask if she wanted to return to Bergen to see her father. He knocked on the oak door of her cosy cottage with its smoking chimney and aroma of venison on the hearth. Astrid opened the door and squealed with delight at the sight of Olaf. He realised at once what a fool he had been. Balanced comfortably on her hip was her little toddler, Anders, son of the unfortunate Renweard, who had been briefly married to Astrid before being murdered in the Northern uprising against Tostig. Kissing Astrid then the toddler on the cheek, Olaf explained the reason for his visit:

"Hej Astrid!" Olaf spoke in Norse to his ex-girlfriend. "I stupidly thought of asking you to join me on the journey back to Bergen. I had forgotten about the little one."

Astrid laughed her high-pitched delivery that always alarmed those who did not know her.

"Oh, Olaf what an ass you are. I mean, herregud, you don't take a tiny toddler across the North Sea in a leaky trading ship. Are you mad? But you can do something for me. Will you go to 'Andershus' and see that my father is well. I hope he has not been driven to an early grave by that harridan hex that he married after Mother died. Tell him that I am comfortable here and we have named his grandson after him, that

I have a cottage and a stipend given by Earl Morcar and that Queen Ealdgyth, Mocar's sister, takes care that I am looked after."

Olaf smiled and was about to leave when he thought of the long cold journey from Whitby to Scapaflow:

"Any chance of some of that venison stew?"

Olaf said his farewells to Astrid, then to Rhys and the Welsh boys followed by Queen Ealdgyth and her ladies Esla and Fionne. With his bow, his sword given to him by Edgar Aetheling, letters and gold given to him by Ealdgyth, Olaf left his life in England behind him.

He met with Gunnar, the ship's one-eyed captain and his motley crew at an inn in York and made his way to Whitby where he was able to fetch a decent price for his horse. He boarded the sixty-foot trader and made himself as comfortable as was possible, grateful of the warm venison dinner Astrid had provided him with prior to his departure. The sails filled and off they set along the coast, past Lindisfarne and up to the coast of Scotland to the Northern tip before tacking right towards Scapaflow. Gunnar, the captain again tacked right before pulling into the port of Barvik (Burwick) for the night. There was a castle and a small monastery there and also an inn that looked inviting. Gunnar led the way and was immediately recognised with rowdy cheers by the revellers inside.

Olaf presented one of the coins he had been given by Ealdgyth to a large lady with beefy forearms, serving drinks.

"Will this cover some hot food and ale for my friends here?"

The gold coin glistened in the firelight as the bar lady held it up to inspect a coin that bore the head of King Harold Godwin.

"English gold!" she whistled through some missing teeth. "This'll buy you meat, bread and a firkin of ale. That's for the six of you plus you, of course, providing you behave. I know that Gunnar, 'ees bin ere before and likes a drink. You watch 'im though or he'll 'ave that gold off thee before yer knows it. I suggest ye rent a nice secure room upstairs so you can sleep with your money under yer pillow. I'll accept a silver coin for that." And with a mischievous twinkle she headed off to fix the vittles.

There was a cheer when Olaf announced he was standing the crew beer and food. Just as he was about to take a seat on a bench, two lean and fit-looking men walked up and peered down at him. They looked familiar.

"Don't we know you? Aren't you the archer from Norway who came to visit Jarl Thorfinn, God rest him?"

"Yes, and you had this squeaky girl with you who killed Einar of Brodgar," said the other. "Well, I never! Been in the wars have we?" he said noticing the scars on Olaf's face and arm.

Olaf didn't laugh very often, but at this he threw his head back and roared to the ceiling:

"In the wars you say? Herregud! I have barely been out of them. Sit down and have a beer with us if you'd like to hear just what wars I have been in, but it might take a while."

The two tall soldiers pulled up a bench as the firkin of ale was wheeled in on a trolley and the beer handed round.

Olaf drank a welcome draft from his goblet and wiped his mouth with his sleeve before commencing:

"Well then, I'll start with my first full battle. It was only six years ago but it seems a lifetime. I was working for Harald Hardråda as an archer-huscarl when we invaded Denmark and fought the Battle of Odense in 1061. Harald beheaded the traitor Kalv Arnesson who had helped to kill his father King Olav II, he had the head thrown into the enemy lines. We utterly destroyed the Danish army and many of their ships. A year later we sailed through the Kattegatt and fell into a trap laid by the King, Sweyn Estridson, at the Battle of Niså in August of '62. Again, we caused great destruction amongst the Danes but again Sweyn escaped."

The assembled company ate and drank noisily but then listened in wide-eyed silence. These two great battles were already the stuff of legends and sagas and yet this storyteller claimed to have been at both.

"So, why were you heading off to England when we last saw you? Why didn't you stay in the service of King Harald?" The voice was one of the two soldiers.

"Ah," said Olaf, "I was on a mission for Queen Consort, Tora, who had letters for her cousin Jarl Thorfinn and also for the Earl of Northumberland, Tostig Godwinson, brother of Harold. The two brothers invaded Wales and I found myself in the service first of Tostig and then Harold after I had saved his life while on the campaign. I took out an archer who was about to kill him from a castle wall in Wales."

Whilst the others were wide-eyed with awe, Gunnar's one good eye was half closed in scepticism:

"You saved Harold Godwin's life? Tchah!"

"Don't sneer," said one of the soldiers, "when we found him and his girlfriend, they were surrounded by a pile of dead bodies including the most wanted cut-throat in the Orkneys, Einar of Brodgar."

"It gets far more incredible, and I don't expect you to believe it, but this is how it happened. I'll only continue if you wish me to."

There was a unanimous chorus of "go on, go on!"

"All right, but here it starts to get complicated. Harold decided to go on a mission to get back his younger brother and his nephew who were being held hostage by the Duke of Normandy and he took me as his servant and bodyguard. During this journey we were shipwrecked in a storm off the coast and I saved Harold's life a second time by cutting loose a mast for him to cling on to as his knights, in their armour, were pulled under the sea."

A ripple of approval went around the room as all who were there had crowded around to hear Olaf's story.

"Then, when we were taken as William's 'guests', we went on a campaign with him and Harold saved two of his knights from quicksand at Mont Saint-Michel. For this William made Harold a knight but of course it was a trap. William was now Harold's overlord, and he made him swear fealty in a cathedral on the bones of a saint to support William's claim to the throne of England. William released us with one hostage, his nephew, not his brother and we returned to England with a character called William Mallett who is really Guillaume de Malet, a Norman spy preparing the location of William's invasion. Back in England, there was a great uprising against Tostig in 1065 when some two hundred of Tostig's huscarls were massacred by the men of Northumbria."

Olaf paused to quench his drying throat with a large gulp of ale, giving one of the two soldiers a chance to pose a question:

"So, what happened to that funny girlfriend of yours who stuck Einar through with a knife?"

"Oh, Astrid you mean? Well, we were lent a cottage in York by Morcar, a Northumbrian noble. Whilst I was away in Wales she was looked after by an English lad who worked for him and was a friend of mine. In my absence they became close and when I returned after a year, I gave my consent for them to marry as I was needed by Harold to go away again. I was given the cottage for my service in the Welsh campaign, but I gave it to them as a wedding present. During the terrible uprising though, many people were murdered if they were suspected of colluding with Tostig. The cottage had been in Tostig's gift, so they took the lad out and hanged him from a tree. He had just become a father too."

Olaf paused and drank again. From the bar came a sniff from the barmaid who wiped her eyes and blinked at Olaf who continued his saga:

"Harold, acting for King Edward, took a small force to meet the rebels who had marched South to Oxford. Unbelievably, although he had little option, Harold agreed to all their demands, the principle one being the immediate removal of his brother Tostig as Earl of Northumbria in favour of Morcar. This enraged Tostig but he had to go into exile where he plotted a return with the help of Hardråda's army. The King was so angered at Harold's giving in to the rebels that he became sick, and shortly after, died in early January 1066. Harold let me go, with a purse and a promise of a title and land. It wasn't to be. I returned to York and lived for a while with Astrid and her baby boy."

"Yes, but what about the battles?" shouted someone from the throng.

"I didn't have to wait long for those," said Olaf. "Three battles, each one greater and more terrible than the last. Whilst I was in York enjoying the September sunshine, a huge fleet was spotted sailing down the coast from the Orkneys."

"That's right!" shouted one. "They stopped at Birsay and took the Jarl's boys, Paul and Erland, with them and left Queen Tora to look after Ingebjørg, Lady of the Orkneys who had recently been widowed by the death of Thorfinn. They left behind Hardråda's daughter Maria, who was betrothed to Tora's brother Eystein Orre."

"Let him tell his saga!" shouted one of the sailors.

Olaf waited for quiet and continued:

"The huge fleet of some 300 ships landed with Hardråda, Tostig, my father Eric Slagbjørn and his huscarl friend Ødger and a vast army of battle-hardened warriors. Morcar had mobilised as many men as he could, and he unwisely decided to give battle outside the gates of York by the marshy ground of Fulford Gate. As many of the Norwegian army were known to me, I was keen not to be involved in killing any of my friends, so I stayed in the rear. From a high vantage point I was able to warn Edwin and Morcar of a ferocious flanking ambush by Hardråda and they pulled back into the city wall and survived. Most of the army were surrounded and massacred within an hour. Edwin and Morcar accepted the demand to surrender and were given two days to accumulate all the gold and silver they had to give, under the terms, along with many hostages to be delivered at a place called Stamford Bridge."

The audience murmured and nodded, for who had not heard of this great battle?

"What Hardråda did not know was that I had sent a message by ship as soon as we had word of the Viking fleet. Harold had his army standing by and was able to make a forced march to York in just five days. When the day of the surrender arrived, Harold and his army were already in the city in full battle armour. A third of Hardråda's army remained with the ships some five miles away. The rest were not wearing armour but were drinking beer and mead and celebrating the great wealth about to be handed over. When Harold appeared with his army there was complete confusion and the Viking army retreated to form up on the other side of the bridge. Harald ordered first my father Eric Slagbjørn and then my adopted uncle Ødger to hold the bridge single-handedly in a suicide mission to buy time to form a shield wall. My father fought ferociously on the narrow bridge, killing some twenty before falling to arrows and axes. Ødger fought in his place with equal ferocity until he was speared from under the bridge by some men in a boat. There were nearly forty English slain on that bridge. I was so distressed to see my father killed I determined to take revenge and in the many attacks on the shield wall I was able to get a shot at the huge figure of the man who sent my father to certain death. The arrow hit the giant king in the throat and he was immediately finished off by English warriors. The battle turned into a rout and most of the Norwegian army were killed including Eystein, Tora's brother and Maria's espoused. The youngsters were spared and Magnus, Paul and Erland who had been guarding the ships were among the survivors who returned in just twenty-five of the original three hundred ships." Olaf paused to drink. One of the soldiers spoke:

"Yes, we were at Birsay when they arrived. Poor Maria fainted when she heard she had lost both her father, the King, and her fiancé on the same day. Strangely, she never awoke from the faint and we believe she might have poisoned herself as she was well acquainted with such herbs, her mother being Elisavetha of Kiev, a famous practitioner of sorcery and medicine."

"I think you all know the rest," continued Olaf. "William landed at Pevensey a few days later and his army started ransacking Harold's lands and property. Harold, having just won a famous victory, believed himself invincible and rushed us all down to London. We were all exhausted and Edwin and Morcar's remaining forces after two battles declared themselves not fit for a long march or another battle. We had all the time in the world to recoup, destroy the Norman ships with our navy and wait for our army to build up to full strength. There were forces coming from all over England. It was already October and soon the Winter would be upon us. William's army was already foraging off the land. Harold had no archers to talk about and fought in the old Viking shield wall style. William's army was modern, well-armed and all professional fighting men. Their cavalry knights were the best in Europe, and they could combine infantry, cavalry and archers as both Harold and I had seen at Mont-St-Michel. Why on earth did he rush to do battle?"

There was much shaking of heads as Olaf paused to have his goblet re-filled:

"But despite all my advice we ended up on very favourable high ground overlooking this formidable army. The slope was steep and their cavalry struggled up the slope time and again. The fighting was incredibly fierce and at one point I thought we had broken them. However, William rallied them and our over-eager fyrd rushed down the hill after them and were cut to pieces by the regrouped cavalry.

After nine hours of intense fighting Harold was struck by an arrow and wounded. William led a killing party and hacked him to pieces. I nearly got him with a shot that glanced off his helmet, I think breaking his nose. The shield wall was now splitting into clusters. The few archers remaining retreated into the wood behind where we set up an ambush by a great ditch and took some two hundred knights down before darkness fell. But the King was dead and William the 'Bastard' had won the field. We had some skirmishes around London but that was it until London surrendered and William was crowned. We ruined his coronation though by setting fire to the houses around Westminster Abbey and I managed to badly wound William's spy Guillaume de Malet. So, I am now a wanted outlaw and fugitive on a mission sent by Harold's mother Gytha Godwin and his widow Ealdgyth to drum up some support from Norway or, more likely, King Sweyn of Denmark. So, that's it, any questions?"

"Yeah, what's the price on yer pretty blonde head?"

It was Gunnar who asked, and a roar went up, with the burly landlady threatening to throw him out.

Olaf took up the offer of a room for security as he was now very tired and very vulnerable. The two soldiers offered their services saying that they were more than happy to post guard outside. Olaf fell into a deep sleep, his bow and sword close by, his wealth of coins and letters under his pillow with a knife. Just telling his saga had been exhausting enough let alone living it. But, at no time had he mentioned his intimacies with Tora or Ealdgyth, the two queens who had helped his path enormously. Their honour must and would be protected at all costs.

The noise downstairs died down as the locals departed and the sailors made the best of the wooden floor by the fire. Soon Barvik fell silent with just the lapping waves on the shore to lull them to sleep. Even the seagulls had fallen silent under a bright moon.

Chapter Thirteen
Return to Norway

Olaf awoke to a knock on the door, which he had locked. Clutching a knife, he slid back the bolt and opened the door to reveal the landlady and the two soldiers. It was clear they had spent the night guarding his room as there were two chairs on which they had lent their weapons. The landlady carried a tray with steaming porridge, some freshly made bread and a flask of milk.

"Grøt!" exclaimed Olaf. "I feel as if I'm back in Norway already! Did you boys stay on watch all night? Let me pay you for your trouble."

The two soldiers bridled at this:

"It was no trouble, sir. You have been a guest of Jarl Thorkinn at Birsay. He was our lord. Anyway, the saga you told last night was incredible and we would not want any thieving cut-throats like Gunnar and his crew stealing away your money. You've earnt it.

Gunnar is not leaving until tomorrow as his crew are too unwell. We've found you a trimmer ship with a small professional crew answerable to the Lady Ingebjørg and the boys, Paul and Erland, who rule the Orkneys. They are sailing up to the Jarl's palace at Birsay and they leave on the tide, which is about half an hour for us to get there."

"Us?" said Olaf. "But, do you know, I don't even know your names!"

"Oh, that's not a problem, mine is Sigurd and his is Ulrik. The only problem is which is which?" he laughed. "You see, we are twins!"

Olaf stared at them. Same height, same features, same speech inflection and they could relay-talk without ever interrupting the other.

"Amazing!" exclaimed Olaf.

"But hurry now we must not miss this boat as we have to be in Birsay to report on our mission in Scotland to Ingebjørg."

Olaf threw his things together and leaving Gunnar and the motley crew snoring on the floor, slipped out into the biting morning wind and down to the harbour wall where Gunnar's tatty trading ship was berthed beside a sleek Karve (a longship used for both war and transport).

A tall muscular man of not more than twenty-five stood by his ship with his long blonde hair being buffeted by the wind. His crew were already in position at their oars and ready to cast off.

"This is Ari, he's the skipper," said Sigurd.

"Come on!" screamed Ari without any introduction.

They rushed up the gangplank and dropped into the narrow hull where there were a few seats not occupied by rowers. Another cry from Ari and the boat moved slowly backwards before turning expertly out to sea where the sailors waited for the great crack of the sail being caught by the wind before putting up their oars. Not until the ship settled and was sailing at speed, heading North up the Islands, did Ari turn his attention to Olaf.

"And who might you be that jumps onto my ship without asking?"

"He's with us," chorused the twins. "He was a guest of Jarl Thorfinn and Lady Ingebjørg when we worked at Birsay. He is trustworthy and will be welcomed at Birsay."

Olaf looked directly at Ari:

"My name is Olaf, son of Slagbjørn. I have served two kings and two queens: Harald Hardråda and Tora Torbergsdattir, Harold Godwin and Queen Ealdgyth of England. I am sailing on business to Norway and thence to Denmark. Thank you for taking me to Birsay. I should like to speak with the Lady Ingebjørg before sailing to Bergen."

Ari stared at Olaf, trying to take all this in.

"The kings you served seem to have met with ill-fortune. Are you some sort of Jinx or Jonah as we seafaring people say?"

"Both kings died in Battle after a lifetime of fighting. It was going to happen one day. Each died sword in hand."

Ari's eyes lit up: "Ah so you are of the old faith then? You are not a Christian?"

"I am baptised since Christmas Day 1065 in York Minster by the Archbishop himself."

Ari's eyes softened into a smile: "Oh thank heaven for that, I was about to get my men to throw you overboard."

Olaf got his cue from the twins who laughed heartily, and he followed suit.

"I now declare you a guest on board this ship in the name of Lady Ingebjørg, who I serve."

Olaf felt much safer now.

As there was no harbour at Birsay, Ari and his crew beached the flat-bottomed karve and climbed out onto the sand. Since they had been sailing all day the sun was just setting and the candles of the Earl's Palace were being lit. The building was set up on the cliffs, but it was just a short walk to the top.

Ari's crew held back so that it was just Ari himself, Sigurd, Ulrik and Olaf who approached the doorway. Ari smote the heavy door with the pummel of his dagger and then waited patiently for the door to open. The scraping of a metal bolt from the inside and the squeal of the hinges revealed an armed man, sword in hand being lit from behind by a tall thin man carrying a candle. The man with the candle called out into the darkness:

"Who are you, strangers, who disturbs us after sunset?"

"It is I, Ari, captain of Lady Ingebjørg's ship with the twins Sigurd and Ulrik who served Jarl Thorfinn. We also have a stranger with us from England who says he knows her ladyship."

The voice from inside replied:

"Ah! Ari, take your men around the back and tell cook that you may eat at the kitchen table. You may use your usual quarters. Stranger, you will remain where you are until we have identified you. Put down your bow and unbuckle your sword."

Olaf moved forward and there in the light was the unforgettable face of Thorkel, his long visage and thick lips twitching.

"Thorkel! It is I, Olaf, son of Slagbjørn!"

"Not Olaf the Fair?" said Thorkel pouting. "Oh no, he was such a pretty boy without scars or beard and a face that has seen a lifetime of battles. Step into the house and let's have a good look at you. It must be five years since you were last here." Thorkel paused, adopting his characteristic dubious pout to have a good inspection before declaring:

"Yes, those eyes, it is indeed you! Lady Ingebjørg and the two earls Paul and Erland are at supper in the hall with a few jumped up nobles from the island. Since Jarl Thorfinn died in 1065, they have taken control and are even more insufferable than they were before. Wait here, they have just started so it might be possible for you to join them."

After a few moments and some shouting from male voices, Thorkel returned with his trademark twitchy smile:

"Her Ladyship would be delighted if you would join her. The boys aren't happy about it, but she has moved a guest so that you might sit next to her. Please remove your bow and sword and I will show you through."

Olaf was announced and shown to the place next to Lady Ingebjørg. He was not indifferent to the glowering stares of the two earls, Paul and Erland. Ingebjørg smiled at Olaf and greeted him warmly:

"I am sorry my husband is not here to greet you. He would have loved to hear how you fared after you left with that very funny girl.... Astrid, I seem to recall?"

Olaf nodded.

"Let me introduce you to my two sons who have taken over from their late father. This is Paul and my youngest Erland."

Olaf nodded in their direction: "Ah yes, we have met already, the last time I was here."

"Yes, we remember you too," said Erland with a sneer, "claiming to be one of Hardråda's huscarls when all the time you were running away from him. Did you know we fought with the King at Stamford Bridge when the cowardly English ambushed us so that we had to fight without our armour? Just one of his huscarls held the bridge against the entire English army and slew forty of their number?"

The chatter was silenced as everyone stopped to hear what Olaf would reply. After a short pause Olaf spoke:

"I do not think you were at the battle Lord Erland, nor your bother. The huscarl who fought on the bridge was my father, Eric Slagbjørn, and he did slay many before being hacked down with his place being taken by another great huscarl, Ødger Skol, who was also killed but not before he had slain many more. There were indeed about forty dead on the bridge when Harold's army finally got across."

Paul rose to his feet and shouted over the table to Olaf: "So, are you telling me then that you were there at the battle, or did you hear others tell of this whilst you were hiding in York?"

Olaf was aware of Thorkel's hand on his shoulder and a sotto voce whisper to not rise to this provocation.

Olaf replied calmly to Paul's insult:

"I had been in the service of Harold Godwin for several years and was at his side when I watched my father being sent to his certain death by Hardråda. So, just as Harold took his revenge on his brother Tostig, I took my revenge on the man who ordered my father to fight a whole army on his own. It was my arrow that pierced Hardråda's throat."

There was a gasp from all at the table. Paul was still standing and his face had turned puce at this shocking revelation.

"What! This is monstrous! The most feared warrior-king in all Europe killed by a little upstart with a bow and arrow? You are lying! Who can vouch for this?"

Lady Ingebjørg raised her hand before Olaf was able to reply that all the witnesses except Rhys now lay dead at Senlac.

"Sit down, please Paul. I will not have you insulting our guests. We all know the story of David and Goliath and I know from those that returned that Harald did not allow any of the younger men such as his son Magnus and you both to take part in the fighting which is a great mercy. Eistein Orre, Queen Tora's young brother, was only nineteen and was killed on that day. Let us eat, now."

The servants came in from the kitchen bearing platers of meat and fish and Lady Ingebjørg turned her attention to Olaf.

"Olaf, you need to tell me how things are in England. Will the Normans try to invade here?"

"England is in turmoil, but the Normans are on the rampage. I think it is highly unlikely they will try to expand North until they have subdued the whole of England. They are building castles everywhere to suppress the people. The only hope to resist the invaders is to try and organise another Viking invasion from either Norway or Denmark and get Scotland to join in the endeavour. Otherwise, Scotland and Scandinavia will find they have a very warlike neighbour in Norman England."

Ingebjørg smiled:

"I may be able to help where Scotland is concerned as King Malcolm III has recently sent me a proposal of marriage! And, another thing, Queen Tora spent some time here when the survivors from Stamford Bridge returned. She confided to me that, with Harald dead, she would seek to make peace with Denmark and even seal the matter by marrying King Sweyn. So, Olaf, I strongly advise you to visit Tora in Oslo and then visit Sweyn to persuade him to invade England. Best do it quickly though as the peace signed between Harald and Sweyn is no longer valid now that one party is dead. Sweyn may very well think an invasion of Norway might be a good idea. Who do we have fighting in England? It will need to be coordinated."

"Well, it's a bit of a mess over there but if we can get the earls Edwin and Morcar to hold the North, rally the people around Edgar the Ætheling, Ealdgyth the dowager Queen and Gytha the mother of Harold and use the fighting prowess of Hereward around Peterborough, we could retake the whole of the North."

Ingebjørg starred at Olaf, her eyebrows raised: "You are quite a remarkable young man Olaf. I have Ari the navigator and my late husband's bodyguards, Sigurd and Ulrik, in my service so I will pay them to take you safely to Norway and thence to Denmark. If you are successful with Sweyn, tell him that his fleet are welcome to stopover here before sailing on to York. Thorkel, can you see to this?"

Thorkel made his most solemn and theatrical bow and, casting his most contemptuous pout towards the young earls, Paul and Erland, left the banqueting hall in the direction of the kitchen with the glad tidings that they were to leave by dawn's early light.

Chapter Fourteen
Anders' Will

Olaf managed to pass the rest of the evening in fascinating conversation with Lady Ingebjørg during which he was able to fill in the gaps in his knowledge of Norwegian history over the last few years. It seemed that Finn Arneson, her father, had escaped the horrors of Hardråda's snake pit and had survived as a prisoner long enough to outlive the Tyrant-King. When Tora returned as Queen Regent for her sons, Magnus and Olaf, one of her first acts was to have Finn returned to Halland which had been bequeathed to him by Sweyn. This move was a smart diplomatic gesture of peace with Denmark by Tora, who had marriage to Sweyn in mind, to strengthen her dynastic line via her two boys.

Thorkel saw to it that Olaf was put in one of the more comfortable rooms where he slept soundly until being awakened by the sunrise. The weather was set fair and before long the boat containing Ari and his crew were making good time bearing Northeast out to Bergen with a diplomatic cargo of Olaf and his letters from England and the twins as bodyguards. It was a day's sailing to the Shetland Island trading post of Lerwick where they sheltered for the night before making the two hundred-and twenty-two-mile journey to Bergen over a two-day period. Olaf missed Astrid's bright idle chatter which so passed the time when they made the journey to England. He decided to visit her father when they arrived and hopefully rest up for the night at his inn. The weather was favourable and by the second evening at sea they spotted the coastline of Norway. Everything seemed so different from the last time he disembarked in Bergen with a wounded Anders and strict instructions to flee from Hardråda by Queen Tora. It was quiet and sparsely populated - unlike when the entire Norwegian army had come through there. Ari broke into his reverie:

"Do you know anywhere where we might stay? This is more your territory than mine and you speak the language."

"What? Oh yes, I think so. If it is still there, it is called 'Andershus' and belongs to the father of an ex-girlfriend of mine who now lives in York."

"Excellent!" Ari slapped his leather-clad thigh. "Then that's where we'll head for a drink and a comfortable bed."

Olaf led the way down the cobbled, narrow streets trying to recall the journey of five years ago with donkey and cart, a wounded Anders and a simpleton named Aksel. As the memory came flooding back, so did Olaf's sense of direction and shortly 'Andershus' the travellers lodge, hove into view and Olaf knocked on the door with his bow. The door opened to reveal a middle-aged woman, whose natural scowl gave way to a frightened expression at the sight of four men she took to be fierce warriors.

"What do you want?" she demanded, half closing the door with one hand and pushing back an inquisitive teenage girl with the other.

"This used to be a welcoming lodge for travellers, where is Anders?" retorted Olaf. The woman raised her eyebrows in surprise:

"You know Anders? Who are you? Anders is very sick but you may stay the night if you pay up front." She opened the door to allow the four men to enter.

"I am Olaf, come from England, and these are good men in the service of Ingebjørg of Orknye. I am a very good friend of your stepdaughter, Astrid, who lives in Yorvick."

"Astrid! That harlot who stole all of Anders' money and ran off with some little goblin whom she had just met."

Olaf's eyes narrowed:

"Can I see Anders? I had promised Astrid to tell him her story. Lads, I'm sure this young lady will fix you some ale whilst I talk to the landlord."

The young girl was more than happy to lead Ari and the twins to a table near the fire and bring them some tankards of ale or öl as the Norwegians call it. The three men understood the Norse language well enough and were happy to chat to the chirpy lass, no more than sixteen, as her sour-faced mother led Olaf up to Anders' bedroom where they had last parted company along with Astrid's dowry.

The door was opened to reveal a darkened room and his wife called harshly into the chamber:

"Anders, wake up - you have a visitor. He says he knows about your thieving daughter, Astrid."

Anders sat up in bed and immediately asked for the curtains to be drawn. The light revealed a painfully thin face with almost grey skin, unkempt hair and beard:

"Olaf, is it you?"

"I'll leave you to talk to the stranger as I've got three others staying the night and I don't want to leave Solvej alone flirting with those young men."

Anders emitted a rattly laugh:

"Ah, you can't stop a young girl growing up. Now, Olaf, pull up a chair and tell me everything."

Olaf sat and gently told of the great saga of Astrid, how she became a heroine in Orkney, enchanted the monks and priests in England and how he let her marry an English lad named Renweard, with whom she had a son named after her father - 'Andersson'. Anders pale blue eyes glistened with tears as Olaf told of the brutal murder of Astrid's husband. Olaf related how he had left her in the care of the Earl Morcar who protected her even though she lived alone in a cottage in York with her son. Anders suddenly became animated:

"Olaf, do you remember my wound from an arrow?" Olaf nodded.

"Well, it never healed and I got some kind of blood poisoning and my wife called the Lech to come and cut off my leg. Since then, I have grown steadily weaker, and my wife often forgets to bring me food. I know I am not long for this world and I know my wife is often out visiting another man. They are just waiting for me to die so they can take control of my business here. Do you remember Aksel, the town idiot?"

Olaf nodded. He was not easily forgotten.

"Well, he comes here most nights around sunset for a flask of ale to try and woo Solvej, my wife's daughter from a previous marriage. Of course, she is not interested in such an imbecile as she is only sixteen and he at least forty. But I need him to do something so that he can finally be of some use to me. Please go down to the hall and wait for his arrival. You can't miss him as he is a gibbering fool. Tell him I wish him to go and fetch the notary and bring him back here as a matter of gravest urgency and Solvej may smile upon him. He's so stupid he should agree at once. When the notary arrives send him to me immediately and, on no account let my wife speak with him. Bring your fellows up here too and let none other enter. I may need them as witnesses. I have coin to pay them for their troubles."

Olaf descended the staircase and sure enough the high-pitched, slightly hysterical voice of Aksel was audible from the hall. From what Olaf could ascertain, Solvej had been rather taken by the long golden locks and nautical swagger of Ari and the gentle and polite manners of both Sigurd and Ulrik. She had no time for Aksel and asked her mother to fetch his ale. Aksel was not happy. Olaf came straight to the point:

"Aksel, do you remember me when I brought Anders home from the battle with his wound and you brought your donkey and cart to help?"

"No!" snapped Aksel.

"Never mind," said Olaf. "Do you know where the notary lives?"

"No!" snapped Aksel.

"Anders has said that if you do this thing for him, Solvej would be very happy and smile on your attentions."

"Come with me," said Aksel, striding towards the door.

The walk was a brief one as Aksel stopped outside a house and pointed to the door. Olaf knocked and was immediately greeted by an elderly, learned-looking man at the door.

"How can I help you?" he asked, looking curiously at Aksel.

"I am sent by Anders who is quite ill and wishes you to make out his final Will and Testament before he dies. Can you come immediately?"

"Well, yes, of course. We shall need three other witnesses besides myself. Can you manage that?"

"Yes, we have witnesses who are trusted men. My name is Olaf and I have taken care of his daughter Astrid on her journey to England.

She now lives in Yorvik, or York as they call it, where she has a son, but her husband was killed in an uprising. I think Anders wants to make sure, as his only child and grandson that their heritage is secure."

"Yes, yes quite so. Let us proceed." The Notary took his coat which was hanging on some antlers in the hall and ushered them out.

In a short time, they were back at Andershus and mounting the stairs to Anders' room. In a quavering voice, but with great determination, he dictated his will leaving all his coin and the power of attorney to his old friend the notary whom he had known all his life. The lodge and all its fixings he left to Astrid plus half of the considerable sum of money. His wife and stepdaughter could remain to run the lodge until such time as Astrid returned. The remaining money was divided up between his second wife and Solvej, less the fee for the notary and a little something for Olaf and his companions. Olaf went down to fetch Ari and the twins who entered the room and witnessed the signing by a very shaky Anders and then by the witnesses.

Downstairs, Aksel was trying to ingratiate himself with Solvej and by doing so revealed that he had taken Olaf to the notary and right now they were sealing Anders' will. There was a shriek and crashing of chairs being knocked over as Anders' wife rushed to the stairs just as the notary was leaving the bedroom with Olaf and the lads. Notwithstanding she managed to push past five men and stood in the doorway screaming at the dying man. The notary left with the power of attorney scroll under his arm and the knowledge that he already had the bulk of Anders' coin safely under lock and key. Olaf and his companions had organised for their tankards to be refilled whilst making it clear to Aksel that he needed to leave Solvej alone. Upstairs, there was no mercy for Anders' last few hours as his wife expressed her rage at not being present for his final will.

That night, sometime in the early hours, Anders passed away, alone and untended by his wife who had left the premises to visit someone and had not yet returned when Solvej discovered his body in the morning and gently closed his eyes.

Chapter Fifteen
Oslo

Olaf and his companions departed the same morning as the lodge was starting to fill up with an assortment of friends and relatives come to pay their respects, a decidedly tousled wife who came home to find she was now a widow, a priest and the notary who presented the lads each with a leather pouch of coins for their service. They bade farewell to Solvej, who was a little tearful, either at losing her stepfather, or of the departing Ari. Anders' widow could barely conceal her delight.

They returned to the boat after buying some stores for the journey to Oslo. Olaf was greatly relieved to be making that coastal voyage rather than the long trip North to Nidaros. The weather was set fair with a fine breeze and Ari and his crewmen cast off, heading South around the coast to the trading town on the Southernmost tip of Norway. Magnus had remained in his father's capital of Nidaros whereas his mother and baby brother quartered in Oslo. It had been an uneventful day's sailing and they hove into the natural port just before sunset. Ari and his crewmen made for an inn to buy some hot food and öl, whereas Olaf, with his two bodyguards, made for the palace of Tora Torbergsdattir and her young son.

Akershus slot or Akershus Fortress was a wooden bastion started by Harald Hardråda in 1065 to protect against invasion from Denmark or, less likely, Sweden. It overlooked the harbour where some of the pitifully few ships of Hardråda's ill-fated invasion of England now bobbed at anchor as the sun set on the horizon. Olaf made his way up the stone path to the wooden gate at the top where torches had been lit to guide their way with Sigurd and Ulrik keeping a close watch on the walls lest there be any archers with a mind to shoot uninvited guests. But it was all quiet with no guards or sentries posted. Olaf thought that if Sweyn of Denmark landed here with a small army he could capture Tora and the five-year-old king without any sort of a fight. At least the gates were locked. Olaf drew his sword as a precaution and beat on the great wooden gate with the pummel. There was no shouting or commotion, just the sound of footsteps of a single person making for the gate.

"Yes? Who is it? Are you expected by the Queen? There is a bell you know." Olaf noticed a small bell with a rope attached.

"Hello! I'm sorry, I didn't see the bell. My name is Olaf. I have come to visit the Queen Consort, Tora. I have business to discuss and letters from England and the Orkneys. I am sorry we are unannounced, but we have been travelling by ship. The Queen Tora does know me quite well." Olaf smiled to himself. "I am the son of Erik Slagbjørn, Huscarl to Hardråda."

"Herregud!" came the oath from behind the gate. "Wait for a moment and I'll inform the Queen. How many are you?"

"Just me and my two bodyguards sent by courtesy of Lady Ingebjørg of Orkney, Queen Tora's cousin."

After a short period, the wooden gate was opened and several unarmed men stood inside with torches, beckoning for them to enter into the square. It reminded Olaf of the courtyard in York with trees and flowerbeds and absolutely no resemblance to Harald's military barracks in Nidaros. At the far end of the courtyard a long hall emitted an inviting glow.

"It's been a long journey from Bergen, do you think we may seek your hospitality for my two companions here? I don't really wish to enter the Queen's presence accompanied by two armed guards."

"No, I can see that," said one of the men. "Don't worry, the Queen has a fine kitchen where we can take you." The twins visibly cheered up and, as there didn't appear to be any threat or danger to Olaf, they agreed with gratitude and peeled off with one of the retainers. Olaf was excited to see Tora again after five years.

The doors of the great hall were opened and the people inside, about sixty of them, were speaking quietly, at a respectful level, as they ate their food. So different to the bedlam of Harald's hall with raucous huscarls shouting at the tops of their voices. The Queen sat at the far end, unmistakable in the dim light. She sat upon an ancient Viking throne of carved stone padded with furs. On her head was placed a band of gold, another Viking work dating back hundreds of years. The elegant and regal beauty that had so captivated Olaf five years ago had been replaced by a haughty stare from sunken eyes that had lost their sparkle. If she was surprised to see Olaf, she hid it very well. There was not so much as a twitch of emotion. Olaf gave a bow that was not much more than a nod and looked straight into her eyes. Neither party faltered. The Queen spoke in a flat voice which betrayed no emotion:

"Are you really that pretty, young boy who came to court in Nidaros just five years ago? Those years have not been kind to you by the look of things." Olaf was thinking just the same thing about Tora.

"Queen Tora, I have fought many battles since then, sometimes on the winning side and sometimes not. I have been sent from England by King Harold's widow and his mother who are planning a great uprising to overthrow the Norman conquerors. They have asked if I can assemble a force from Norway and Denmark. It is said that you have an understanding with King Sweyn?" At this she twitched:

"You are well informed Olaf. Where did you hear this?"

"From your cousin by marriage, Lady Ingebjørn, wife of Thorfinn."

Finally, the porcelain cracked, and Olaf was relieved to see a barely perceptible smile:

"She must really trust you to divulge such information. Come closer as this is for your ears only, not these charming noblemen of Norway."

Olaf approached close to the Queen as the hubbub of conversation ensured that only he would be party to what she had to say:

"Olaf, dear boy, it is so lovely to see you, even though you have lost your looks. I have a son who is nearly six and is sleeping now. He is fair and gentle and will rule Norway as Olaf III. I will marry Sweyn and there will be peace between Denmark and Norway. My eldest son Magnus has a terminal illness and, even though he is only twenty, is not expected by the Lechs (doctors) to live much longer. He refuses to come to Oslo but stays in Nidaros and is much like his father,

Hardråda, unlike my son Olaf who will bring peace and stability to this country."

"Is he really my son?" whispered Olaf.

"Well, you only have to look at him to see there is no Hardråda Sigurdsson blood there. But I can tell you that no one must ever know of this, no one. If this gets out there will be civil war and I would have to have you killed. Have you told anyone?"

"Only my father, but he was killed at Stamford Bridge." Olaf thought it best not to mention he had told Freya.

"Good," she said relaxing, "you do understand, don't you?"

Olaf nodded.

"Is it true, the rumour brought back by Magnus that two giant huscarls held the bridge and slew forty English warriors? You were there, I gather, at Harold Godwinson's side?"

Olaf nodded sadly, "Yes, my father Erik Slagbjørn and a close friend, Ødger Skoll. It was a suicide mission when Hardråda discovered I was on the English side. But I did take my revenge."

Queen Tora's eyebrows raised sharply: "I heard that my husband was slain by an arrow through the throat fired by an archer at Harold Godwin's side. I saw you take out that warrior's eye when you first came to Nidaros, and a drunken clod offended you. Was it you who killed my husband, King Harald III of Norway?"

Olaf looked her straight in the eye:

"Yes, it was me."

"Well, that's two favours you've done for me in my life. God, I hated that man. Such a brute, a monster. And what of my poor, sweet brother, Eystein?"

"He died so bravely. He ran five miles from the ships to join the battle and was utterly exhausted when he arrived to fight. I am so sorry; he was my friend."

"So, I suppose you expect me to get another army and sail out for revenge? Well, I haven't any warriors to speak of and all the huscarls are dead. You will have to come with me to Denmark as I am due to visit Sweyn to discuss peace and marriage. At least I can't have any more children. Do you know he has fathered twenty children? What an animal! From Harald III to Sweyn II and all in the name of politics. It will protect Olaf's position here in Norway. Come, let's feed you and get you something to drink. I am a terrible hostess. A small table and two chairs were called for and Tora left her throne and sat with Olaf as victuals were provided and they talked long into the night.

Tora Torbergsdatter

Chapter Sixteen
Roskilde

The next day Olaf woke in a comfortable bed to the noise of seagulls and waves breaking. He was relieved that he had not been compromised once again by the Queen, given that she was betrothed to the King of Denmark. That might have been awkward.

He re-joined Ari and the crew members and waited for the twins to appear. Looking out to sea, Olaf drew in his breath as a huge longboat appeared out of the morning mist and Olaf immediately remembered when he had first laid eyes on it at anchor in Nidaros and his oath of "Fae Faan, it's huge!" That was in 1061, when he was eighteen and the boat was King Harald's flagship 'Ormen' (Serpent). Now, here it was, returned from England and ready to transport Queen Tora to the Danish capital of Roskilde. A shout distracted Olaf from watching this magnificent ship sail into the harbour.

"Olaf wait for us!" It was Sigurd and Ulrik.

"We weren't going to go without you," laughed Ari from inside the boat, "but you are always late."

"The Queen and her entourage are right behind us", said Sigurd, pointing up the stone pathway to the fort.

Ormen and its crew had already reached the jetty and manoeuvred in beside Ari's ship, which it dwarfed. The crew were busy making fast and lowering a gangplank when Queen Tora hove into view with a bevy of ladies in waiting and a few noblemen but not a single man at arms. Seeing Olaf, she veered off in his direction.

"Olaf," she called out, "we've been looking for you. You need to travel in this ship if we are to arrive at the same time. If you travel in that boat, you will arrive in Denmark about two days after us."

Ari bridled at this but there was some truth in what she said. They couldn't hope to keep pace with Ormen sailing through the treacherous Kattegat waters.

It was then that Olaf realised it was time to let Ari and the twins return home:

"Thank you for your service and your friendship Sigurd and Ulrik and Ari, thank you for your great skill in sailing and navigation. I must travel with Queen Tora now to Roskilde. Please report back to Lady Ingebjørg my thanks for her help on this mission. I hope our paths will cross again soon."

Sigurd and Ulrik looked crestfallen and disappointed, but Ari had a jaunty air.

"Alright then Olaf, we'll say our farewells, but I'm going back to Bergen to take Solvej away from that ghastly mother. She can come and live with me in Orkney." They all laughed, and the sad moment was gone. They bade each other farewell and the twins asked if Olaf would collect them on his journey to England, which was not a promise he could make, but said he would try.

Olaf boarded the great longboat and was invited to sit on fur rugs next to Queen Tora. There was much shouting of orders as the skilled crew pulled away out of the harbour. The Ormen had thirty-five rowing benches so the crash of seventy oars hitting the water was impressive. Olaf watched the shore as the figures of Sigurd and Ulrik waving on the levy grew smaller. He remembered his first journey on this boat, standing in the aft castle with the other Byzantine archers, including the legendary Urbicus Acropolites, who fell at Stamford Bridge - along with all the others. Then he had been sea-sick but now he was a seasoned sailor and he relished being seated next to Tora, breathing in the sea air and smelling the trademark scent of her alluring Jasmine. Olaf was alone and seated next to a queen who, last night, had threatened to have him killed, but he understood the gravity well enough and was as comfortable as he had ever been whilst crashing through the Kattegat to Denmark.

They finally reached the coast of Denmark, and the sailors lowered the great bloodred square mast and navigated the dragon ship into the Roskilde Fjørd where the crew rowed slowly to the waiting reception committee. Tora's ladies in waiting fussed around her, fixing her windblown hair and making her look as regal as they could on a dragon boat. Olaf took a backseat as the gang plank was lowered and Tora disembarked with her entourage.

The levy was crowded with Danes to greet them from the Royal Household and among their number was a face that Olaf recognised. He gasped in astonishment to note that the person who came forward to greet Queen Tora was none other than Finn Arneson! But if Olaf was astonished, Tora most certainly was not. Harald, having personally decapitated his brother, Kalv, at the Battle of Odense in 1061, had later captured the traitor Finn at the Battle of Niså in 1062. Harald had him kept in chains next to a snake pit but was prevented from enjoying watching the agonising death of the slippery advisor by two awkward facts. Firstly, Finn was Tora's uncle and, secondly Finn's daughter Ingebjørg was married to Thorfinn, Jarl of Orknøyar. King Harald desperately needed the Orkneys as an ally to use as a staging post for his planned invasion of England. So, Finn was spared and one of the first actions by Tora after hearing of Harald's death in 1066, was to free her uncle and allow him to return to his land in Halland in the service of the King of Denmark. It was a shrewd move as Finn was now the architect of the diplomatic marriage between his niece, mother of the new young Olaf III, King of Norway and peacemaker between Denmark and Norway. The stories of Finn's death in 1065 were quite untrue as Olaf could now attest and it seemed that Finn, as Tora's closest living relative, was going to 'give her away' at the wedding.

Finn greeted Tora as an uncle by first kissing her hand to acknowledge her status and then throwing his fur covered arms around her. Tora stood expressionless and as straight as a sapling as she disengaged herself from his hug:

"Where is the King?" she asked.

"Ah, he is with his warlords and councillors and is keen to meet the envoy from England. Is he here? I am instructed to make you and your entourage comfortable before the dinner tonight."

"The envoy of whom you speak is just here behind me, the blonde warrior carrying a bow,"

Finn peered past his niece into the setting sun and squinted to focus on the figure who had just disembarked.

"Olaf, son of Slagbjørn! How in the name of Thor and Odin have you survived? I heard you were all killed at the bridge near Yorvick, along with Hardråda."

Olaf smiled mysteriously:

"Ah, it's a long story. I was there at that terrible battle where my father and all the Huscarls perished, but I was in the service of Godwinson and was also there at his side when his housecarls were slaughtered near *Hastingas* by the Normans. I am here at the behest of Ealdgyth, dowager Queen, and Gytha Thorkelsdóttir, a Danish noblewoman, mother of the King Harold. All her sons were killed in 1066 and now she appeals to King Sweyn to help free England from the Norman tyranny."

"Yes, of course I knew Gytha, she had close family ties with Canute the Great, back when we really did rule England. So, I think it is time for these warriors to take you to speak with King Sweyn."

At a nod from Finn, two enormous Vikings carrying spears, stepped forward and smiled awkward craggy smiles. They gestured for Olaf to follow them up a steep slope to the castle while Finn excused himself with an obsequious bow to go to tend to Tora and her entourage.

The guards stopped at a large heavily studded double door and banged their spears on the stone floor, twice. The doors were swung open to reveal a Great Hall in the Viking fashion which was not so different to Hardråda's hall in Nidaros. At the far end was a long oak table surrounded by a bevy of men who, judging by their fine clothes, were Danish nobility. The tall man in the centre was clearly the King. He wore a band of gold around his head and his large hands were bejewelled with heavy rings set with precious stones. Looking up from the maps on the table, King Sweyn called out to Olaf in English:

"Ah, our visitor from England! Approach us friend, you are most welcome."

Olaf replied in the common language spoken by both Danes and Norwegian Vikings:

"Thank you, gracious King. My name is Olaf, son of Eric Slagbjørn. I am sent here by the late King Harold's widow, Ealdgyth to tell you now that the English would support your claim to the throne if you would join forces with Edgar Ætheling. Your uncle was Canute the Great, King of England and Denmark. You have a strong claim and a right to overthrow the hated Normans."

The King took a few steps closer to peer at Olaf who, clearly, was no Anglo-Saxon. He had a strong feeling he had seen this envoy before and in very different circumstances. He reverted to his native Norse:

"And why would Edgar Ætheling wish to support my claim when he is the last remaining heir of the Anglo-Saxon Royal house?"

Sweyn moved with a slight limp as one leg seemed shorter than the other and made it awkward for him to move his large frame smoothly. He looked older than Tora, which he was, and although in younger days he must have been handsome – handsome enough to have sired no less than twenty children, all with different mothers, and only one within wedlock, but now the years had taken their toll. Olaf thought the chances of Tora providing him with a legitimate heir were exceedingly slim, she in her early 40's and he just turned 50. It provided Olaf with the answer he needed:

"Well, my Lord King, forgive me for saying, but I know that you were born in England in 1019 which makes you fifty years of age. Edgar is still not yet twenty. He would be happy to grant you the throne of England if you named him as your rightful successor."

Sweyn threw back his head and roared with laughter and turned to his nobles and generals:

"Do you honestly think that, after I am dead, any self-respecting Viking calling me father would pay any attention to whom I had declared as my rightful successor?" The nobles joined in the mirth.

"This Edgar Ætheling, is he much of a warrior?"

Olaf couldn't lie on this one:

"No, great King. Indeed, he is not. I am wearing his sword which he gave to me saying that he was not worthy to wear it having signed away his birth right to the Godwin's and then the Normans.

"Good," roared Sweyn, "then I think we should proceed with our invasion plans. You must give me all the intelligence I need. Names of allies, strength in numbers and equipment, everything. You will join us for the next few months to plan this and I shall rely on you. If it works out, you will be rewarded. But first, I have a beautiful Queen to bed, erm I meant 'wed'..ha-ha."

The nobles, keen to flatter, joined in the laughter. Olaf thought to himself: *you have no idea who you are taking on, that's for sure.*

Olaf took his leave and was taken to his quarters, which were sparse. He hoped Tora's were fit for a queen. That night, Sweyn and his nobles gave a great feast in honour of his future wife. Olaf thought how radiant and regal she looked and how much younger than Sweyn when in fact there was only six years between them.

Seated at another table by the top table at a forty-five-degree angle to the King was another long table with some eighteen rowdy youngsters, expensively dressed. It turned out that these were all the offspring of Sweyn and his many concubines, except the one child with his first wife who had died young. On the other end of the top table was the third part of the square where both Olaf and Finn were seated along with some dull nobles and Tora's twitchy ladies-in-waiting. Tora sat beside the King and smiled regally but with nothing of the twinkle in her eyes that Olaf had so admired. This was duty, pure and simple. At least tonight she was safe, but tomorrow, she would have to take her marriage vows, presided over by Bishop Vilhelm in Roskilde Cathedral before a huge multitude. After that, Tora would have to endure the lust of Sweyn in the obligatory consummation after tomorrow night's wedding feast.

Bishop Vilhelm it was who had refused to allow Sweyn into the cathedral for mass on New Year's Day as a few party guests had got drunk and ridiculed him behind his back on New Year's Eve. Sweyn had them killed in a church the following morning. Bishop Vilhelm, stood at the doors of the cathedral to prevent the King from entering using his crook and calling the King a murderer, condemned by God and excommunicated him from the church. Sweyn's men drew their swords to hack the bishop down, but the King prevented them. He departed to his castle and returned barefoot wearing sackcloth and lay down on his face at the door of the cathedral begging for abject confession. Bishop Vilhelm stopped the mass and went and heard Sweyn's confession and repentance which was so sincere that the bishop helped him up and lifted the excommunication with the words 'Te absolvo" before leading the King into the cathedral.

This story was recounted to Olaf by Finn who marvelled at the power of the Church of Rome over even kings. In the Viking days, Vilhelm would have been hacked to pieces.

The following day, Tora became officially Queen in Denmark as well as being Queen Regent for the young Olaf III back in Oslo. The service was grand but compared to the services Olaf had witnessed in York Minster, Westminster Abbey and the Cathedral in Rouen it was a rather backward and plain affair. Olaf, of course attended and did his best to suppress his yawns as the Latin mass droned on and on. Finally, it was all over, and the 'happy couple' walked down the aisle to the great West Door to the sound of bells and a large cheering crowd outside.

The wedding feast though was far more like an old Viking wedding with much music and laughter and drinking of mjørd and öl. Olaf befriended a very attentive young noble lady from the direction of where the great youthful noise emanated from Sweyn's many offspring. They were all very drunk by this time and Tora had slipped away to prepare herself to do her duty. This particular daughter of Sweyn was singularly beautiful and fresh-faced and revealed that her name was Ingerid of Denmark, daughter of the King. She told Olaf that she was promised in marriage but that the boy was very young and as she was nearly seventeen, she couldn't wait that long. She then rather drunkenly confessed that she would like to experience her first love with Olaf until the boy was old enough. Olaf, having also imbibed a considerable quantity of mjørd and, having from an early age, no actual Christian morals, was not altogether indifferent to this idea provided that Sweyn did not find out. Ingerid stroked his blonde beard and face and said:

"I hope my future husband will look just like you with your beautiful hair and the bluest of eyes. Do you not have a wife?"

Olaf thought for a moment:

"Erm, I suppose I don't, actually. But tell me, who is this boy you are pledged to marry. Have you seen him?"

"No, but they assure me that he is very pretty and will grow up to be very handsome and kind."

"And who told you that? Was it King Sweyn?"

"No, he has not seen the boy, but Queen Tora has told me and she should know."

"Oh, why is that?"

"Because she is his mother! He is King Olaf III of Norway!"

Olaf choked: "Oy Herregud!" He now realised he had come close to an intimacy with his son's betrothed wife.

Olaf smartly managed to disentangle himself from this beautiful maiden with some very sound reasoning:

"If you were an ordinary person, you might well be able to have some fun before you marry. However, a marriage between the Royal Houses of Denmark and Norway is quite another matter, now that the Christian Church has such a hold on people's lives, and you would need to prove your chastity and purity on your wedding night. I think you know what I mean."

Ingerid's large blue eyes widened in realisation that the strict ethics of the new religion which would not have bothered the pagan Vikings, were very much to be obeyed. She left Olaf to rejoin her party of siblings, with a backward, doleful glance.

Chapter Seventeen
1069 – Invasion of England

Olaf remained a valued guest of Sweyn at his court in Roskilde where he saw in a Danish Christmas and New Year. It was now 1069 and although neither Olaf nor Sweyn knew it, a great massacre had been perpetrated against the Normans on 26th January in York resulting in the deaths of some 900 soldiers.

What had happened, it seems, is that William, realising that he needed to tighten his grip on the rebellious North, decided to appoint a new Earl named William Cumin to replace the unfortunate Earl Copsig, decapitated by Oswulf. In light of this remembrance, Cumin, a Flemish mercenary from Comines marched North with a strong force of nearly one thousand mercenary soldiers, many of them being Flemish. His orders were to govern the territory beyond the River Tyne using as much force as was deemed necessary. Cumin took this as carte blanche to pillage the local countryside along the way. Normally, the villagers would flee as news of the soldiers' approach was learnt, but, on this occasion, during an especially harsh Northumbrian winter, the snowfall was so thick they were unable do this. Instead, the men of Northumbria banded together into a sizeable force, determined to kill the earl or die in the attempt. The Bishop of Durham sent a messenger to Cumin warning him that he was in grave danger of being ambushed. Cumin, with a cold and hungry force of mercenaries spurned this good advice and marched into Durham, killing and looting and finally feasting and drinking late into the night. As the sun rose over the white fields, the Northumbrian men burst in through each of the city's gates and surrounded Cumin and his men. A massacre ensued with the streets choked with bodies. Cumin himself had been sleeping in the Bishop's Palace where a small bodyguard put up something of a fight until the rebels decided to set light to the building. Many were burnt alive, with Cumin rushing out through the front door, his lavish clothes burning, and was impaled by a well-aimed javelin. The earl and his entire force were wiped out on the morning of 31st January 1069.

All across the North, encouraged by the massacre of Cumin's men, the general uprising continued with an ambush of the governor of York Castle and many of his men, who had been marching toward Durham in an attempt, it seems, to hook up with Cumin. But the Norman Sheriff remained in the newly built castle of York and prepared for a siege.

Word had reached the three brave exiles in Scotland, Mærleswein, who had been a steward of the Fyrd at Hastings but left the field early, Edgar Ætheling, who had submitted his rightful crown to both Harold and William and finally, Gospatric, the earl of Banenburgh, and one who collaborated with William as often as he rebelled against him. Also, among the English leaders were, of course, earls Edwin and

Morcar, who had surrendered to Hardråda and failed to support King Harold in his fight against William.

Between them they fielded a sizeable army and, during the Spring, laid siege to York Castle. Somehow, the Sheriff managed to get a message to London telling William that, if he did not come at once, he would be forced to surrender. William did more than that. By the end of March, he had gathered a large force and, in a swift lightning strike came upon the unsuspecting rebels with such suddenness that they were quickly overwhelmed and put to flight. Many were killed or captured although all the key figures escaped, including Edgar Ætheling, and returned to the safety of Scotland. York was ravaged and put in the custody of William fitz Osbern, William's no-nonsense right-hand man. A second castle was started on the West bank of the River Ouse and William returned South to celebrate Easter in Winchester Cathedral.

What the Normans did not realise was that Queen Ealdgyth, her lady-in waiting Fionne, Esla the maid and of course Astrid, were all in York. Ealdgyth had taken a cottage in the close, near to Astrid which she shared with her two retainers, and Astrid remained as a widow with her son, Anders. It was a very dangerous place to be at this time, but they kept a low profile and weathered the storm as William had very strict laws regarding his soldiers abusing women and the punishments were eye-wateringly painful - enough to discourage such wrong doings. As they were close to the Minster they were left alone whilst other parts of York were not so fortunate.

Meanwhile the Godwin boys, Godwin, Edward and Magnus took the Northern unrest as a good time to cause William some grief of their own. They sailed from Ireland on midsummer 1069 with a fleet of sixty-five vessels and landed not far from Barnstable in North Devon.

There was a fierce fight against the occupiers commanded by Brian the Breton the local lord. Both sides suffered heavy casualties but it was the Godwins who, once again, were defeated and forced to return to Dublin.

Meanwhile, back in Denmark, Olaf had seen the winter months melt into Spring and then Summer as the work on the invasion was put in place. It transpired that Sweyn himself had decided to remain behind and put his trust in Olaf and several Jarls, his brother Asbjørn, Jarl Thorkild and his two burly sons, Harald and Cnute. They had assembled a sizeable force and had persuaded Tora to send some men from Norway to make it a real Viking coalition. Olaf had been hugely frustrated by the incredibly ponderous speed of the recruitment, shipbuilding and planning. He had hoped they would have set sail by early Spring. As it was the fleet didn't depart until 20th August with some of the boats not leaving until 8th September. Instead of sailing straight to Orkney, where he had hoped to pick up his two friends, Sigurd and Ulrick, the plan was some bizarre journey down to the South coast of England, starting at Dover and working their way up the East coast as if they were a Viking raiding party. Apparently, this was the route they always took. The element of surprise would be completely lost and William would have all the time in the world to assemble a large force to meet the Viking fleet. It was insanity, as Olaf repeated often, but it fell on deaf ears.

The huge Danish fleet of some 300 ships set out from Roskilde on a fine morning on the long journey around the Danish peninsula, sailing North through the Kattegatt and then hugging the coastline past the Northern tip of Skagen before turning West and taking the Southerly route back down towards the mouth of the Elbe at a small fishing village called Cuxhaven. The first ships, which included Olaf and the Danish leaders, sailed down the Elbe to Hamburg where they re-supplied and met with clergy from Hamburg-Bremen who blessed their voyage as William was now out of favour with the Pope. After resting, they continued to sail along the coast of High Germanie and on to Flanders between the Fresian Islands and the Flemish coast. This all seemed to be taking an age as Olaf became more and more frustrated. Had they gone to Bergen, Orkney and Northumbria, they would have been there by now. Some more political shenanigans occurred as they met up with Baldwin VI of Flanders who had recently inherited the position from his father, the ever-welcoming Baldwin V who had died in 1067.

Finally, they reached Calais and turned North to make the relatively short journey across the Channel to Dover. After a small foray and a bit of looting with the Normans not venturing out of their castle against such a vast hoard, they continued on. Next, on to Sandwich, Ipswich and Norwich where they met little or no resistance. But, although William was away near Chepstow, hunting in the Forest of Dean, messengers arrived with the news of the Viking invasion.

Just as Hardråda had done three years earlier, the great fleet sailed up the Humber and anchored there, a short march to York of around 7 miles. But, instead of being met with a defending Norman army, the Danes were greeted with euphoria by a large army led by Edgar Ætheling, Gospatric and Mærleswein. Asbjørn led a party out to greet them, including Olaf, who spoke both English and Norse although all the men of Northumbria and Yorkshire spoke Norse. After shaking hands with Asbjørn, King Sweyn's brother, Edgar spied Olaf behind him and let out a cry:

"Olaf! My fwiend Olaf! I am so pleased to see you back here to help our cause. And you have kept my sword safe I see. Please keep it, I have another. Gospatwic you know, and this is Mærleswein who commanded the fyrd at Hastings."

Olaf nodded at Gospatric of Banenburgh and looked at Mærleswein:

"Ah, yes, I did see you with the fyrd at the outset of the battle. I was with the housecarl archers, and we stayed by the King to the end and, even after the army broke, we caused heavy casualties to the Normans. It was a pity the fyrd couldn't have held."

Mærlswein had turned puce:

"They were but peasants against knights. They had no training in holding a line and just rushed down the hill to their deaths every time the enemy withdrew. I did what I could, but it was hopeless."

Olaf, knowing full-well that he had fled the field at around four in the afternoon, said nothing more on the subject other than:

"Well, I'm sure we're all very keen to wreak our vengeance on those Normans who have treated the people of England so shamefully."

There was general nodding at Olaf's diplomatic reply.

Edgar spoke up:

"Well, I suggest we march to just outside York and pitch camp. They won't dare attack us with these numbers."

Asbjørn was all set for a celebration:

"We have had a long journey so a night of feasting in earshot of the defending garrison of Yorvick might persuade them to come out and surrender?" There was unanimous agreement.

That night, about two miles South of York, the noise of a great host feasting and drinking could be heard from the battlements of the two castles and by the inhabitants of the City of York itself.

Olaf was fretting about the army storming the city and slaying all inside which may very well include Astrid and Queen Ealdgyth.

During the night, a further body of men arrived led by the two brothers, Earls Edwin and Morcar. No sooner had they arrived than they learnt that Olaf had returned with the Danish fleet and hastened to find him by the firelight.

"Olaf! Welcome back, my friend!" It was Morcar.

"Well, I do seem to be very popular here, I'm pleased to be back. My worry is probably the same as yours. Your sister Queen Ealdgyth is holed up in the city along with my very close friends Astrid, Esla and Fionne. We must extract them safely if they are still alive."

"They are," affirmed Edwin, "we have spies in the City and they can get messages out. They are all safe in the square by the Minster which has its own wall and gate. But as soon as this fight gets underway we cannot be sure of their safety. We must get them out." There was general nodding.

Inside the walls of the city Minster, the distant noise of a large army at revels could be heard. Astrid and her son had gone over to Ealdgyth's much larger cottage to be with the others. As they sat talking about how they might get out before the full battle took hold, there was a knock on the door. Astrid opened the door to find a clergyman was standing outside. It was a face she recognised from their first meeting all those years ago when the three bishops stood outside in the rain and she invited them in to dine on venison and dumplings.

"Bishop Wulfstan?"

The bishop was momentarily confused:

"Astrid, my child? Have I come to the wrong dwelling? I was seeking Queen Ealdgyth."

"No, your Grace, you are in the right place, she is inside with Lady Fionne and Mistress Esla. The boy is my son, Anders."

"Yes, yes," nodded the bishop. "Terrible business about his father. But I have come here to ask help for Archbishop Ealdred. His mind has gone and he is sick with fear about the Viking army. I know that Lady Fionne has healing skills and would ask the Queen if we might avail ourselves of her talent to try to heal the Archbishop?"

Fionne appeared behind Astrid in the doorway with a wooden box of herbs and a cloak over her arm:

"The Queen has given her consent as she heard your conversation. Esla will stay here with your son if I might bring Astrid along too, we can leave right away."

"Yes, of course, he is with the monks at the Bishop's Palace by the Minster."

Astrid also took her cloak and the three of them went out into the evening, over the cobbled paving, toward the great Minster and the Bishop's Palace. There were people everywhere with a great deal of shouting and a general air of panic. All the Norman men now wore armour and helmets in preparation for battle. The Sheriff was standing at the top of the steps of the Great Hall that belonged to Edwin and Morcar and, indeed, to Ealdgyth, their sister. He was flanked by two knights holding lances with pennants embroidered with dragons.

Pushing their way through the throng of Norman soldiers, Bishop Wulfstan led the way up the steps to the Bishop's Palace and thence into the incense-filled chamber of the Archbishop of York. The heat from the many candles was palpable as it was 11th September, and the air was still warm. The monks and a congregation of clergy surrounded the huge, canopied bed with heavy curtains and a round tent-shaped apex. The monks droned their chants.

"Are they trying to suffocate him?" asked Fionne to Bishop Wulfstan. The bishop called out to the crowded chamber:

"Everybody out into the hall. Open some windows. He needs air!"

The sight of a woman being allowed into the chamber met with mutterings of disapproval from the monks, but they complied. Fionne moved straight to the enormous bed and placed her box on a table. Removing the Archbishop's arm from the covers she placed two fingers on his wrist and then moved them up to his neck.

"He is sleeping now," said one bishop. It was Æthelwig, who had so admired Astrid's dumplings back in 1062.

"Will he be all right?"

"Well, he has nothing to fear from any Viking army," said Fionne, "he is in the hands of God now. You may say your requiems, I am too late to help him."

"Requiescat in pacem", chanted the clergy as they fell to their knees and Bishop Wulfstan made the sign of the cross over his forehead. The great tenor bell of the Minster tolled a mournful message to the people of York, every five seconds, that their archbishop had departed this life.

York Minster

Over the River Ouse, about three miles South of the fortified wall of York, around 9,000 Anglo-Danes were enjoying the mild September evening in the meadows surrounding the village of Badetorps (Bishopthorpe). The leaders each stood up and hushed their men. As the hubbub died down, all were able to hear the doleful death knell being sounded from the Minster on such a still night where the water carried the sound. There was much muttering as to what this could signify. It was suggested that perhaps it signified an execution and immediately rumours grew that the Normans had discovered Queen Ealdgyth and were preparing to have her put to death. This much agitated her brothers and Olaf who immediately started to put pressure on Asbjørn and Edgar Ætheling to have the men ready for a dawn assault before the execution could take place. Asbjørn declared that he was reluctant to interrupt his men enjoying the feasting after their long journey. This really angered Edwin and Morcar and even surprised Edgar Ætheling regarding his newfound ally. Just as tensions were beginning to mount, a rider entered the encampment and quickly dismounted. He was pointed to the gathering of the leaders where he recognised the two Earls, Edwin and Morcar.

"My lords, I bring news." This was clearly one of the agents on the inside that Morcar had spoken about with such confidence.

"The Queen," said Morcar, not giving the panting messenger a chance to speak, "is she all right?"

"Yes, my lords. But the Normans are planning a pre-emptive strike out of the city at first light, believing you will all still be drunk and asleep from tonight's revelries."

"But what of that death knell we've heard tolling for the last hour?" enquired Olaf. "Is there to be an execution?"

"No," replied the galloper, "it is for the Archbishop of York, he has died."

There was palpable relief from the commanders. If the Normans were going to come to them, they wouldn't have the high risk of an assault on a fortified city with two Norman castles giving excellent killing-zone sight to the Norman archers.

Olaf, ever the military thinker, put the question:

"Do you have any idea of their numbers in terms of cavalry, foot soldiers and archers?"

"Well, it was chaos in the city this evening, close to panic, but I estimated around five hundred archers, the same, perhaps less of mounted knights and the rest, Norman foot soldiers. Just over three thousand in total and commanded by a very arrogant and puffed-up Sheriff who has never commanded an army in his life. If he marches out at dawn into a shield wall of nine thousand warriors, I think he might just wet himself !"

There was general laughter from the commanders and it was agreed, even by the Danes, that they should stop the revels, get some rest, and be ready to move out at five o'clock next morning, giving them two hours to march under cover of darkness to set up ready for sunrise at seven. They didn't want to arrive too early, or it would give the Normans the chance not to sally fourth. They would probably set out at six thirty and be about half a mile outside the gates before they noticed nine thousand hairy and boisterous Anglo-Danes coming out of the woods in full battle formation.

"Thank you, God, Thank you Thor!" said Olaf as he went off to check that his quiver was fully stocked and those of the Danish archers in his charge.

"Another day, another battle" he mumbled to himself.

Olaf Slagbjørn aged Twenty-seven

Chapter Eighteen
1069, Ambush at York

Olaf managed to catch a few hours sleep and awoke damp and cold from the heavy dew. Fires had been lit and many were drying themselves and finding pleasant warmth from the burning logs. The leaders, Asbjørn, Edwin, Morcar and Edgar Ætheling were all mounted and ready to move out. There was hot grøt, freshly made to fill the stomachs of the soldiers and all seemed in good humour since the colossal hangovers that would have ensued had the feasting continued, had been averted until after the fight. Olaf had served with Edwin and Morcar at the Battle of Fulford and had saved them from getting slaughtered but he hadn't been impressed by their disastrous tactical leadership. Asbjørn frankly hadn't a clue above forming a shield wall and crashing into the enemy and Edgar just wanted to be recognised in battle but had little idea how to achieve this. Secretly they were all relying on Olaf to have a clever, or even, cunning plan, which, of course he did.

It was not so much a plan as a theory that involved hoping that the Normans would be marching in a long, drawn-out line with the cavalry at the front followed by the infantry, then the archers. There was a thick wood that ran alongside the road about two hundred yards to the Normans' left. If they were stretched out along this road, Olaf could take one thousand men, comprising six hundred archers and four hundred infantry, as protection from cavalry should they not be too far up front, and circle around the column to be in the rear with the Norman archers' backs as targets. As it was nearing the Autumn Equinox and the sunrise was to be around seven o'clock, due East, the whole column would have the rising sun to their left and would be squinting into the sun, as a force, three times the size of their own, emerged from the forest. The shock of this would render them oblivious that their archers, some five hundred strong, were being wiped out in the vanguard.

It all happened exactly as Olaf had predicted or hoped. The Anglo-Danish force was quietly ensconced in the forest a half mile down the road from the gates of York. At half past six the gates opened and out came the procession, led by the puffed-up Sherriff, flanked by his two horsemen carrying the dragon banners. Behind him, no doubt in order of importance, came the mounted knights, the foot soldiers and then the archers and several carts of supplies including food, wine and arrows. They marched between the two castles of York on the West of the Ouse and Baile Hill on the East, built by William in 1068 and 1069 respectively. It was these two castles that Olaf had no wish to be caught between attempting a frontal assault on the city.

Olaf signalled that his cohort should move out as the carts and archers began to pass by. Fortunately, there was a reverse slope behind the copse and they were able to proceed swiftly to be in position behind the column. The Norman archers were still drowsy as they had been kept awake all night by shouted orders and preparation, not to mention the tolling of the bell. If they did notice any movement behind them, they just assumed it was more of their own column joining them. That was until Olaf and four others loosed their arrows into the last of the column. Five men fell to the floor with a clatter alerting the men in front of them who were instantly dispatched by five more of Olaf's team. This repeated itself with murderous effectiveness until it became clear to those at the back that they were under attack. At his signal the remainder of Olaf's archers fanned out into a wide crescent running forward to outflank the Normans whilst Olaf's foot soldiers crashed into the rear before the Normans could even string their bows. At this point the sun broke in a dazzling sunrise over the line of the woods as eight thousand men with the sun at their back came crashing out, banging their shields. The Norman archers were caught on three sides by a hail of arrows or throwing axes. They broke and ran up the road, disrupting any attempts by the Normans to form a defensive line. Many had their hands to their squinting eyes to try and determine what sort of enemy they were facing to their front as another thousand warriors charged down from behind the reverse slope to reinforce Olaf and prevent any from running back to York.

The warriors advanced down the slope in two ranks, the second rank forming a shield wall three deep in preparation to receive cavalry when they finally woke up to the fact that they were under very serious attack. For the fleeing archers and foot soldiers, it was a cauldron of death, with Olaf's relentless rate of fire into the infantry who were now being hacked to pieces from the rear and from the front rank from the forest who had smashed into them in a hundred-yard dash down the slope. It was a slaughter and was only compounded when the mounted knights, finally realising they were being attacked, attempted to relieve their infantry by charging up the slope into the second rank who were stood firm, three deep, their shields locked, with the second and third lines, hurling javelins and axes into the few hundred horsemen.

Within the hour, the bright Autumn sunshine lit up a scene of such devastation that, out of a Norman army of some three thousand soldiers, only a handful had survived around the Sheriff. He was permitted to return to York to collect his wife and family and return to London to tell William to fear the North.

"Now that's more like it!" said Olaf, leaning on a supply cart and trying to catch his breath whilst quenching his thirst on a flagon of Rhenish wine, clearly once the property of the Sheriff, currently being escorted to York.

The large and victorious army marched back to York with a few surviving prisoners, most of whom were wounded, and the Sheriff, whose arrogance seemed to have completely deserted him. His two burly spearmen both lay dead by the road with their Norman colleagues. Olaf had mounted up once more and was riding towards York with Edwin and Morcar when great billows of smoke began to swirl up into the morning sky from the buildings around the moat of the city.

"What's going on there?" Edwin shouted at the hangdog Sheriff.

"I, I gave orders that if we needed to pull back, the guard inside were to set fire to the outbuildings to prevent you crossing the moat," stuttered the Sheriff.

There was a gusty Southerly wind blowing that quickly fanned the flames and blew burning wood sparks up into the air and over the city wall onto the thatched roofs within.

"You bloody idiot! You'll burn down the whole city! Come on, we must save the Queen." And with that, Edwin, Morcar and Olaf spurred their horses into a gallop to cover the quarter mile to the city gates.

"W-What queen?" called out the Sheriff, holding up his manacled hands. "What queen?"

They reached the gates with fire raging around the wall. Several Norman guards on the gate tower were terrified to hear that Edwin and Morcar were outside with nine thousand men coming up the road behind them. One even tried to negotiate but Olaf was in no mood for discussions. An arrow went flying up and caught him on the shoulder, hurling him off the rampart with a yelp and a thud as he hit the ground. Almost immediately the outer gate swung open. Entering the city, there was already an air of panic with people rushing about with buckets of water. The inner gate was also barred to prevent the fire from spreading to the palace and the Minster, but this gate was manned by Northumbrians who recognised both Edwin and Morcar and immediate access was granted. Riding into the courtyard, Olaf dismounted and went straight to Astrid's cottage to find it cold and deserted. He rushed back outside, shouting:

"Astrid's not here. Where might the Queen be hiding?"

"Not the palace for sure," said Morcar. "We own all those larger cottages. See if any are occupied." Olaf ran up to the door of the one closest to Astrid's home. There was a fire burning inside. Before he could bang on the door, it was opened and out peered a face eager to see if the hiatus outside would reach them. She gasped:

"Olaf!" Olaf started back to get a look and identify the familiar voice:

"Esla! You are here! Thank God and Thor and Odin! Do you have the Queen and Astrid?"

"Yes, yes, there are all inside." said Esla who was being pushed aside by a tall lady.

"And the one who saved your life! Am I so quickly forgotten?"

"Fionne! You are all here. This is wonderful. I have Ealdgyth's brothers outside. You must grab what you can and get ready to leave. Not only will the fire spread here but there is an Anglo-Viking army about to enter the city with a mind to loot, pillage and celebrate their great victory. All the Normans are dead." At this there was an ear-piecing squeal as Astrid charged through the doorway and into Olaf's arms.

"Olaf! You've come to save us and kill all those horrible Normans. I told them you would."

Olaf, slightly winded by Astrid's charge, tried to stay focused:

"Astrid, you and the ladies have precious little time. You must gather clothes and anything of value. Load them into carts and get the Queen's carriage. I think we may have one hour. The pillaging will centre on the Norman properties, the Bishops Palace and Minster. But we must get out quickly. Tell Anders to get your things from your cottage." Olaf turned to find Edwin and Morcar behind him.

"We will go up to our great hall and save what we can and then gather the carriages from the stables. We can greet our sister later."

The earls had not dismounted and now trotted off in the direction of their palace at the other end of the close where the stables housed the carriages.

Edgar Ætheling and his Northumbrians along with Asbjørn and his considerable force of Norwegians and Danes had just reached the gates of York. There was black smoke everywhere. Edgar was having difficulties trying to persuade Asbjørn that they should not look to pillage from the Church. Asbjørn laughed at the idea of this:

"How do you think the Normans have been funding their mercenaries and their castle building? I have heard that York Minster is one of the few that has not been emptied of its gold and treasure. God has no need of such things but we Vikings can use it."

All in earshot laughed and a cheer went up. Asbjørn raised his arm in a signal and as it dropped, there was a roar as thousands of soldiers ran over the drawbridge into the suffocating smoke in search of Norman loot.

Inside the second wall, the gates had been closed again to prevent the fire from spreading but also to buy time for the Queen and her entourage to load up their belongings, including a sizable quantity of gold coin which the Queen had cunningly hidden under a tree in Astrid's Garden. Inside an hour, two carriages and a baggage cart had been assembled and drivers employed to drive the teams. Outside the gates the noise of the soldiers made it clear that they would soon be forcing their entry. The earls and Olaf had the gate opened and they rode out into the throng. Edwin spoke to the soldiers, their faces blackened by smoke:

"Soldiers! You know me. I am Edwin, Earl of Northumbria. You fought a brilliant victory today planned by young Olaf here. The Normans didn't know what hit them!" A great roar went up. "I have here, ladies from the royal household of King Harold, including our very own dear sister Queen Ealdgyth who have hidden here in York under the very noses of the Normans without them knowing anything of their whereabouts. I would like an escort to see them safely out of the city after which, everything inside these palace walls is yours for the taking. The cheers were followed by the crowd opening up a path for the pale blue carriages to proceed towards the outer gatehouse. Many Northumbrians doffed their caps and the Danes stood still in respect. The pillagers rampaged long into the night as the fire, inexorably continued to spread. Once it reached the wooden Minster it took hold of the nearby Bishop's Palace. Ealdred, Archbishop of York, who had crowned both Harold and William as kings, lay still on his deathbed as the flames caught on the silken canopy and effected a cremation as, by this time, all the clergy had fled.

Outside, as York and its archbishop burned, Olaf led the Queen's procession down to the Humber where the plan was to evacuate if Edwin, Morcar and the Anglo-Danish army could not prevail against the Norman reprisal.

Across the other side of the country, King William was trying to enjoy some hunting in the forest of Dean. Insurrection was breaking out everywhere and, as word reached the Southern counties of the fate of York, the men of the West renewed their attacks on Norman strongholds. Exeter, Yeovil, Chester, Shrewsbury all suffered attacks with great losses being sustained on both sides. William could not be everywhere at once, so he sent William fitz Osbern to subdue the revolt in the West while he took personal control of a force to meet the Danish and Northumbrian forces. He sent his half-brother Robert to the Humber while he dealt with a large force of rebels at Stafford. Again, losses on both sides were significant although William emerged the victor. William marched on to Lincolnshire where there had been reports of the presence of the Danish army.

It was true that a small detachment had ventured South. It was Olaf and a small force who were on a mission to make things difficult for the approaching Normans. The Normans approached the River Aire which, as it was mid-November, was swollen by the Autumnal rains. The bridge had been smashed using axes and the Normans were forced to find a ford further up-river. It was the trap Olaf had planned for and he and his archers were able to rain down arrows on the knights just as soon as their horses entered the freezing waters. Olaf had delayed the Normans by three weeks and when the Normans did arrive in force, Olaf's men had melted into the forest with many a Norman night lying dead or wounded and all were cold and wet. The route that Olaf had forced the Normans to take was through dense woods and much marshy land. It wasn't until mid-December that the beleaguered Norman army reached the outskirts of a blackened and charred York only to find that the Danes were not there. Having destroyed the two castles that the Normans had built to protect the main gate, the Danes thought it prudent to retire to their ships where William could not get at them.

On 15th December, a party of Normans arrived at the point where the Danish ships lay at anchor. They were led by a disfigured knight who walked with a limp when he dismounted. He announced himself as Guillaume de Malet.

The bridge which was so effectively sabotaged by Olaf and his Danes was later to be known in the district as Ponte-fract (broken bridge).

Chapter Nineteen
The Harrying of the North

The Danes had no intention of fighting a pitched battle with William's forces since the Northumbrians had scattered and returned to their homes with Edwin, Morcar and the Ætheling all heading for the safety of the Scottish border. It was with pleasant surprise to Asbjørn, therefore, when he learnt of a body of Normans come to offer very favourable terms for a peaceful Christmas.

Asbjørn gathered together several warriors including Earl Thorkild and instructed Olaf and twenty of his Norwegian archers to attend and cover them. It was dark when they left their ships and made for the tent and torches that the Normans had erected for the treaty. A party of ten Norman knights stood around two tables. One contained several parchments and the other a large heavy looking chest.

It has to be said that Olaf's relationship with Asbjørn had never been a particularly friendly one. When Edwin and Morcar, together with the Ætheling, put their confidence in Olaf to oversee the military planning of the ambush of the Sherriff of York and the subsequent overwhelming success of said ambush, the resentment and feeling of inadequacy that Asbjørn harboured had now given way to the green-eyed monster: jealousy. These feelings were then given the opportunity to show themselves. It was as Guillaume was reading the parchment, written in French, and being translated by a Franco-Dane, that one of his knights, a survivor from the disastrous pursuit of Olaf to London, looked into the torchlit faces of the Norwegian archers and recognised the unmistakeable good looks and short stature of Olaf Slagbjørnson, the wanted outlaw. Moving close behind Guillaume, he whispered in French into his ear:

"Olaf the Outlaw is here, just before you."

Guillaume de Malet had been a well-trained spy and his experience allowed his face to emit only the slightest twitch as he continued reading. As he came to the end of the terms, he looked up and spoke in English, in the dialect spoken in York which was very similar to Norse:

"This very generous payment of Danegeld contained within this chest and this Christmas peace agreement allows you and your ships to Winter here peaceably. You may forage, unmolested by the King's men, on the understanding you obey the King's laws which includes any outlaws you may be harbouring. The most wanted of these is Olaf, the Norwegian archer who, I see, is standing behind you with his bowmen."

The Norman knights instinctively began to draw their swords. Olaf had seen Guillaume but had hoped that in the dark he might not be recognised so thought it wisest to keep still. Now he realised the game was up he called out in Norse:

"Nock! Draw!"

With a swish, twenty arrows were 'nocked' onto their bow strings with de Malet and the knights within a second's relaxation of two fingers on the word 'loose!' and certain death. Asbjørn was also in the line of the arrows and looked round with horror:

"Archers! Put down your bows now! If Olaf is an outlaw, then we must abide by Norman law. My brother, King Sweyn of Denmark, will completely understand. We must hand him over and retire with our gold."

The Norwegian archers did not flinch. Earl Thorkild spoke up:

"Archers, relax. Olaf is working for the King of Denmark and is in no way subject to any Norman law. He has proved himself a loyal and valuable asset. Asbjørn, you behave with little honour. Bad enough to accept a Norman bribe, but to betray one of our own? The King will not be pleased. Normans, we will accept your peace offer and take the Danegeld, but Olaf stays with us, no matter how much trouble he has caused your King. There can be no law against fighting in battle against an invader."

This took a moment to sink in, but Guillaume nodded to his men to sheath their swords as he signed the parchment and passed the quill to Thorkild. Asbjørn also signed, his hand shaking with rage at this public humiliation. Olaf had made yet another enemy. The heavy chest was transported onto the leading longboat and the Normans returned with the signed parchment. Guillaume couldn't wait to convey to King William that Olaf, who the King had declared the most wanted man in England, was just a short distance away, having returned with the Danish fleet. The pain from the wounds inflicted upon him by Olaf had never ceased to trouble him and he wrongly assumed that this would be likewise for his King. In this he was entirely mistaken.

William was looking forward to Christmas at York as this would mark the third anniversary of his coronation as King of England and he intended to show the people that he was the rightful king, anointed by God. He sent to Winchester for all his coronation robes and his crown to be delivered to York where he would celebrate Christmas in the burnt-out minster and billeted himself in what used to be the palace of Edwin, Earl of Northumberland. He was interested in Guillaume's news, of course, but no, his broken nose was a distant memory and he had bigger fish to fry. The North of England had constantly revolted against his authority and despite being put down time and again they just rose up again. No, this time they would feel the wrath of William the Conqueror, as known as William the Bastard. He planned a horrifying genocide against his Northern subjects on a scale that had never been perpetrated before. But first he would celebrate Christmas in York.

Whilst William was celebrating Christmas in the charred remains of York Minster, his lieutenants were out and about with the army gathering intelligence as to the whereabouts of his enemy. In the last week of 1069, William had enough information to set out across the frozen and trackless wastes of North Yorkshire in an attempt to confront and destroy all who opposed him. Earl Gospatric surrendered and swore an oath of fealty whereas the Ætheling, Edwin and Morcar fled into Scotland. William's strategy was clear enough; he would destroy the North so completely that they could never rise up against him ever again. The army was split into small raiding parties that would scour the villages and hamlets, the woods and the hills and kill any they came upon. More than that, William ordered that all cattle, sheep, pigs, chickens and any food stores be burnt. All crops were destroyed and the whole area North of the Humber completely stripped of any means of feeding its population. The winter of 1069 into 1070 saw a terrible famine so brutal that deaths from starvation accounted for more than 100,000 of men, women and children. Chroniclers at the time referred to this genocide as 'The Harrying of the North'. William pushed his army very hard in this murderous work in terrible conditions and, as many of his force were mercenaries from Brittany or Anjou there were bitter complaints and many desertions. Finally, as the Winter turned to Spring, having narrowly avoided a mutiny, William turned his army South. At Sarum they were disbanded with many of them being deployed to garrison the castles that were being built up and down the country.

Olaf wintered with the Danish fleet by the Humber and stayed with Queen Ealdgyth and her ladies, including Astrid, Anders and Harold. It was cold and uncomfortable but Ealdgyth with her great wealth was able to order in food and wine from the monastic foundations South towards Peterborough, so they were better off than the disgruntled Danes. Tragedy struck, however, and baby Harold contracted a strain of pneumonia which not even Fionne was able to cure and he passed away at the tender age of three.

The Normans kept their bargain and they were left in peace. But the Danish army had come to conquer England not to be bought off by Norman bribes of which they would receive little. Asbjørn had signed an agreement to leave as soon as the Winter passed, but now it was nearly Easter and the leaders showed no sign of departing. Olaf had forayed as far South as Ely and had visited Father Leofric. It was there he met Hereward the Wake – an Anglo-Saxon nobleman who had been in exile during the Norman invasion but was now back home and very keen to hook up with the Danes to cause as much trouble for the Normans as possible. It seems the Normans had killed his brother and seized all his possessions. Olaf acted as the go-between Hereward and the Danes.

Hereward the Wake 1070

Chapter Twenty
Hereward the Wake and the arrival of King Sweyn

Shortly after Easter, May 1070, the Danish king arrived to join his brother Asbjørn and the Danish army. His arrival was greeted by both Danes and English alike with great joy. Nobody could have been happier than Hereward who immediately suggested to Olaf that a base should be set up at Ely. He and his followers were planning an attack on Peterborough and in particular, the Cathedral. The archbishop installed by the Ætheling during his pitifully short reign had been displaced and a new ferocious Norman Abbott named Turold, who behaved more like a knight than a man of God, was given the position.

Sweyn dispatched Olaf and a very sulky and resentful Asbjørn, who had been given a rough dressing down by his brother when he learnt of his acceptance of a bribe, instead of taking York, and of his willingness to hand Olaf over to the Normans. They left the ships with three hundred huscarls and twenty Norwegian archers and set up a camp in Ely.

William had been short of money after the Yorkshire campaign as he had paid off the many mercenaries at Sarum with what coin he had left. William fitz Osbern had come up with the idea that many English nobles had hidden their coin and gold within the abbeys and cathedrals which they believed would be places of safety. Subsequent searches proved this to be the case and William ordered that all such buildings were to be searched. However, Peterborough had yet to be searched by Norman knights and Hereward was aware that he must move swiftly against the Cathedral to prevent the Normans from getting their hands on its wealth. Hereward, aided by the Danish contingent, forced his way into the town and, despite the best efforts of the monks, broke into the abbey church and carried away a sizeable quantity of gold and silver in the form of crosses and shrines and a large amount of gold coin. This was transferred to the Danes camp in Ely. But if Hereward believed that this wealth was to be used to finance a major uprising, he was mistaken. Sweyn was appalled by the state of his army. Without the large Mercian and Northumberland force which had been scattered, his army was in no fit state to take on a Norman force. The Harrowing of the North had meant that there was precious little food and many of his men were nearing starvation. Asbjørn was holding Peterborough with some three hundred huscarls and Olaf's twenty archers. The new and warlike Abbott Turold arrived at the outskirts of his diocese with a force of one hundred and thirty mounted knights. With his large force, Asbjørn could easily have held a defensive position but instead, he chose to withdraw to Ely and ordered that Olaf and his few archers should hold the marshy route to the island lest he and his huscarls should be ridden down whilst retreating. This infuriated Olaf but as Asbjørn was the King's brother,

Olaf obeyed and placed his men in an ambushing formation. No riders came from Peterborough as the Abbott Turold was keen to enjoy a hearty meal provided as a welcome for their new Abbott and to atone for losing most of the abbey church's treasure.

Having been in England for less than a month, and during the attack on Peterborough on 2nd June, Sweyn was again offered favourable terms by a messenger from William and a second payment was accepted. Sweyn ordered an immediate evacuation taking with him both the Norman payment and the loot from Peterborough. Olaf returned to Ely at sunrise to discover Asbjørn had left to rejoin the fleet. By the time they reached the mouth of the Humber, the entire fleet was on its way down to the Thames Estuary where they stopped to reprovision for two days. They then sailed back to Denmark taking Ealdgyth, Fionne, Esla and Astrid.

Olaf and his twenty archers were left high and dry with only Hereward as an ally. With heavy hearts, they trudged back to Ely to explain to a horrified Hereward the infidelity of his Danish allies.

Chapter Twenty-one
The Fortress of Ely

The island of Ely was surrounded by water and marshes. The Danes had chosen it well as their camp, so that William's army could not get at them. But now that they had gone William began to think that all would return to peace given the horrendous punishment he had meted out against the people of the North during the 'Harrowing'. In this assumption he was mistaken. Whilst William sailed to Normandy to try and restore order in Flanders, his wife's home, Hereward and Olaf busied themselves during the Autumn by fortifying the island of Ely. For this venture, they were assisted in their organisation by the redoubtable Father Leofric, who organised the local monks into a workforce to build a great wooden causeway across the marshes to bring in weapons and provisions to last out the Winter.

Olaf and Hereward got on incredibly well insofar as they had much in common. Hereward was an outlaw, so was Olaf. Hereward had served as a mercenary with Baldwin V of Flanders, Olaf had served with both Harald Hardråda and Harold Godwinson. Furthermore, Olaf had shot William de Warenne out of the saddle who was pursuing Hereward in a revenge attack.

When Hereward returned to his lands in 1067, he was met by his trusted retainer, Father Leofric who explained that his brother had been taken by the Normans, who killed him and placed his head upon a spike whilst they remained in drunken revels inside his hall. In a great rage, Hereward rushed into the hall and slew all twelve seated at the table, ably assisted by Leofric. The ringleader who had murdered Hereward's brother was Frederic, William de Warenne's brother-in-law. William swore revenge on Hereward and sometime later launched an ambush while they were escorting supplies from Peterborough to Ely. Olaf's Norwegian archers kept the soldiers at bay whilst Olaf shot de Warenne out of the saddle at a distance but only winged him in the shoulder. The Normans withdrew taking the wounded hero of Hastings with them. Hereward was delighted:

"Ha! They told me you could shoot a bow better than any man in Europe and you only winged him!"

Returning to Ely, the provisions were transported by boat whilst Hereward's men made their way over the marshes using the newly laid causeway that remained partially concealed by the rushes. Olaf noted that when large men walked over it, carrying heavy shields and armour, the causeway sank about a foot into the water but still carried the weight of the foot soldier. He wondered if this structure, made by monks, would hold a mounted knight or wagons laden with swords. Father Leofric had noticed the same thing and, for now, all provisions were transported by boat.

The camp at Ely was growing daily and was a hive of building activity as more and more dispossessed and disgruntled exiles and outlaws threw their lot in with Hereward, now becoming something of a local hero. Blacksmiths were setting up, traders, food vendors, fletchers and carpenters were turning the island into a fortified village. Olaf and his Norwegians had built themselves a 'longhus' in the Viking style, with skillfully interwoven branches covered with skins and managed to stay warm with a central fire. There were women on the island too who helped prepare food and offered services such as washing clothes and other such temptations as were inevitable where a large body of men were gathered.

One day, early in the new year of 1071, a number of ships sailing along the coast and up the River Ouse, approached the island of Ely with what appeared to be around two hundred and fifty armed men. There was a call to arms, but Hereward and Olaf agreed that the Normans would never attack with such a small force and so the ships were welcomed to land, and the people to come ashore. One man stood out by his fine clothes. It was none other than Æthelwine, Bishop of Durham. Hereward and Olaf were astonished and greeted the bishop as an honoured guest rather than as an outlaw on the run.

"My Lord Bishop, how very welcome you and your men are. We have more people arriving every day but not usually in such numbers and with a bishop at their head."

Hereward laughed heartily joined by cheering from his men or those who were in earshot. Æthelwine smiled sheepishly:

"Is there somewhere we can go to get warm? Having sailed from Scotland I am very cold and would welcome a fire and a warming draught."

"Of course, your Grace. Olaf and his Vikings have been teaching us the art making a longhus and because I am the chieftain here, I have the grandest! My people will extend you hospitality and you are welcome to join our fight against the oppressors. We were expecting Edwin and Morcar any day, so the hall is prepared for their 'noble' arrivals. Come, let's go and drink some Norman wine we stole from them in Peterborough and you can tell us your story."

Hereward led the way with Olaf followed by the Bishop, Mærleswein, the erstwhile Sheriff of Lincoln, and a formidable warrior of the house of Bamburgh and a dispossessed landowner named Siward Barn. They entered the cosy wooden interior of the longhus where a good fire was burning, and two ladies were on hand to pour the ale, mead and Norman wine imported by Breton traders for the Norman army.

When all were seated and goblets filled, Hereward and Olaf leant forward in anticipation to hear the story of Æthelwine, Bishop of Durham:

"Gentlemen, my story is long so I will strive to make it very brief. When the North rose up in the Winter of 1068/69, I was implicated and outlawed for this revolt against the Normans. William's army came across Yorkshire in the bleakest of winters and laid waste to every living thing in their path. Hearing of the great slaughter heading our way, I took my people, such as they were, out of Durham and headed towards Lindisfarne in the hope of some temporary refuge. I remained there until early Summer when a letter in reply to mine arrived from the Bishop of Cologne, offering me a safe stay away from the malignant Normans. I set sail but was blown back to the Scottish coast by an ill wind. It was there that I met the Ætheling and Mærleswein and heard news of the revolt in Ely. Being a Fenland boy myself, I felt strongly that I had a duty to go and join this uprising and aid the cause, as it were. I brought as many as I could muster including a great warrior in Siward Barn. And here, on this island, you find me with my people pledged to help your cause."

There was a long silent pause as the fire flickered and people took in this remarkable story. Olaf broke the silence with a question that was vexing him:

"So, what has happened to Edwin and Morcar? We were hoping they would arrive with all the forces at their disposal."

Æthelwine looked up as he had news of the two earls:

"Having been held as 'guests' by William and their lands given over to Norman governors, Edwin and Morcar decided to make a break for it. I have no other news but for the fact that they were trying to raise support in the North but with very little success. You see, when you are an earl of great districts such as Mercia or Northumbria, it comes with great responsibilities to the people who pay their taxes there. Neither Edwin nor Morcar took any steps to resist the Normans or help King Harold. When William took his ire out on the poor people of the North in the so-called 'Harrowing', there was no sign of the earls. And now they are asking these same people for help. I haven't heard any more other than that the uptake was very slim indeed and that William has now declared them outlaws."

By a strange quirk of fate, a warrior entered the longhus to announce that Morcar, erstwhile Earl of Northumbria, had just arrived with a very rag-tag force of half-starved fugitives who had appeared more as refugees than a relieving fighting force. He was requesting permission to cross the causeway onto the island of Ely and join with Hereward. Of Edwin there was no word. Morcar joined the assembly in Hereward's longhus but as one of the ladies came forward with a goblet of ale, she drew back with an expression of repulsion which turned to laughter as she held her nose.

"Dear God, if you really are an earl, you need a bath urgently, you stink!"

Morcar looked sheepish and embarrassed at the general laughter.

"I know, I expect I do. We have been living rough, hiding in the forests for some months now and I have only these clothes."

Olaf intervened:

"Lord Morcar, we have all been there. Across the way you will see another Viking longhus built by Norwegians and of course we have a sauna there. Tell them I sent you and that you are the dispossessed Earl of Northumbria. Leave your clothes outside and the ladies from the wash station will have them cleaned."

"Oh, you have a sauna? That is wonderful. Astrid built one at York. I had never heard of such a thing, but she insisted I used it during my visits to her. I was the most fragrant man in the whole city."

"Go quickly," said Olaf, "you smell like a dog who has rolled in foxshit."

Morcar was ushered out by two warriors towards the Norwegian archers' longhus.

Olaf reflected on how Morcar was happy to be a patron to Astrid, who was after all, a widow, and use her as a mistress but was too lofty to make an honest woman of her. 'How are the mighty fallen', he thought to himself.

⤖

Chapter Twenty-two
The Siege of Ely March 1071

William had been in Flanders trying to prevent a civil war when a messenger arrived with news from England. Edwin and Morcar had slipped away from court in London and were attempting to hook up with the rebels, under Hereward the Wake, who had set up camp on the island of Ely. In a fury, he ordered the messenger to return immediately with a note to state the two earls be declared outlaws and that an army of Normans and mercenaries be ready for his return when he would personally lead the assault on the rebels' stronghold and put down the uprising once and for all.

Arriving in London mid-February, William was pleased to discover that a sizeable army was in full readiness, having been called up by Ivo Taillebois aided by the wounded but vengeful William de Warenne who carried the scar given to him by Olaf when he had attempted to ambush Hereward. The King wasted no time and marched up to Peterborough and thence to a small hamlet called

Bromdun (Brandon), where they made camp and began preparations for a frontal assault on Ely. Whilst in Peterborough, a Norman monk had asked to see the king's commanders and had told them of a secret pathway through the marshy fens and the concealed causeway which the English monks had built with Father Leofric. Taillebois was delighted with this news and suggested that they attack immediately. William gave the order for a full-frontal assault using the hidden causeway which the Norman monk had so usefully revealed. William was exhausted after his crossing from Normandy and his long marches to London and thence up to Brandon, so he entrusted the attack to the fierce and martial Ivo Taillebois.

Now in complete command, Taillebois marched out with a good-size force, nearly twice the number of the defending army that Hereward commanded. But the island had been skillfully fortified and they were well prepared for the first assault from the direction of *Aldreth*. The foot soldiers went first in a long line with the late winter sun sparkling from the muddy water and onto the helms and drawn swords. Olaf and his twenty Norwegians hid behind an earthwork where the wooden causeway's ropes were attached to stout wooden poles driven into the mud. Directly behind them was a shield wall of housecarls commanded by Hereward with Siward Barn, Morcar and other noble warriors. Should the archers be unsuccessful in stopping the first Norman attack with arrows, they would quickly withdraw behind the shield wall. Hidden in the shallow marshes were the main body of Hereward's army – poorly equipped but being so lightly armed, at a great advantage over Normans in chain armour floundering among the reeds and the mud. Olaf looked back at Father Leofric who smiled and winked at him, shouting:

"You mark my words, if they put armed knights on that causeway there's many a Norman who'll learn the efficacy of Fenland mud!"

Olaf grinned.

Across the meadow, opposite the island of Ely, the Normans appeared through the mist in orderly battalions each under the banner of his lord. The line was then broken down into ranks of three as the armoured men stepped onto the causeway. The causeway sank under their weight, just as it had for Olaf and Leofric, and, over on the island Olaf heard the creak of the ropes attached to the great poles sunk into the earthen works built by Hereward's men. The Norman soldiers moved forward relentlessly despite the muddy water seeping around them up to their knees. As more and more came onto the causeway, it began to sway from side to side. Eager to get off the bridge before they drowned in the foul mud below, the knights pushed forward earnestly. Hereward shouted out from behind the earth work:

"Olaf! Cut one of the ropes."

The Normans were close to reaching the end of the causeway so this would be a perilous operation to be caught at the base of the earthwork but, without hesitating, he slid down the muddy bank, sword in hand, shouting in Norse to the archers to cover him. The splashing and yelling of the Normans made it clear that he had less than a minute before they would be on him. He held his sword two-handedly and thrashed at the sturdy rope closest. From above came the whistle of a flight of arrows which struck the first of the Normans and threw them off the bridge. The action of this was to cause the bridge to sway even more violently and, when Olaf's sword had all but cut through, the rope gave way and snapped apart, causing the bridge to topple and throw a great many knights into the water and the mud. With some difficulty, Olaf managed to clamber back to his archers at the top of the earthwork. There he reclaimed his bow and joined in the devastation of those who had fallen. From the Norman side they managed to right the bridge and continued to charge across it. A very few managed to reach the muddy embankment, slipping on the piled bodies of their comrades. Then, from the opposite flank, there came a great shout as a body of English, not in the shield wall behind, rose out of the shallow fens and charged into the flailing knights. The death and destruction in the next twenty minutes was absolute, where the Normans, either pierced with arrows, trampled into the mud by their own colleagues, or hacked to death by great war axes, could do nothing but die in great numbers. Over one thousand knights perished that day.

First Battle of Aldreth

Chapter Twenty-Three
The second battle of Aldreth

Taillebois limped back to Brandon with his much decimated and completely humiliated forces. He was seething with rage but realised he must control himself and prepare for the inevitable fury of his King, who had entrusted his army to him, a third of whom, a thousand armoured knights, this night lay wallowing dead in the black mud and peat of Ely. This was not going to be pleasant. And neither was it. William listened in disbelief to the recounting of the massacre of so many of his men whilst Hereward had suffered barely a single fatality. Taillebois stumbled and stammered whilst de Warenne did his best to persuade the King of Taillebois' unique incompetence.

"My Lord King," said Taillebois, "I believe we were not properly prepared for this attack, and I think the monk was working for Hereward to lead us into a trap. He must be executed. I have also heard that Hereward's wife, Torfrida is deeply religious and is considered to have great powers much akin to witchcraft and magic. I strongly urge that we fight fire with fire, magic with magic and hire a witch to work for us, cursing and frightening the defenders into surrendering. We also need to build a sturdy bridge that we may use, that will take the weight of horses and siege machines. We need siege-towers and we need to build bulwarks to house our balistas, catapults and divers siege artillery to get over their defences."

"Bridges and siege engines I can manage but, as a Christian king, I do not have connections with the black arts and do not keep witches at my court," replied the King. "Is this something you know about Taillebois?"

de Warrene snorted in derision.

Taillebois raised his hand to silence his mockers:

"As a matter of fact, I have made some inquiries in the village and there are a pair of terrible hags who live together, as they are sisters. They are known for their curses and spells but also for potions both healing and poisonous. If we hire one of them and put her in a siege tower close by Hereward's defences, she can scream her curses on them from up there."

"I doubt your strategy", replied William, frowning, "but if, as you say, they have a witch to help them then I suppose we had better match them with some devilment of our own. Tell the hag we have need of her evil services but only pay her half of what she asks until she has proven her powers."

Taillebois bowed feeling smug at having regained the King's support after his recent disaster and smirked at the fuming de Warrene.

"It shall be done, my lord."

William moved his army to Cambridge where he could obtain the supplies he needed to make a great causeway that would not sink. His planners came up with the idea of attaching inflated goatskins underneath the wood to give the causeway far greater buoyancy. Carpenters worked for over a week building towers and catapults.

Back on the Isle of Ely, Olaf and Hereward watched with interest as Norman engineers built great earthworks on their side of the water and began to erect a tower from where they could look over the English defences. Olaf asked the question:

"Will these reeds burn?"

Hereward and Leofric smiled but Olaf's question was answered by Torfrida:

"It has been a very unusual March, Olaf. We have had no rain for three weeks and the reeds are very dry. Yes, they will burn as long as we have something substantial to light them with. Just over there in that swamp, there is a bubbling in the peat that releases a foul-smelling gas. That's swamp gas, Olaf, when lit by your fire arrows it will ignite with sufficient force to set all the reeds alight. We must pray to God that it does not rain and that the wind is from the East. If so, we have the gift of fire to stop the Normans."

Olaf emitted a low whistle: "I'm glad you're on our side Lady Torfrida".

Father Leofric laughed, "It is not witchcraft Olaf but science. Methane is a flammable gas known to the ancient Greeks and used to make Greek fire for their balistas."

Olaf had heard of Greek fire from Urbicus Acropolites, the Byzantine master archer who had fallen at Stamford Bridge. He had said that if Harald Hardråda had possessed Greek fire at the Battle of Niså, Sweyn's Danish fleet would have been so much firewood. But Viking kings thought that such a weapon was unmanly and declined to use it.

Cerridwyn had drawn lots with her older sister who drew the short straw and fumed as her sister cackled with glee and snatched the small leather purse from Taillebois. Her name meant 'bent' or 'crooked' derived from the Welsh word 'cyrrid'. Her mother had been Welsh and had given her this unkind name due to her deformity, but locally she was known as 'the Witch of Brandon'. Two soldiers placed her in a cart and made off in the direction of Ely.

Early the following morning, the defenders of Ely, peering into the marsh mist were regaled with a foul-mouthed drunken rant from the tower across the water. She had spent the night in the Norman camp with a flask of her own brew made from sloe berries and ginger. It was pleasant and warming and only a small amount was needed to induce drunkenness. Cerridwyn had not consumed a small amount and mounted the ladder of the tower with some difficulty.

Down below the new bridge was being rolled onto the water. Catapults and balistas were heaved up onto the earthworks. Several mounted knights rode onto the bridge which bobbed a little but held, sturdy and strong. Having seen the two horsemen safely onto the bridge, William decided that it was time to lead from the front and spurred his horse onto the causeway. A cheer went up of 'Dex Aie' as the Norman army marched forward to support their King. Rushing past the screaming Cerridwyn, who had now taken to exposing her buttocks to the English in her drunken stupor, the Normans pressed forward and charged over the bridge.

On the mound opposite, while the witch screamed and railed, Torfrida, dressed in white, stretched out her arm and pointed towards the Norman soldiers struggling in the waters. As their own witch jabbered her curses and cantrips using foul and blasphemous language, the Saxon lady, by contrast, looked fair and powerful, chanting Christian doctrine so as to encourage her own people and put the fear of God into their enemy, floundering about in the waters and swamp.

William, flanked by Taillebois on the bobbing bridge, asked what the fair woman could be pointing at. Torfrida had by now begun singing in a strong, clear voice, almost drowning out the screeching of Cerridwyn. William squinted in the morning light before exclaiming:

"There, there, she is pointing at that spot where the ground pushes up gas. It's a trap, we must pull back immediately!"

Olaf and his archers, guided by Torfrida's calm instruction saw the spot in the bog where the gas pushed up and duly fired their flaming arrows onto the mark. The gusts of wind from the East were exactly what Torfrida had prayed for and very quickly the tinder dry reeds were igniting and moving speedily Westwards towards the Norman advance. William had at once spotted this dilemma and ordered his men to withdraw in good order. But the wind was quicker and soon the flames licked right up to the causeway. The Norman soldiers tried to turn about but were caught from behind by a shower of arrows and spears. Olaf suddenly spotted William on the bridge and readied his bow for another chance. At the last second, with chaos breaking out on the bridge, William turned his horse to steady his men and in doing so saved his own life. Olaf had relaxed his fingers, and it was too late to stop the release. The arrow hit the King's shield with force, piercing it so far that the arrow struck through his chain mail. With a cry, William galloped off the bridge in full sight of his soldiers who thought he had been mortally wounded. The flames engulfed the bridge and many a Norman soldier plunged into the muddy water to relieve the burning of limbs only to join their colleagues from a previous conflict a week before in the depths of the swamp.

Finally, the flames reached the end of the causeway and up to the tower where Cerridwyn had sobered up to the sight of so many men drowning and burning. Quickly, the flames licked up the tower to the screaming witch whose costume at once caught alight. In her burning agony she threw herself from the tower and plunged to her death, her neck broken by the fall, a smouldering bundle of lifeless rags. Thus, perished Cerridwyn, the Witch of Brandon in March 1071.

William was in some pain but only the tip of Olaf's arrow, stopped by both William's shield and his expensive chain mail, pierced his flesh, there was some bleeding and much bruising. It was his pride though, which had suffered most as his men had seen the King driven back by Hereward's army in ignominious retreat. In his pain and rage he railed against the folly of Ivo Taillebois and his own folly for listening to him. Taillebois himself snuck away meekly but inside he too was raging and ordered two knights to accompany him to Mildenhall, where Cerridwyn's sister dwelt. They dragged her out of her cottage, screaming, and hanged her from a gnarled oak that grew by the Sloe tree that the sisters relied upon for their berries. As the bough creaked and the second witch fell silent, Taillebois realised his rage had not been sated. But there was nothing left to do but return to the camp and face the anger of the King.

Chapter Twenty-four
Fall of the Isle of Ely

The following day, the defenders, waiting for a third assault, were delighted to see the siege machines being dragged off and the entire Norman army pulling back to Brandon. The Normans had no desire to face the fire of the marshes a second time having seen so many of their fellows die a horrible death amongst the burning reeds and sucking mud. William left half the army at Brandon and withdrew to make his headquarters at Cambridge to recover from his slight wound.

Olaf sat with a fellow Viking named Ranald Sigtrysson, the Viking King of Limerick, married to an Irish princess, but fighting for the English cause. They chatted in their native Norse until they were joined by Hereward, Leofric and Morcar.

"The men are in very high spirits," said Leofric, "but I'm afraid that Morcar has some very sad news."

Morcar came forward:

"It seems that the monks of Peterborough have heard that three men of my bother Edwin's household betrayed him to the Normans, who ambushed his party, they all died fighting. The traitors cut off my brothers' head and took it to William yesterday hoping for a reward. They were forgetting that Edwin was the fiancé of William and Matilda's daughter, Adeliza. All three are currently hanging from an oak tree on Brandon's village green."

Olaf remembered well the beautiful young Adeliza, when she was just eighteen, from his visit to Normandy with Harold. She had been very taken by Olaf at their meeting over supper, so much so that Matilda, William's wife, had taken great care to ensure that the two never got the chance to be together alone. But he also mourned the treachery which led to the death of his friend Edwin, Earl of Mercia, elder brother of Earl Morcar and Queen Ealdgyth. A handsome warrior of the dwindling line of Saxon nobility, what tragic news to be so betrayed. Olaf rose and put his arm around Morcar, still in a state of abject shock.

Ranald broke the awkward silence:

"Come my brothers, let us take the Viking philosophy in this moment and remember that Edwin was betrayed, outnumbered, and surrounded and yet refused to yield but died fighting with his sword in his hand. I heard he slew many Normans before going down with great courage. He died a true English hero. Let us go and drink his entry into Valhalla. Though he lived a Christian, he died like a proper Viking."

Father Leofric twitched somewhat at this but concurred that what was needed was a good wake to send off this noble earl as befitted his heroic death. Perhaps you could feast in Valhalla before going to Heaven? Leofric didn't know and right now, didn't care:

"Let us salute your noble brother, Earl Morcar, and God rest his soul."

The party of warriors and noblemen made their way to Hereward's longhus and there they drank deep and late into the night to the memory of the Earl of Mercia.

Several months passed as William tightened the blockade of Ely. One day during the Summer, a monk was rowed to the island by a posse of armed Norman soldiers. William had instructed Taillebois to deliver the monk with a message to Hereward. It was costing William dearly to keep a standing army and the losses from another frontal assault could not be countenanced. The message was a simple one: "Surrender to me personally and stand down your rebel army. I have great respect for you and your courage. As King of England, I will grant you a pardon if you will join with me and accept me as your King, your lands at Bourne will be returned to you and your followers will be granted safe passage to return to their homes after swearing allegiance to me as your rightful King, anointed by God in Westminster Abbey."

Taillebois read this message with horror. He held such hate for Hereward that he could not possibly accept him being forgiven after the slaughter he had wreaked on the Norman army.

Taillebois had the message re-written to include a proviso that his wife Torfrida be handed over to the Church to be tried under canon law for the suspected offence of practicing magical arts tantamount to witchcraft. The monk knew nothing of this edited version and delivered it to Hereward in good faith.

On reading the parchment, Hereward flew into a berserk rage and threw himself at the Norman soldiers hacking at them with a war axe.

Siward Barn was with him doing likewise with a double handed sword. The soldiers were quickly dispatched, leaving the monk standing in the water shivering and quaking with fear. Hereward handed back the parchment to the monk:

"Hand this back to the King in person and see that no one else sees this parchment. I suspect treacherous deeds in the Norman camp. William is, above all, a diplomat and this is not the way of a diplomat. This has all the fingerprints of a clumsy second such as that idiot Ivo Taillebois."

At this the monk's eyes widened in terror.

Hereward nodded, "Ah, yes, I thought so."

Anglo-Saxon axeman defending Ely

Torfrida heard the news from Hereward and was greatly disturbed by its implications, that they seemed bent on burning her as a witch.

"So, they mean to burn me, do they? Hereward you must not let me be taken. I could not bear it. Kill me first."

"They will not take thee my love, I vow it. We will get you to safety off this island and break the Norman blockade by night. We must plan your escape and find you a safe convent to take refuge."

In Cambridge, William had spent months planning his next move but had hoped that a diplomatic solution could be reached. On reading the parchment that the monk returned to him, and learning of the murder of his couriers by Hereward, he, likewise, flew into a rage and screamed at Taillebois:

"How dare you think to interfere with my messages in suchlike manner?"

Taillebois had his defence cunningly prepared and argued that Torfrida was a well-known sorceress to the monks of Peterborough and was therefore not to be included in any amnesty, as she would be subject to ecclesiastical courts.

Puce with anger, William knew that he was correct in what he said.

"And in any event, my Lord King, Hereward has sworn a solemn oath to oppose you and would never surrender, let alone allow his lady to be burnt. But it puts the monks on our side for the first time."

William growled inwardly and drank a draught of wine whilst waving a hand for them to leave him to ponder.

As Hereward assembled some of his most able people to smuggle Torfrida through the Norman blockade, William activated his third and most ambitious plan to take the island. He would ride out from Cambridge at sunset and create a torchlit procession to alert all the defenders of Ely to expect another attack. This army was only a portion of his forces, however, made up mostly of shocked survivors of the two previous assaults, whose morale was rock bottom. But travelling by night and guided by a number of treacherous monks who had gone over to the Normans, a full, fresh army was sailing from the seaborne side using all the ships at William's disposal. Whilst the defenders looked Westwards to the torches of William's army, the main force would land by night on the Eastern bank of the island and set light to the houses to cause utter panic.

By coincidence the appointed time was the same as chosen by Hereward for Torfrida's evacuation. The chosen men in the boat were Hereward, Leofric, Olaf and a few housecarls of trust. When the Normans landed therefore, the leadership of Hereward was not there and the panic created by William's sea invasion was more than the minds of Morcar, Siward Barn and Ranald Sigtrysson were able to control. After a struggle, both Siward and Ranald sold their lives dearly and, with the Norwegian archers being overwhelmed, Morcar raised his arms and screamed to the defenders:

"Stop! Enough! We cry quarter! We yield!"

The Normans pulled back ten paces and signalled for the English to lay down their arms, which they duly did, and were kept under careful watch until sunrise when the King and Taillebois would cross over to identify any nobility and look especially for Hereward and Torfrida, oh yes, and Olaf. William had neither forgiven nor forgotten.

Splashing quietly through the reeds, Torfrida looked behind her from the boat and gasped.

"Yes, I know" said Hereward, who had been rowing and had noticed the fires lighting up the night sky from the direction of Ely. "We must just pray they hold until we can get you safely out of here."

Olaf shrugged doubtfully. If buildings were burning it meant that the Normans were in the village and at the rear of the defence works. The defenders would be surrounded. Leofric muttered a prayer and was joined by Torfrida. The housecarls gazed silently, counting their blessings that they were not part of what could well be a massacre.

As the sun rose, an ominous black pall of smoke was discernible from a distance over the island of Ely, as William and Taillebois with the army made their way onto the dry land among the many dead bodies of Norman and Saxon alike. The Norwegian bowman had taken quite a tally and had fought ferociously to the last man as had Siward Barn and Ranald Sigtrysson. But without Hereward to lead them, the instinct for survival overcame many who, if they had known their fate, may well have preferred to die sword in hand with some honour. But, once Morcar had surrendered, the battle was lost. William set aside the few nobles including a wounded Æthelwine, Bishop of Durham. The rest were sent in groups of thirty or so to the ships over on the Eastern side of the island where they were told they would be pardoned and set free. This was the case although not before William's men, organised by Taillebois and de Warenne, had cut off the hands of the unfortunate survivors and gouged out their eyes. The women were spared and ordered to steer the boats to the mainland to warn off any others who might contemplate a revolt against the King. William then had de Warenne search through the bodies for Hereward and Olaf. There was one Norwegian archer with long blond hair matted with blood and staring blue eyes. De Warenne was sure that it was the same man who had shot him out of the saddle. William was not convinced that this body was indeed that of Olaf Slagbjørn.

"Guillaume de Malet told me in London that this Olaf carried a beautiful sword given to him by the one they call 'the Ætheling' who claims my throne. This dead archer carried an axe like any Viking."

The Bishop, Earl Morcar and a few other lesser nobles were taken away to be imprisoned for life.

And thus ended the last of the English rebellions against the Norman conquest.

Chapter Twenty-five
Return to Norway

Olaf was as heartbroken as Hereward at the loss of the army, although they did not then know how complete that loss was. They landed the boat and made their way on foot to a Benedictine nunnery called Chatteris Abbey. Torfrida was known there and would be relatively safe. Hereward had a tearful farewell as his belovéd disappeared into the cloisters escorted by a kindly Abbess and several young novices who comforted her.

Olaf, Hereward, Leofric, and the housecarls were now in a bit of a quandary as to where to go next. All agreed that York by boat would be the quickest way out. They returned to their skull and made off for the coast and North up to the Humber. Now that Guillaume de Malet had been driven out of York by the Danes, it was a much safer place as the new Sherriff of York was a certain Hugh fitz Baldric, a pious man who, more importantly, would not recognise either Olaf or Hereward.

The boat landed up the Humber estuary and past Ricall where the Viking invasion of Hardråda had landed their three hundred ships. Given the small skull, they were able to get to within a mile of York before they disembarked. Once inside the city, the burnt-out Minster, and other surrounding buildings were evident, but the town seemed to have restored itself with dwellings and shops and the occasional inn. Olaf and his group headed for the rowdiest inn, obviously. Entering the dimly lit drinking house, there was no immediate recognition of a famous warrior, a Norwegian archer, a priest and four men at arms. This boded well until some idiot in his cups called out:

"Hereward! You are Hereward, the saviour of England!"

Hereward's four housecarls immediately silenced the idiot by pushing him into a corner and shoving a cloth into his mouth.

But the damage was done. People began murmuring and pushing their way towards Hereward in order to get a better look.

"Yes, it's Hereward for sure!" cried one.

Father Leofric took the floor:

"Listen, you fools! Are there any Normans or Norman spies here?"

The crowded inn laughed:

"Ha! They wouldn't last very long in here. Are you he though? If so, Lord, you are amongst friends. We know everyone in this inn except those three foreigners in the corner over there. They came in from Orkney just this morning. They are known in York and, I believe, may be trusted."

Olaf peered into the gloomy corner. He squinted slightly as he thought he recognised the party, it was Ari the mariner and the twins, Sigurd and Ulrik who had protected both he and Astrid in Orkney.

Olaf was delighted to see the answer to his problems:

"Ari, Sigurd, Ulrik! We meet again!"

The twins arose shrieking in joy to toast Olaf, whereas Ari placed his hand on his forehead:

"Oy Herregud! Where are we going this time?"

"What a timely meeting," laughed Olaf. "I need a lift out of here quite urgently. The Normans are after my blood. I have, once again, done some serious damage to the King's pride!"

The four retired to the quiet corner to plot Olaf's extraction from a disastrously lost cause.

"We sail on the tide to Orkney. Don't be late this time. Glad to have you back with us. Sigurd and Ulrik, do not get drunk this night nor allow our honoured guest to do so either."

In another corner of the rowdy inn, Hereward the hero, was negotiating his own extraction with his men to Scotland. He would live to fight another day and Father Leofric would live to write his saga or history.

The following morning, after sleeping at the inn, Olaf arose early and bade an emotional farewell to Hereward, Leofric and the housecarls. He had arranged to meet Ari on the River Ouse and hastened over to Astrid's cottage, hoping against hope that it was still empty. Incredibly, in the square, under the shadow of the burnt-out

Minster, the cottages stood intact and, judging by the overgrown ivy around the door, it looked very much as though nobody had dared to take over someone else's property just yet. Everything was overgrown but Olaf still had the key given to him by Astrid when they left York in flames. The lock was rusty but it turned. Forcing open the door against the strands of ivy, Olaf entered the dusty living room finding it just as Astrid had left it. Making his way to the hearth, Olaf removed the cauldron and wobbled a particular stone behind it. It moved reluctantly and Olaf helped it out with his dagger. To his great joy and relief, there were the papers from Harold Godwinson promising him an earldom and land, the letters of introduction from Tora to Thorfinn Earl of Orkney and from Thorfinn to Tostig. Behind them, at the back of the hole, was a leather bag containing a sizable quantity of gold coin, some featuring Harald Hardråda's head and the rest featuring Harold Godwin's head. This was a small fortune and would get Olaf home. He thanked God and then, putting his hand on the small hammer around his neck, thanked Odin too, just for good measure. Olaf left the cottage and carefully locked the door with his bag of precious items, including the deeds as given to him by Morcar, but which Olaf had given to Astrid and Renweard as a wedding gift. So many memories, but Olaf hastened away to the River Ouse at Fulford several miles away. There was Ari, standing astride his vessel shouting orders as supplies were loaded on. Olaf pressed a gold coin into Ari's hand.

"Next stop, Orkney and then Bergen!"

The twins Sigurd and Ulrik gave a loud cheer claiming this to be like old times, being part of Olaf's great saga. Olaf pulled a fur over him. It was a glorious Summer's day, but the wind was like a whetted knife. The sail filled and fluttered as the men on the riverbank cast off the ropes. Olaf breathed a sigh of relief, in a few hours he would be out into the North Sea, out of sight of England and out of reach of the Norman's clutches.

It was a beautiful day and Ari's sleek ship ploughed North past the John O'Groats tip of Scotland and out East towards Orkney before turning due Northwest into the islands and the little port of Kirkwall.

Olaf disembarked to stretch his legs:

"Are we stopping here the night?" he enquired.

"There's a nice inn here where we can rest up, let's go."

It looked inviting. Ari signalled for them to go inside where a large, smiling lady brought them flagons of ale and some bread.

"I think we've earned a drink and a warm bed. I would have gone up to the Earl's palace at Birsay but as the Earl Thorfinn died a while back and the Lady Ingebjørg passed in December 1069, the rule of the islands is being shared by those two spoiled brothers Paul and Erland. They hate you it seems almost as much as they hate each other so we won't be going there on this trip. The two earls wanted me to return this ship that had been gifted to me by Lady Ingebjørg. So, I left my home in Birsay and took my young wife with me back to Bergen. That's why I'm headed there. Do you remember that pretty young girl in Bergen who had the ghastly mother who was married to the dying man called Anders?"

'Yes, of course. Astrid's poor father. We arranged his final Will I remember," said Olaf.

"Well, this terrible woman went wild with rage when she discovered Anders' Will had left her practically nothing. She took her rage out on Solvej, so I vowed to return and bring her to Orkney as my bride. We lived happily in Birsay under the patronage of the Lady Ingebjørg until she sadly passed. I received a written order from the two brothers that my ship must be returned as I was no longer in Lady Ingebjørg's employ on account of her having died. That ship was originally given to me by Jarl Thorfinn and I continued to use it to keep Lady Ingebjørg supplied, especially when she was sick. That boat is my livelihood, so we left and returned to Bergen where we rented a small place. Solvej's mother would not let us use Andershus as she needed the rooms to rent to passing travellers and sailors. But we have had word that Astrid has now returned with her son who she named Anders after her father. The notary was summoned, and the old woman was given notice to quit, whereupon she moved in with some lover she had been seeing when Anders was dying. Astrid has now taken back that which is rightfully hers and has the money to do the place up and restore it as a popular inn and guest house. She has invited her stepsister Sølvej back to help her run the place and look after little Anders, who is now eight years old."

"This is wonderful news!" Olaf had been listening intently and was going to ask of any news regarding the ladies that Sweyn had all but abducted. "So, Astrid is back home in Bergen. But what of the others? Queen Ealdgyth with Fionne and Esla, where did they go?"

"I am not sure," replied Ari. "I heard a rumour that they had gone with Sweyn to his court as his wife Tora was having a difficult pregnancy."

Olaf's eyes widened: "Queen Tora expecting? But she must be in her mid-forties! She is far too old to be having babies!"

Ari raised his palm, "That is only what I have heard, Olaf.

But the big story is that, after they left Bergen, Sweyn's fleet hit a terrible storm on his journey to Denmark. He lost seven ships, particularly two that were carrying the gold from Peterborough Cathedral and the substantial bribe he had accepted from King William." Olaf exploded with laughter.

Ari, being a devout Christian, quoted from St Paul to the Galatians:

"'Be not deceived, God is not mocked, for whatsoever a man soweth, that shall he also reap.' I heard that one at Lindisfarne, but it seems to fit the fate of Sweyn."

They chatted into the late evening with the twins constantly asking Olaf to tell them more about his battles with the Normans. They especially liked the bit about the Witch of Brandon.

The following morning, the skies were dark and the sea looked rough and forbidding. Olaf looked doubtful.

"Don't worry Olaf, I've sailed in rougher seas than this," laughed Ari, "and anyway, call yourself a Viking?"

The journey was rough, but Ari's ship was used to ploughing through the vast waves of the North Sea. Olaf had not been sick at sea since his first time on Harald Hardråda's dragon ship 'Ormen' but he controlled his queasiness and didn't disgrace himself. Finally, the storm broke, and seagulls could be heard overhead indicating that the coast of Norway would soon be in sight. As Bergen hove into view Olaf felt a slight butterfly sensation at the thought of seeing Astrid again. She might be one horn short of a helmet, but Olaf had always been very fond of her, she made him laugh and kept him cheerful.

They sailed into Bergen to a magnificent sunset, slightly north of 'due east', it was late Summer and the solstice had passed and the Autumn equinox was fast approaching. The sun dipped behind the mountains, lighting up the green slopes and the distant white peaks. Securing the ship on the waterfront, they headed directly to Andershus with Ari pushing the pace in his eagerness to be reunited with his young bride. Knocking at the door produced a fresh-faced young lad of about eight or nine. Ari had not seen him before but Olaf knew him to be Anders, son of Astrid and Renweard.

"Olaf!" he shouted in delight. "Móna (*mummy*), come to the door quickly. It's Olaf!" A high-pitched squeal indicated that Astrid was inside. She rushed to the door followed by Solvej and another, if anything, higher-pitched squeal as she recognised her beloved was standing next to Olaf. Anders put his hands to his ears:

"I think the wheels of the cart need greasing." The twins found this very amusing as Astrid hugged Olaf and Ari hugged Solvej. The twins did what they did best, they stood and grinned without feeling awkward.

"Oh Olaf, I'm so glad you're alive and here. That beast, King Sweyn, and his hideously unpleasant brother, Asbjørn, just upped anchor and sailed off taking me and little Anders like captives. Queen Ealdgyth was furious! Why did he leave you behind with just your twenty Norwegian archers. Are these two of them?"

Olaf was aware that Astrid had stopped to draw breath:

"No, I suspect the Norwegians are all dead. These fine men are Sigurd and Ulrik from Orkney. Don't you remember them?"

Another high-pitched squeal from Astrid indicated that she did.

"Oh yes! All those years ago when those ghastly bandits were trying to kill us. You came and rescued us."

Sigurd coughed and Ulrik smiled:

"Well, you didn't seem to need much rescuing" started Sigurd,

"As all we found were dead bodies," finished Ulrik.

They both laughed in unison.

"Well, they were annoying us and trying to kill Olaf. Did you hear what happened to Sweyn?" continued Astrid. "Having agreed to drop me off at Bergen, he set off south to Denmark and ran into a terrible storm in which all the money and loot he had stolen from England sank to the bottom of the sea. It got worse. Having lost a fortune, he stopped at Oslo to check that young King Olaf was being taken care of. He was, but it was there he learnt from the eleven-year-old king that his mother Tora, Sweyn's recent wife, had died and had lost her baby in childbirth."

Olaf looked profoundly shocked. Ari had told him about the shipwreck but not about Tora. He closed his eyes for a second and in that moment, he imagined he smelt the aroma of Byzantine jasmine.

"Shall we go inside?" said Olaf quietly, turning away to avoid a tear in his eye being noticed. Despite this, everyone did notice and the atmosphere became subdued. Never one to be downcast, Astrid invited them into the hostel with the great tidings that she had been teaching Solvej how to make Norse dumplings. Some Laps had recently passed through and sold her some tender reindeer meat, the aroma of which was extremely pleasing.

"Solvej, pour our lovely men some øl and I will light the wood for the sauna, and we will sweat the sea salt from their bodies." The men gave a cheer and Olaf managed a smile.

The men emerged from the sauna, cleansed, and tingling with an appetite for some more øl and a bowl full of Astrid's delicious reindeer stew. They talked long into the evening, catching up with all the stories. Astrid had a good one:

"Oh yes, I haven't told you about Asbjørn....I think you'll like this one Olaf," said Astrid, giggling behind her hand. "I have heard that Sweyn was so furious about losing all his money and his failure to take York that he asked his brother why his alliance with Edwin and Morcar had fallen apart without a battle. Asbjørn told him that he had accepted a bribe from William not to fight. Sweyn was so furious he banished Asbjørn from his court and declared him a traitor and an outlaw!"

At this, Olaf roared with laughter: "Oh! That is just too good. It couldn't have happened to a nicer prince!"

And so they talked and drank as the candles guttered. Eventually, they all began to yawn and the twins wandered off, Solvej was keen to take Ari upstairs and Olaf was left looking at the mischievous smile and twinkling eyes of Astrid.

"For old times' sake?" she asked.

Olaf smiled: "I am your guest; it would be rude to refuse."

Olaf stayed as Astrid's 'guest' for nearly a month. Ari and the twins sailed off on various trading trips until, one evening, Solvej mentioned that their next trip would be down to the new capital, Oslo. Olaf picked up on this at once. He had been wondering if he would get a chance to visit the young King Olaf III of Norway, son of Queen Tora and, in all probability, himself. Astrid was very understanding. She had enjoyed having Olaf to stay but she knew of his *vandrelyst* (wanderlust), of his low boredom threshold and, while he had no surviving relatives, he did have various offspring scattered about, one of whom it seemed, was the current King of Norway. And anyway, he was starting to get under her feet, so it was with mixed emotions that she bade him farewell one more time.

Chapter Twenty-six
Oslo

Olaf disembarked at Oslo just as he had several years before when visiting Tora. Ari and the twins said goodbye as they peeled off to an inn they knew on the waterfront. Ari waved, calling out:

"If you are not welcomed, come back and find us. You know where we'll be!"

Olaf laughed and began the trek up the steep stone pathway to Akershus slot, the wooden fortress built by Hardråda to protect his boatbuilders from Danish forces. As before, he had to pull the bell rope and wait for someone to come out to the gatehouse. No soldiers were apparent on the walls. Finally, a small window opened in the door and a bearded face called out from inside.

"Who is it? What do you want?"

"My name is Olaf Slagbjørn. I was a guest here of Queen Tora. I should like to speak to the King."

"Queen Tora died in Denmark a year ago and the King is but a boy of eleven years. You may not speak to him." He was just about to slam the window shut when Olaf called out:

"Alright, tell me who is looking after him or acting as regent and I will speak with them."

The bearded soldier growled:

"Some weird bloke Queen Tora sent for from Orkney. Apparently, he looked after her cousin, the Jarl, until he died. Now he's looking after the royal lad whilst four Jarls rule as a council until the King is old enough."

Olaf laughed with delight:

"Tell me, is he tall and twitchy with a long nose and a habit of pouting sideways when he looks at you down his nose?"

"Herregud, yes that's him alright, in every detail! Who did you say you were again?"

"Tell Thorkel that 'Olaf the Fair' awaits him outside."

"I think you had better come in, sir. Are you armed?"

"I am carrying a bow, as always, having been a huscarl archer to King Harald and I have a sword given to me by Edgar Ætheling, claimant to the throne of England."

The guard continued to be impressed by Olaf's bearing and realised that he was in the presence of someone who had seen a fight or two.

"I'm afraid you'll have to leave them at the guardhouse, sir. It was a strict rule with Queen Tora, and this has been continued by Thorkel."

Olaf shrugged, "Yes, I remember," and unbuckled his sword and quiver.

Entering the great hall, the torches and fires were already lit as it was September and the Autumnal nights were drawing in. The guard closed the door behind him as Thorkel rose from a chair.

"Ah! The Prodigal Olaf returns to Norway. My dear boy, how lean and hard you look. I would not have recognised you but for the fact that I have an exact copy of how you looked when I first met you on that journey to Nidaros, before you grew a beard!"

"An exact copy? Hello Thorkel and what do you mean?"

Thorkel smiled: "Your Majesty, may I introduce you to an old friend of mine and, indeed your mother's, who he served recently in Denmark".

In the dim light Olaf was only vaguely aware of other people in the room. Occupying the throne, that Olaf had last seen being used by Tora, was a boy of about ten or eleven years of age wearing a small golden band around his head in lieu of a crown. Sat beside him was an old man with white hair and a long beard. Olaf put him at around sixty-five to seventy years old. The boy stood up and was already as tall as Olaf. He was going to be tall, he thought to himself.

"You knew my mother?" The boy spoke clearly with an, as yet, unbroken voice, which revealed a gentle confidence and authority so different to that of the young Edgar Ætheling. "Then please approach us so that I may see you better."

Olaf made a small bow and approached. The likeness was uncanny and Thorkel turned his head and pouted to the old man as if to say: "I told you so."

Olaf and King Olaf III of Norway stood and stared at each other. For Olaf it was like looking into a mirror around 1062. For Olaf III there was something familiar about the face:

"Have I met you before?"

"No, your Majesty, I don't believe we have met."

"Well, you may stay, and we will offer you our hospitality but, as for me, I have to catch up on my Latin grammar as two bishops are coming tomorrow including Asgaut, Bishop of Oslo, and I want to impress them. We have plans for a cathedral in Bergen. Thorkel and Jarl Arneson will discuss the reason for your visit here."

Olaf's eyes widened: "Finn Arneson? I thought you were long dead?"

"Hello Olaf, it's been a long time. Yes, I survived despite being captured at Niså, fighting on the wrong side, and was imprisoned near the snake pit. I thought my days were very numbered. My daughter Ingebjørg and Tora, my niece, made it almost impossible for Hardråda to execute me. I languished there for nearly four years until he set off to conquer England, taking Tora's brother with him. At Stamford Bridge I gather that he sent your father on a suicide mission to hold a bridge against the whole Saxon army. Then some incredible marksman of an archer got him through the throat. I don't suppose you would know anything about that, Olaf, would you?"

Olaf's face remained inscrutable.

"Tora was devastated by the loss of her younger brother and my nephew, Eystein Orre, but never shed a tear for Hardråda. I was set free and was allowed to return to Denmark and served Sweyn until Tora came over for the wedding. It was here that she drew up a document stating that if anything happened to her before her son Olaf had reached maturity, I was to return to Norway and act as regent with Thorkel here acting as his tutor. But here's the problem. Given the astonishing resemblance that young King Olaf has to you and Tora, you cannot possibly remain here at court for the other Jarls to spread gossip. We will pay you a stipend and you will be looked after but, as far as Norway is concerned, the King is the son of Hardråda and the dynasty will remain intact. Mercifully, King Olaf not only has none of the looks of his 'father', but he also has none of the violence and cruelty which Magnus inherited. Under Thorkel's guidance, he will grow up to be a fair, intelligent, and peaceful ruler, far more interested in building cathedrals than building empires. Of course, Tora never told a soul about her little venture to your bedroom but, when the baby was born Thorkel heard word that it was a very fair and blond baby and began to realise why the Queen had given you money and letters to flee from Nidaros before Hardråda had time to piece together his suspicions. It was Elizaveta of Kiev who was adamant that Tora's baby was illegitimate. But she is now dead, as are Hardråda and my niece, Tora. Nobody needs to know – especially not our young King. As I mentioned, you will not be able to remain here in Oslo but you may return to your home, either here in Norway or in England. You must never mention this to a soul. In return the treasury will pay you a generous annual stipend until you die. You may be called upon to serve the King but that is highly unlikely in the near future. Do we have an agreement?"

Olaf nodded.

"Thorkel here has a pouch of one hundred golden 'Hardråda-mynt' coins so that his face may serve as a reminder. Next year you will receive the same if you tell us where you are living, only this time the coins will feature the head of Olaf III, King of Norway and son of Harald Sigurdsson, known as Hardråda. Come let us drink on this and then you must be on your way."

Thorkel clapped his hands and a serving lass appeared carrying flagons of beer. Thorkel placed the heavy leather pouch on the table which chinked pleasingly.

After downing the ale, Olaf thanked them both and said that he would be heading to Lillehammer to visit his son also called Olaf. Ignoring their wide-eyed astonishment, Olaf picked up the bag of gold coins and made his way to the guardhouse to collect his bow and his sword. He expected to see neither Thorkel nor Finn Arnesson again.

Chapter twenty-seven
Return to Lillehammer

Olaf made his way down the stone path away from Akershus slot with the heavy pouch tied to his sword belt. He hoped to find Ari and the twins still there. The sign outside the inn read 'Havfrue' and to prove it there was a painting of a beautiful mermaid with long blond hair covering her ample breasts. Olaf entered to find the place noisy and crowded. A loud cheer betrayed where Ari and the twins were enjoying the local Oslo øl.

"No, joy then Olaf?" Ari called out. "Never mind, come and join us in a drink of this fine Oslo øl."

"On the contrary, Ari," said Olaf, smiling. "I met, of all people, Thorkel who you know from Orknye. Also, Finn Arnesson, the traitor to Harald and brother to Ingebjørg. He survived! But most interesting of all, I met the young King Olaf III and, I must say, the resemblance is quite striking except for the beard. But enough of that, I have agreed not to mention it again, for which I have been generously bribed."

Olaf laughed and patted the large leather bag attached to his hip. The twins roared with approval and shouted that the drinks were on Olaf. Moving to the bar and clutching a gold Hardråda mynt Olaf asked the landlady if she could change his gold coin.

"One Hardråda mynt gets you ten silver pieces. For five silver pieces I can provide you with a room, some food and I will keep your flagons topped up until you sleep. One more silver piece will buy your three friends another flagon of ale each."

Olaf returned to his table followed by the burly lady carrying a tray with four flagons of øl and a sharing plate of meat, fish and bread.

"I need to buy a horse tomorrow for a journey to Lillehammer. Can you help me with that?"

"Oh, of course," the landlady replied. "I can get you one of those comfortable Icelandic ambling ponies, complete with a fur saddle and tack."

Olaf nodded enthusiastically and recalled the eventful journey with Erik and Ødger over ten years ago.

He paid the landlady in advance and offered to pay Ari and the twins for the travel, but they shook their heads, saying:

"No, no, we were coming this way to trade anyway and as you are practically family, we are pleased to have brought you this far. It's only a pity we can't take the ship to Minnesund and then sail up the beautiful fjørd 'Mjøsa' all the way to Lillehammer. Will you be alright on your own, Olaf?"

Olaf was touched by Ari's concern but reassured him:

"The last time I travelled from Lillehammer to Nidaros it took seven days during which time I killed a man and was surrounded by a wolf pack who didn't attack us. I was seventeen but was accompanied by two of the biggest men you have ever seen, one being my father. This time I will travel alone, and may the gods forgive anyone who tries to steal from me, because I certainly won't."

The twins laughed and the flagons were emptied and refilled.

Finally, it was time to turn in and Olaf once again thanked them and bade them farewell as Ari wanted to sleep on the boat to guard their trading wares. Olaf unloaded all his belongings from the boat and took them upstairs to his room including the two pouches of gold coin from York and from Finn and Thorkel. The night sky was clear and the stars twinkled in their millions over the fjørd of Oslo. Olaf wondered whether Freya's elderly husband was still alive and what her response would be to his turning up. He remembered his name was Bjarke, a kindly, wealthy merchant who had given Freya and her son a comfortable home. If he was dead, as was likely, she would be a wealthy lady and the suitors for a rich widow would be many. These thoughts and many others were blurred by sleep, which descended onto his consciousness and forced his rest.

The bright sunlight and the crying of the gulls woke Olaf from his deep reverie. Someone was knocking at the door, which he had locked. It was the landlady and another girl carrying a steaming tub full of hot water and some soap, that rarest of commodities. The landlady appreciated Olaf's custom and said that she made it for Queen Tora by appointment. Olaf was astonished:

"You knew Queen Tora?"

"Oh yes", said the landlady, "she was a very special lady and was lucky to get shot of that awful Harald Hardråda. I was so sad to hear she had died recently. The man looking after the new young King has asked me to continue supplying soap to the castle. I've never known young boys like soap very much."

"No", said Olaf, "that'll be for Thorkel."

"Yes, Thorkel, that's his name. Now how did you know that?"

"Never mind," said Olaf, "now let me wash in peace."

"Right you are, sir. Your Icelandic pony is outside all saddled up and he's been fed and watered."

Olaf came downstairs with his belongings and his coins in saddlebags. Peering out through a window, he spotted the dapple-grey pony munching contentedly on a bucket of oats. Suddenly it all came flashing back.

"*Vanir!*" exclaimed Olaf out loud. "My pony looked exactly like this one and I called him *Vanir* after the Norse god of wisdom. I left him at Nidaros ten years ago. This could be his son."

The landlady was washing flagons and pretended to be interested. Olaf loaded the saddlebags, blankets and other items of clothing including a waterproof coat Astrid had given him. After a bowl of grøt and a mug of milk, Olaf set off on his two-day journey comprising about twelve hours of actual travel time. The horse was just as comfortable as Olaf remembered and his saddle, like a fur armchair, rocked by a sure-footed amble.

"Freya and Lillehammer, here I come!" shouted Olaf to the people on the jetty. Ari and the twins had sailed at sunrise.

Olaf had worked out a map with Ari the night before. He was planning to avoid the roads and use the ships compass so favoured by the ancient Vikings. He reckoned with his sturdy horse, he could make Bjørnholt, heading due North, in about four hours at a gentle amble. After a short rest he was planning to make the long journey Northeast to Minnesund at the base of the great Mjørsa fjørd. It was a clear autumnal day, his horse, Vanir II, had clearly enjoyed his oats and was keen to walk off the extra pounds by ambling at almost twice a brisk walking pace. Olaf felt happy and relaxed to be going back to his village at Dalby and was hoping that all may be well with his wish to reunite with Freya.

They had been travelling for about two hours when Vanir II began to get somewhat troubled and petulant. Olaf stopped at a small lake to allow him a drink and to check that his horseshoes were all in order and that he hadn't injured his hooves. Vanir was throwing his head about as if he sensed some danger. Olaf picked up on this and walked him into a wooded area where he stood for a while, calming the horse by stroking his nose, but whose ears were up and alert. Sure enough, after a few minutes, the sound of a horse's neigh and voices had Olaf's senses sounding alarm bells. Two riders were coming down the track, one carrying a lance and the other, a hunting bow. The track meant they would pass very close to Olaf and his mount. He planned to just let them pass but, as they drew closer, he could hear their voices. It seems they were no random local hunters, but bounty hunters who had seen Olaf paying with gold coin at the Havfrue Inn. They had tracked him ever since he left Oslo and were keen to relieve him of his gold.

"He's left the track here." said one, wearing a hood.

"Looks like he headed towards the lake," said the second nocking an arrow onto its string. At that moment Vanir let out a whinny of alarm and, instinctively, the mounted archer loosed an arrow towards the sound. It flew through the branches still thick with leaves. Olaf felt his horse start with pain as the arrow thudded into his hindquarter. Releasing the bridle, Olaf quickly removed an arrow from his shoulder quiver and sent the missile with his usual unerring aim at his attacker who was calling to his accomplice:

"Got 'im, come on lets guh...!" The last word was strangled as Olaf's arrow pierced his lung and threw the gurgling rider onto the grass spluttering out the last few seconds of his life. His hooded accomplice looked in shock for a few seconds at the kicking body until it fell still. Emitting a vengeful shout, he couched his spear and spurred his horse to charge at the wooded area where Olaf was concealed. Olaf had had ample time to nock a second arrow and stick his sword point into the turf. The arrow caught the rider in the shoulder, but he kept his saddle although badly wounded. Olaf crouched down by his injured horse with his sword in his left hand. Coming through the branches, the rider finally caught sight of his quarry and attempted a clumsy stab with his spear. But his shoulder contained a steel tipped arrow and there was no power in the lunge. Olaf sprang up, parrying the spear with his bow and executing a textbook fencing 'parry-reposte' by driving the thin blade deep into his assailant's torso. The rider slumped from the saddle, not dead but not long for this world. Olaf sped up his journey to the next world with a merciful *'coup de grace'*.

Olaf paused to draw breath and check on his unfortunate horse. Nearby, a branch had been scored by the arrow which had ricocheted into poor Vanir's hindquarter but with much of the impact taken by the tree. The arrow, therefore had not penetrated too deeply.

Although Vanir was in pain, he was still able to stand. Nearby, the two bandits' horses were chewing on the rich green grass, quite oblivious to the recent debacle. Olaf collected them both and transferred everything from Vanir onto the two horses, especially the heavy saddlebags. Mounting the stronger of the two horses, he set off slowly with the other and the wounded Vanir. Olaf had gently cut off most of the arrow-shaft but had left in the arrowhead to prevent extensive bleeding from the wound before it was properly dressed by a horse-doctor, hopefully an hour's ride away at Bjørnholt.

Olaf approached the small hamlet of Bjørnholt leading the wounded Vanir at a walk. He was hopeful that there may be a doctor who could help the pony. The villager he asked shook his head but pointed down the track to where a blacksmith was audibly hard at work on his anvil. Olaf tethered the two horses and walked Vanir to the sweating blacksmith:

"Do you need a shoe?" he called out without looking up.

"No," replied Olaf. "I need an arrow removing from the hindquarter of this pony."

The blacksmith stopped what he was doing and looked up:

"Oy Herregud! How did that happen? It's my wife you'll be needin' then. Jorunna! Come outside! You are needed!"

A rotund lady with rosy cheeks emerged from a hut wiping her hands on her apron.

"Is your darling pony lame?" she asked.

"No, 'ees caught an arrow in 'is arse!" shouted the blacksmith before Olaf could answer.

"Oh, he has, has he? Well oil see if oi can fix thaat." And with a nod she bundled back to the hut and busied herself preparing things. Minutes later she reappeared with a knife, a basket of herbs and some wet clay. In no time she befriended Vanir, who was looking nervous, and proceeded to cut out the arrowhead. It was done with some expertise and Vanir bore his pain bravely before she inserted various herbs into the wound and sealed it up with the clay.

"So, what happened?" asked Jorunna inspecting the blood-stained arrowhead, was it a hunting accident?"

"Sort of," replied Olaf, "it was me they were hunting, a pair of brigands but got my horse instead."

"Brigands, was it? Well, I hope you saw them off, shooting a poor horse loike that. Oym afraid he won't be good for travelling for a day or two. We can let you have the barn for your horses while he rests up. My husband could do with some help around the anvil."

And so it was that Olaf became a blacksmith's apprentice and, for several days, toiled around the anvil learning the arduous skills of metallurgy. Vanir healed quickly and soon was able to walk without a limp. Olaf gave one of the horses to Jorunna as a thank you. She was thrilled:

"Did you know moy name means, *she who loves horses*?" she laughed.

"Just as 'e was startin' to get the 'ang of it," said the blacksmith regarding Olaf's apprenticeship.

Olaf waved them goodbye from the horse's saddle while Vanir walked alongside laden with lighter things. After four hours they reached the river crossing at Minnesund where Olaf was able to get a ferry that would take horses across the great Mjørsa fjørd up to Lillehammer. The journey would take a whole day.

It was around six in the evening when the ferry made its final stop at Lillehammer and Olaf led Vanir and the other horse over the wide gangplank and onto terra firma. It would have been impossible to have made that journey overland with a wounded pony and Olaf could not leave him behind as he believed he owed his life to Vanir's vigilance preventing him from getting an arrow in his back. The light was still good as Olaf entered the centre of the town. It had been over a decade since he had visited Bjarke's house, but the town had not changed very much other than extending outwards. The centre of town was very much the same and Olaf was pleased to see the lanterns of Bjarke's, or hopefully, Freya's house, were lit and a wisp of smoke was spiralling from the stone chimney. Olaf walked on past to the small hotel at the end of the street to enquire about a room and stabling. The landlord and his wife were courteous, and a boy was sent for to take Vanir and his equine colleague to a warm stable for a drink and some oats. Olaf retained his saddlebags over his shoulder. Leaving his other belongings in his room he enquired about a strong box which, by luck, the hotel had. Extracting a few coins, he placed the saddlebags in the trunk-like box and turned the key which he then kept in his leather pouch. The landlord became even more helpful now that he had evidence that his guest had ample means to pay his bill. Olaf left his bow and sword in his room and so looked like a traveller more than a warrior.

Seated by the fire and wearied from his travels he wanted to rest and bathe and go to see Freya when he was refreshed, and a little more fragrant, in the morning. His beard was unkempt too and his hair needed cutting. A flagon of øl and some bread and smoked fish was placed on the table by a pretty waitress who fluttered her eyelashes at him. From behind, the landlord, her father, was thinking 'don't even think about it' which must have been picked up by Olaf's subconsciousness as he was thinking, 'don't even go there!' He just needed to concentrate on making the best possible impression on Freya in the morning. He smiled at the pretty waitress, and she made a small bow and withdrew. Gradually the inn began to fill with guests and soon Olaf was just another inconspicuous man with a flagon of øl. When the waitress came to fill his cup, he asked her if she knew Bjarke from the big house up the road.

"Oh, yes sir. He was the wealthiest man in the town. He took a very young wife, but I think it must have been all a bit much for him though, as he died a number of years back. His widow is called Freya and is rather haughty and high and mighty but she is a skilled healer. All the single men and probably many of the married ones in the town want to marry her but she hasn't even let anyone woo or court her. She has a son by another man, so she was very lucky that Bjarke agreed to marry her." At this point the waitress was called away by her father to attend to customers waiting. Olaf scratched his beard and planned for the following day.

Freya aged 30

⌇

Chapter Twenty-eight
Freya

Olaf enjoyed sleeping in a bed for the first time since leaving Oslo. Before nodding off he pondered on why he was unable to make the relatively short journey from Oslo to Lillehammer without having to add another two kills to his already considerable tally. He decided that he had had enough of wars and killing and would wish only to settle down peacefully with his first love - if she would have him. In his favour, he was the father to her son. Not in his favour was the fact that he had left her as a single unmarried mother with baggage. Also not in his favour was the fact that he had had many affairs including two queens and, most recently, Astrid. How, he wondered, had Freya changed in the past ten years.

The following day, Olaf went on a spree. He had his hair washed and his beard trimmed, he ordered a new pair of boots from the cobbler and a new set of clothes and a cloak from the seamstress as he only had the clothes he stood up in and they were travel-stained with mud, blood and smelt of horse. Within a few days Olaf became a familiar face to the trades people of Lillehammer and, as the boots, the clothes, the cloak and general tidying up of his hitherto unkempt appearance developed, he became an object of great interest to the young waitress in the hotel whose fascination with Olaf was only exceeded by her curiosity. Each evening as he sat by the fire, she would serve him food and øl and stay to chat and, despite Olaf's attempts to protect his privacy, she managed to learn quite a bit of his plans to ingratiate himself with Freya. Her name was Anja and although being at least ten years younger than Olaf, she was pretty and effusive and kept him amused. She rather reminded him of Astrid when he first met her. One piece of useful information she was able to impart was the fact that Bjarke had asked Freya and her son to become baptised Christians and she had continued to visit the church with her son every Sunday after he died. As it was Saturday evening, Olaf was delighted to hear this news, as he wasn't sure that just going and knocking on her door would be the ideal way of re-introducing himself.

Viking Church - Lillehammer

The town of Lillehammer had only in the past decade converted from Paganism to Christianity and a church had been built. It was rumoured that the new young King was a devout Christian himself and so it became fashionable, particularly among the middle classes.

Sunday morning was a beautiful sunrise with the sun reflecting brilliantly off the Mjørsa fjørd and lighting up the mountains. Olaf, looking more like a merchant than a warrior, with his new boots and clothes, his orderly coiffure and his regal sword, set off towards the wooden Viking church on the slopes of Lillehammer, leading his Icelandic pony, Vanir. When dealing with a single mother, he thought, always best to bring a gift for the child, especially as he was the father of that child! He arrived at the church just as the bell began the single toll to announce that the mass was due to start.

Tying up Vanir by a water trough, Olaf entered the little church, just as the priests and altar boys were entering, and slipped into a pew at the back. Near the front pew, Olaf spotted a lady in a rich blue costume with beautiful gold embroidery and a white shawl, which covered her head, but not all of the long red plaited hair which fell from her shoulders down her back. Beside her sat a young lad with identical hair colour. That could only be Olaf the younger, his first son, conceived in the year 1060 which would make him nearly twelve. Hopefully, he wouldn't yet have a pony of his own.

The mass went through its course from the Kyrie to the Agnus Dei with the congregation not having a clue what was being said or chanted but who knew the words by heart. Finally, the priest called out in Norse:

"The mass is ended, go in peace."

The people from the front filed out first and Olaf waited to catch her eye as she walked past. No hope there as Freya looked steadily ahead ignoring all on either side. Olaf jumped out behind her and followed closely before being stopped by the priest:

"Hello, I haven't seen you here before, you must be new to Lillehammer? Are you a baptised Christian?"

Olaf stopped and replied:

"Yes, I am a Christian. My name is Olaf, born nearby in the village of Dalby and baptised in Yorvik, England by the Bishop of York."

"Really? Well, you are most welcome. What is your name, my son?"

Olaf replied in a loud clear voice:

"I am Olaf, son of Erik Slagbjørn, huscarl to King Harald III. I have come home to find some people who might remember me."

At this, Freya spun round with an expression of abject shock on her face as she recognised at once her first and only lover.

"Olaf! Olaf!" Her whole demeanour changed from cold aloof to a melting joy and she flung her arms around him. She still stood a good few inches taller than him, but he could feel the tears from her cheek on his. The priest's jaw dropped in astonishment and young Olaf took a step back, his eyes wide, lacking any sort of comprehension. Olaf could not believe this reception as he had, for days, expected a well-deserved rejection. The embrace lasted for what seemed an eternity to young Olaf until they finally released each other.

"Freya, we have so much to talk about, but first you must introduce me to this fine young man."

"Yes, of course, Olaf meet Olaf, son of Olaf."

The boy had by this time clicked as to who this stranger was as she often talked about his errant father who was away fighting wars across the seas:

"I suppose you must be my father then? Have you come back to take care of us?" Olaf coughed and looked embarrassed:

"Well, yes, if you'd like me to." He replied, glancing at Freya.

"Mamma, does this mean I can have a proper father like the other boys?"

"Kjære(darling), you've always had a proper father, he just hasn't been around lately, but I expect he'll have a great long saga to tell us in the evenings. Shall we walk down to the house?"

Many people had stayed around the church to gawp and gather gossip to take down to the town, but now they began to wander off, including the priest, who at once began to think that there might well be a marriage service in the offing to make an honest woman out of this wealthy widow.

Olaf remembered that he hadn't come alone:

"I had forgotten that I brought a friend with me. I shall have to call you Olafsson to avoid confusion. So, Olafsson, do you ride?" The boy shook his head. "Well, I should like to make a gift of my Icelandic pony to you. He is called Vanir, after the Old God of wisdom but don't tell the priest that. He is very dear to me as he saved my life in a recent fight where he was wounded by an arrow, so we must be very gentle with him as he is still very sore."

Olafsson jumped up and down with excitement:

"Herregud! Is he for me? Can I ride him now?"

Olaf laughed and Freya frowned at Olafsson's language, but she was too happy to say anything. She had never seen her son so animated and, while there had never been a bond between her elderly husband and her son, this was quite different. As Olaf helped the boy into the saddle and Vanir gave a snort there was already a natural bond between father and son developing.

They walked down to the town with Olafsson loving his ride on the sure-footed Vanir and Freya with her arm through Olaf's to hold him close as if to say, 'don't even think of ever going away again'. Olaf explained he had been staying at the hotel as he didn't know if she had remarried or had someone in her life. She explained that after Bjarke died, her father also fell ill and died, so there was no one in her life but her son and, despite the loneliness, she could not contemplate a relative stranger coming into her home despite the many suitors. She was sure that Olaf was dead in some battle or other and had had no news whatsoever, but she still dreamt and hoped that one day, he might return.

"But Herregud Olaf, you took your time!" And, for the first time in an age, she laughed out loud, unable to contain the huge surge of joy and happiness that were now contained within her.

"Can I call you 'Far' or Pappa?" Olafsson called from his pony.

"I think 'Far' will suffice. You are soon to be a man and Pappa is for children."

"Ok, 'Far' it is then." laughed Olafsson.

It was a short walk to Bjarke's house which was now Freya's house and Olaf was keen to see how it looked inside. He had a vague memory of when he had met with Bjarke that it was quite luxurious. The house had a stable which contained a carriage and one horse so there was plenty of room for Vanir. Olafsson tethered him up near to the solitary horse for company and they all went into the house. If it had been luxurious before, four years of Freya's 'woman's touch' had turned it into something exquisite. Olaf thought it more palatial than the King's palace in Oslo. There was also the smell of cooking coming from the kitchen. Freya had four staff living there to cook, clean, look after her son and to tend the stables and drive the carriage.

"Olaf, we eat on Sundays in the afternoon, please will you stay for our luncheon?"

"Thank you, Freya, I would be honoured." Olaf had never heard the word before but if luncheon meant eating then luncheon would be fine. Freya had invited several of the leading figures in the town to join them: councillors, åldermen and the priest, Father Benedict, who she placed opposite Olaf. No öl or mjørd was served but instead Frankish red wine and white wine from the Germanic states. It was very unlike a Viking feast and more like the dinner he enjoyed as guest of Thorfinn in Orknye with the three bishops in attendance. Father Benedict said grace and Freya was very impressed that Olaf knew all the protocol and had perfect manners. Father Benedict quickly picked up on the fact that Olafsson was referring to Olaf loudly, for all to hear, as 'Far' and was concerned enough to ask Olaf why he did that. Olaf had been enjoying the wine and was in no mood for secrecy:

"Well, Father Benedict, Freya and I were young lovers when we grew up together in the village of Dalby. There was no Christianity then and we enjoyed each other's company under the freedom of the pagan gods. Inevitably, a child was conceived. I had hoped to marry Freya in a hand-fasting but I was summoned to Nidaros by King

Harald Hardråda along with my father. I returned after the child was conceived and Freya had already made arrangements to live under the protection of the kindly Bjarke. A Viking wedding was held, and it was all official. I met Bjarke and gave the match my blessing even though he was so much older than she. It was agreed that she should re-marry after his passing. I have returned to Lillehammer now as all the king's and earls I have served are either dead or in exile, to see if she will allow me, the legitimate father of young Olaf, to continue as her husband and protector. So far it looks promising."

The priest frowned:

"I don't think I would use the term legitimate. If Freya wills it, you may legitimise your paternal status with the boy by being married in a Christian church and become Freya's lawful wedded husband."

Olaf nodded enthusiastically:

"Oh yes, I'm quite happy to do that. You see I am nearly thirty now. I fought my first battle in Odense in 1061 when I was just 18. The following year I fought for Hardråda at the Battle of Niså. I campaigned with Tostig and Harold Godwinson in Wales and in Normandy. I fought at Stamford Bridge and Hastings, in London and, finally, at Ely with Hereward the Wake. I am weary now. Just recently I was ambushed and nearly killed. I need to settle down to enjoy a peaceful existence with my son and the first lady in my life."

The priest stared, his mouth open with unconcealed incredulity:

"Sweet Jesus! I have heard of some of these battles. They are the stuff of legends. And you survived all of these to be with us now. It was obviously meant to be and therefore if it is the will of God and

Freya is happy to take you as her husband, then I shall make all the arrangements and clear it with the Bishop in Oslo."

"Oh, that's good," said Olaf, "perhaps I could invite Thorkel to attend the wedding as the King's representative?"

Father Benedict laughed:

"Ha, so now you are going to tell me that you know the young King and his extraordinary tutor, Thorkel? These stories are getting taller by the minute!"

"Oh yes," said Olaf, in a matter-of-fact voice, "I was speaking with them just recently, and also Finn Arneson, the senior regent of the council."

Father Benedict wanted to say 'Oy, Herregud' but given that he was a priest and that Olaf was seated beside his eleven-year-old boy, he restrained himself.

Freya was seated at the head of the table, surrounded by some stuffy looking åldermen and councillors, who nodded and smiled at everything she said. She looked comfortable holding court much like Tora and Ealdgyth used to in their regal way. Looking up she caught Olaf's eye and her face warmed into a beautiful smile. Olaf thought to himself that he had much to discuss with her before the priest went at it like a bull at a gate.

As the meal came to a conclusion, the guests gradually said their thanks and were seen out by Freya, but not before they had shot inquisitive glances to the stranger in their midst. 'Who was he and why was he here and why was he seated beside Freya's son?' These were the thoughts uppermost in their minds, but they were too polite to ask. Finally, Father Benedict got to his feet and thanked his hostess:

"A splendid meal, Freya. I shall take my leave now as I expect you and Olaf have much to discuss. Olaf, it is important that you are seen leaving the house of this widowed Christian lady before it gets too late. Lillehammer is well-known for its gossip and tittle-tattle."

"I think we are quite old enough now to know how to behave, thank you Father Benedict," replied Freya reproachfully. The priest accepted this put-down with a nod and raising his hood over his head, he left the building.

"Mamma, I would like to go and look in on Vanir and give him a brush. I want him to be my friend. Then I will go to bed. Goodnight, Mamma, goodnight, Far."

Freya and Olaf both replied almost in unison:

"Goodnight Sønn."

Olafsson skipped off to the stables laughing. For a moment there was an awkward pause as they looked at each other alone for the first time in ten years. Without a word they fell into a passionate embrace and held each other in silence. The stillness was broken by a whinny from the stables.

"That's Vanir enjoying his grooming. I think they'll be the very best of friends," said Olaf laughing.

Freya broke from the embrace and looked straight into Olaf's eyes:

"Right, tell me what that conniving old priest had to say. You seemed very deep in conversation."

"Well, he practically booked his trip to Oslo to seek the Bishop's blessing on our nuptials."

"Herregud, Olaf! Did you not travel all the way from England hoping that we might be married?"

"W'well, I was hoping for that, yes," stammered Olaf.

"Then why in the name of Odin's trousers did you not think to ask me first before getting that meddling priest involved."

"Well, I haven't had the chance to get a word in. Freya, I have always loved you and I love you still and I wish to be your husband and proper father to our son. Will you be my wife?"

"Of course I will, you idiot," And with that she wrapped Olaf in her arms and planted a passionate kiss upon his mouth until he nearly ran out of breath. They parted, panting for lack of air and Freya smiling:

"There, that wasn't so difficult, was it? Now trot off to your hotel before the priest starts banging on about the sins of the flesh."

Freya saw Olaf out, her face flushed and beautiful. Overhead, a clear night sky dazzled with a million stars. He passed the stables and called out:

"Goodnight Vanir!" From within came a snort followed by a whinny.

Chapter Twenty-nine
Self-defence?

Olaf walked back to his hotel in a daze. He could never have imagined, in his wildest dreams, to have received such a welcome home. He understood that in such a small, newly Christianised town, that the religious fervour of the townsfolk and particularly Father Benedict, would preclude any intimacy with Freya until after the wedding. Having lived in England where they were far more lax about such things, Olaf realised he would have to respect the pious ways of the good people of Lillehammer.

Entering the hotel, most of the town's folk had left to turn in as it was a Sunday night. The fire was burning and Anja, the waitress, was sweeping the floor. Her eyes lit up at the sight of Olaf:

"You are back! Finally! I've been waiting for your return all evening. How did it go? What happened, tell me everything. Were you accepted?"

"May I kindly have an øl and, if you'd like to join me as there are no prying ears around, I will tell you about my day - but not a word will you get until I have øl on the table. Freya served only wine which is not good for any self-respecting Viking." Anja hurried off and returned with a large flagon of øl for Olaf and a small flask of mjørd for herself.

"Well," began Olaf, "having not seen Freya for a decade, I was not sure what to expect. But I never expected that she would throw herself into my arms outside a church with the congregation and the priest all watching, not to mention her son. But that is exactly what happened, tears and all. It seems she had been fending off a small army of suitors in the hope that one day I would return, and that day was today."

Olaf then told of the gift of Vanir to Freya's son, the luncheon party and the enthusiasm of Father Benedict. Then he described the parting and Freya's passionate kiss. Anja sniffed and her eyes glistened in the light of the fire.

"Oh Olaf, that is so beautiful, you have made me cry" she said, half laughing, half sobbing. "Her loyalty has been rewarded. God has truly smiled on you both."

"I doubt he smiled much on me!" said Olaf laughing, "my sins have been too many to number. As a warrior I have slain a great many, more than I can remember and, as a lover, well let's just say there have been occasions when the Pagan in me took its natural course." Anja stopped smiling and her face grew serious.

"Well, if you weren't going to be reunited with Freya, I should have been very pleased if the Pagan in you would have taken its natural course with me."

Even though the light was dim, Olaf could see that Anja was blushing very prettily, somewhat shocked at what she had just blurted out. Olaf laughed gently and put his hand on hers on the table.

"Dear Anja, I am about ten years older than you and although I am very flattered that you, a very attractive young lady, should find me of interest. Where are all the fine young men of Lillehammer?"

"That's just the point," she replied, "they are either dull farm hands or fishermen. All the interesting young men leave Lillehammer and head off to Oslo, Nidaros or Denmark."

"Ah, yes I did notice how few young men came in here to drink."

"That is, until you arrived. But now you are spoken for and I shall be alone." Olaf laughed again, not so gently this time:

"Remember I have a son here in Lillehammer just a little under your age also called Olaf. Give him a few years and he'll grow into a fine young man given his parentage." Anja's eyes widened,

"Freya's Olaf is your son! Oy Herregud, of course, it all makes sense now! But he's only about twelve."

"That may be, but in five years he'll be seventeen and a fine-looking Viking. I was just that age when I was first with Freya and just eighteen when I was taken off to battle. Do you ride?"

"What?" Anja was taken aback at this change of direction but managed to nod.

"I shall be teaching Olafsson, as we now call him, to ride. Why don't you come with us. Borrow your father's horse. You can get to know the boy then the man. Time for bed now. Goodnight Anja."

He left Anja by the fire with her mouth open in mild shock.

The next day Olaf called on Freya and was let in by a maid who explained that she was in a meeting with Father Benedict. Olaf assumed he had got there early to check that Olaf hadn't stayed over, when in fact the priest had been summoned by Freya to come and discuss the forthcoming nuptials. Olaf smiled to himself; she wasn't wasting any time. Father Benedict stood up and smiled at Olaf:

"Ah Olaf, wonderful news, wonderful news. Freya has great plans for the wedding. We are hoping that Bishop Asgaut, Oslo's very first Bishop, will come and grace us with his presence. He is quite elderly but a wonderful man, much admired by the young King."

Olaf wasn't really paying attention as Freya had risen from her chair and put her arms around his shoulders and planted a kiss on his cheek. A maid emerged from the kitchen with a flagon of warm milk, sweetened with honey and offered it to Olaf. Before long all three were deep in discussion regarding the church service and the guest list for the reception, which was to be held in the house for the privileged few, and in a large tent for the remainder. There was to be much drinking and feasting, as was essential in pagan times, and there were to be musicians for dancing. Unlike Olaf, Freya had attended many weddings and knew all about the traditions and customs that were to be observed, most going back to pre-Christian days.

The first thing on Freya's mind seemed to be the *brudekrone* or bridal crown. Although she still had the silver crown given to her by Bjarke on her first wedding day, she wanted to have a Christian 'brudekjole' made. It would feature a delicate veil made of silver, which represented the Virgin Mary and her purity, given that Bjarke was not able to consummate his wedding, which he had made clear to her at the outset. The one lover she had, was the one she was planning to marry. The veil would contain delicate silver bangles that would chime against each other whenever she moved her head. In pagan times these were to ward off any evil spirits and Freya wanted to keep as many old Norse traditions as possible, whatever Father Benedict thought. As Olaf was still pagan at heart and still had his Thor's hammer around his neck, he was delighted. Another strange custom was that the bridesmaids were all to dress the same as the bride. This was again to confuse the evil spirits and protect the bride. As per the Christian tradition, 'gifteringer' (wedding rings) would need to be crafted and exchanged in the church and worn on the right hand. All this and much more was discussed with Father Benedict, Freya displaying a great talent for organising and a keen eye for detail. Finally, Father Benedict stood up and declared that he must go and prepare for his journey to Oslo the following day. Olaf was concerned that the priest would be travelling alone and imparted the story of how he had been attacked by robbers who had tried to kill him. Freya looked shocked: "So, what happened Olaf? Did they rob you?"

Olaf laughed: "No, they managed to wound poor Vanir, but I discouraged them after that."

"And did they depart from you after that?" asked Father Benedict.

"Yes, in a manner of speaking, they did depart."

"Well, I'm sure they wouldn't attack a priest," said Father Benedict.

Olaf smiled, "Oh they won't trouble you; I can guarantee."

With the priest gone, Olaf stayed and chatted with Freya who was keen to learn all his news. However, he suggested that there was so much of it that it might be best to keep it for the evenings in front of a fire where he could unravel his saga in episodes. At this point, Olafsson appeared from the stable direction where he had been with his new best friend, Vanir.

"Hej, Far! I'm all ready to go for a ride."

"Ah, hej sønn. I don't have my horse here. I came on foot. But we can walk with Vanir back to the hotel. There's someone there I should like you to meet. She can come riding with us."

"She?" asked Freya. "Do I know this girl?"

Olaf laughed: "She is the daughter of the innkeeper where I am staying. Her father keeps a strict eye on her, so she has no friends. She's about nineteen and just needs some company."

Freya conceded as she had always doted on her son and had very rarely refused him anything.

And so it was that Olaf, his son and Anja became regular riding partners and soon it became clear that Olafsson had developed a bit of a crush on this pretty, much older young lady. Anja had impressed Freya on her visits and was now invited to be a bridesmaid. Olafsson was thrilled. Anja found Olafsson a pretty boy but much too young to consider, even though he was now taller than her.

Meanwhile, on the road from Oslo there had been developments.

Father Benedict had taken his horse onto the ferry from Lillehammer to Minnesund. Being very well known in his own parish the other passengers were all happy to chat with the priest and share any gossip. When they learnt that Father Benedict was headed for Oslo, one of the travellers frowned and said:

"'Ere Father, you be careful on that road. I've heard there's been a double murder down there. Two men found dead; their 'orses were stolen too. One with an arrow through the throat and the other wounded in the shoulder then run through twice with a very thin blade, not like a Viking sword at all. They've held a *Gulathing* (legal assembly) and two of the King's law-keepers 'ave been sent to search for the culprit or culprits. They found one 'orse when they reached the blacksmiths at Bjørnholt and 'is wife said it were given to her by a shortish blond feller whose 'orse had been wounded by an arrow. She said 'ee carried a bow and a fine aristocratic sword. Sort of fits the description of that new stranger in town come to think of it."

Father Benedict listened in horror. It fitted exactly what Olaf had told him the day before.

Back in Lillehammer, Olaf returned his son and horse safely home and trotted off with Anja to the hotel. Freya watched as they rode away, Anja chatting and laughing with Olaf and wished this wedding could be sooner rather than later. She wasn't comfortable with her fiancé being in the company of a very attractive young woman who was clearly quite taken by Olaf. On arrival, Anja slid gracefully from the saddle and said she would stable the horses. Her father was inside and would fix him an øl. Olaf entered the inn and encountered the landlord inside looking very nervous and twitchy. Olaf's experience told him something was very wrong, but he was totally unarmed.

"Ah, Olaf. There have been some men here today asking after you. It seems they would like to ask you some questions." He signalled with his head for Olaf to go through to the main hall where the fire was. As he did so, a large powerful man swung out from behind an arras and wrapped a strong forearm around Olaf's neck. At the same time another large man appeared from the other direction and placed a knife blade under Olaf's chin. The first man then released his grip and proceeded to tie Olaf's hands behind his back. The pressure now removed from his windpipe; Olaf was able to speak:

"Is there anything I can help you boys with or have you come here to rob me?"

"Shut up and sit down. We are here as law-keepers on business from Finn Arnesson acting regent for the King in Oslo. Now, answer these questions: Did you stay at the Halvfruh Inn in Oslo where you bought an Icelandic ambler for your journey here?"

"I did," answered Olaf truthfully.

"And, on that journey, did you encounter two travellers who you murdered and stole their horses?"

"I did not. I defended myself from two murderous brigands who had followed me, tried to kill me, wounded my horse and attempted to steal the gold given to me by none other than Finn Arnesson himself for my services to the crown. I took the horses, yes, as the two riders were dead and I gave one to the blacksmith's wife for the kindness of tending my poor wounded ambler and the other is currently being stabled next door by the landlord's daughter."

"So, you are asking us to believe that you were ambushed by two large, mounted and armed brigands whilst you were on an Icelandic ambler and yet you, a half portion, were able to dispatch these two killers without a scratch on you?"

"They wounded my ambler with an arrow meant to kill me."

"These two were dispatched by a highly trained killer. An arrow through the throat. A second into a moving target and then a sword thrust followed by a coup de grâce. Would you be that professional killer? Who are you?"

Before Olaf could answer, there was a high-pitched scream as Anja had just entered from the stables:

"Olaf! What is happening! Who are these men and why are they hurting you?"

Olaf spoke calmly: "They are not hurting me Anja they are just asking me some questions, albeit with unreasonable force. Run to Freya and ask her to fetch the Ålderman and some councillors and bring Vanir as a witness."

"Wait there!" shouted the big man behind Olaf who ran towards the door to prevent Anja from leaving. Olaf swung round and stretched out his brand-new boots to catch the big man in the shins and sent him sprawling with a furious oath as Anja slipped quickly out of the door and down the street.

"Right," said Olaf, "I think we need some semblance of *Gulathing Law* here." The big man arose, his face red with fury, and prepared to strike Olaf a massive blow across the face, when the other man with the dagger, raised his palm to signal his colleague against such an act. Olaf was cut free and the questions continued in a far more congenial manner. With the senior citizens of Lillehammer on their way, the two men working for Finn Arnesson knew they needed to tread carefully, especially as Olaf had told them he was paid in gold by Finn Arnesson as well. If he could produce the wounded ambler, then that may be considered as enough evidence to suggest self-defence. But the question that irked them remained, who was this stranger?

In a remarkably short period of time, probably just twenty minutes, Freya had managed to summon all the councillors and the Ålderman along with Olafsson riding astride the ambling Vanir, led by Anja. They all made their way up the steps and into the hotel where it was announced that there would be an official *Gulathing* assembly as they had enough to make a quorum. Freya gave a character reference having known Olaf since he was a child, the landlord produced the Hardråda-mynt gold from the strong box as proof of Arneson's payment and Olafsson rode Vanir up the steps and into the inn as the prime witness that he had been the victim of a pre-emptive strike and that his master was quite within his rights to defend himself. Olaf answered the question the oafish law-keepers most wanted answers to; that Olaf had served two kings and had fought as a royal huscarl in five historic battles and was a highly experienced warrior and considered one of the most lethal archers in England. The Ålderman, who just last Sunday had sat next to Freya as a guest in her house had no doubt that her fiancé had been the victim of an ambush and, given his military skills, it was of no surprise that the brigands had received their just rewards. The two large law-keepers were made to seem ridiculous for their violence towards Olaf who was fêted as a hero. They were given a flagon of öl each and told to make their way to catch the last ferry back to Minnesund. Meanwhile the hall in the hotel became a scene of great celebration and Vanir was allowed to remain whilst the great and the good enjoyed the mjørd and øl.

It was at this time that Anja began to contemplate on the real possibility of waiting for Olafsson as, by then, he would be quite a catch having the height of Freya and the handsome features of Olaf.

The two law-keepers did catch the last ferry and rode hard from Minnesund to Oslo, overtaking Father Benedict to deliver the news of the assembly. Father Benedict, who had been in a terrible funk as to how he was going to ask the Bishop of Oslo to preside over the wedding of a murderer, was greatly relieved when he was told that Olaf had been cleared on the grounds of reasonable self-defence and the brigands who had been unfortunate in their choice of victim, had reaped the consequences of attacking a royal huscarl.

Icelandic Ambler similar to 'Vanir II'

Chapter Thirty
At Court in Oslo

On arrival, Father Benedict's first course of action was to report to Bishop Asgaut at the Bishop's Palace. He was informed by a monk that the Bishop was not at home but that he was in conference with the King over at Akershus fortress about a mile away. They were discussing plans for a new and first Cathedral in Oslo, dedicated to St. Hallvard to be built next to the Bishop's Palace. Father Benedict did not need all this information, but the monk was still talking as the priest walked his horse off in the direction of Akershus down by the sea front.

Father Benedict was greeted by the same guard who had divested Olaf of his weapons but, as a priest, he carried none. He was ushered into the Great Hall where King Olaf III, Bishop Asgaut, Finn Arnesson and Thorkel where all gathered around a table, gazing at some architectural drawings beside a wooden mock-up of a cathedral.

The guard coughed politely and they turned their attention to the travel-stained figure of Father Benedict.

"Your Majesty, my Lord, your Grace, Father Benedict, priest of Lillehammer, requests an audience with Bishop Asgaut."

"Your Majesty, forgive the intrusion", said Father Benedict with a bow to the young King.

"No, no please approach us. We are all in agreement here that Oslo needs a cathedral, a coronation place for kings and the Bishop here wants it built by his palace so he won't have so far to walk!" The King laughed a schoolboy laugh and everyone in the room followed suit except the old Bishop, who smiled.

Father Benedict approached somewhat nervously.

"Thank you, your Majesty. I have travelled here to ask Bishop Asgaut for a special favour by presiding over a wedding in Lillehammer." The bishop raised his eyebrows. Lillehammer was a two-to-three-day journey.

"As the priest of the town, why do you not preside over the marriage yourself. I'm far too old to go rushing around Norway taking weddings."

"Quite so your grace, but this one is a little exceptional. A wealthy merchant named Bjarke and his young wife converted to Christianity about seven years ago and donated a large sum of money for the building of a fine Viking-style church in the town which led to most of the inhabitants converting too. I now have a full church every Sunday. He died around four years ago and now his widow is to remarry. She is the most influential lady in the town and is planning to marry Olaf Slagbjørn, once a huscarl to King Harald."

There was a loud snort of laughter from Finn Arnesson:

"Ha! He doesn't waste any time does he. We've just had word from two of our law-keepers that he pleaded guilty to killing two brigands on the road to Minnesund but that a *Gulathing* in Lillehammer cleared him after he produced his wounded ambler to prove it was self-defence. Now he's marrying the richest girl in town! You've got to admire him, haven't you."

Father Benedict smiled: "They were both born in the village of Dalby, just outside Lillehammer and grew up together as childhood sweethearts until Olaf was taken off to Nidaros to join King Harald's army. He has only just returned. Apparently, he is a wanted man in England, having fought against the Normans."

At this point a door opened and a guard announced the arrival of a lady with beautiful long black hair:

"Your Majesty, please receive Ealdgyth, dowager Queen of England."

Everyone, even the King, rose to their feet as the widow of King Harold Godwinson swept majestically into the room and was welcomed by the smiling assembly. Ealdgyth made a small curtsey to the young King out of respect and her lady-in-waiting did likewise. Ealdgyth spoke in Anglo-Norse:

"Good afternoon your Majesty. I had come to ask you about my carriage, but I was intrigued to overhear you have someone here who has fled from the Norman persecution, as I have. Is it someone I may know?"

Thorkel spoke on behalf of the King:

"I believe your Majesty will know him. He is a Norwegian who has been in England serving your late husband King Harold and, more recently, King Sweyn of Denmark over in England. His name is Olaf Slagbjørn."

Fionne, the lady-in-waiting had to put her hand to her mouth to hide her amusement, but Ealdgyth remained inscrutable:

"We are delighted he has survived. He had twenty Norwegian archers with him when we last saw him in England. I had heard that they were all slain by the Normans along with Edwin, my brother and Morcar being imprisoned. At least Olaf got out alive."

Father Benedict spoke: "He has returned to his native town and has been accepted in marriage by a wealthy widow. I am here to ask the bishop to conduct the ceremony."

"And I am here to say that I am too old to make such a journey on horseback," interrupted Asgaut.

"I have a carriage," said Ealdgyth, "and I'm sure Olaf would like us to be at his wedding if he knew we were here. My lord Bishop, the carriage was a gift from King Olaf III but needs a new wheel which is why I came here this afternoon. If we can get it fixed you would be very welcome."

"The young King laughed and clapped his hands at the resolving of the problem: "There it is, let it be done. Thorkel, can you arrange for that?"

Thorkel nodded. Thorkel arranged everything for the King which reminded Father Benedict that there was one thing more to ask:

"Oh yes, Thorkel, Olaf has asked if you, as his oldest male friend, would kindly act as his *forlover (Best Man).*

Thorkel smiled and addressed the King:

"If your Majesty could do without me for a few days?"

King Olaf had no trouble answering that one:

"I'm sure the Kingdom of Norway will survive your absence for a week."

Finn laughed and Thorkel pouted. The Bishop looked like he had been check-mated as there seemed no way out but to accept Ealdgyth's invitation to share her carriage.

"Wonderful!" exclaimed the boy-king, delighted not to have Thorkel fussing around for a whole week. "Then it's all settled. I think we need to bring in some food and øl for a little celebration. Thorkel, can you organise another leather pouch of gold coins as a wedding present from the treasury of the Crown of Norway to the happy couple?"

Thorkel nodded: "Of course, your Majesty."

Viking Pouch of Coins

Chapter Thirty-one
The Wedding

Father Benedict returned to Lillehammer in the happy knowledge that he had achieved something of a diplomatic coup. Not only had he fixed the Bishop of Oslo to preside and Thorkel as Best Man, but he had also added English royalty to the guest list and he had secured the King of Norway's blessing with a gift from the Treasury. Not a bad days work he thought as he disembarked from the ferry. But most fortuitous was that Olaf had been cleared of any murder charges which would have made the marriage impossible. Heading straight to Freya's house he imparted the news. Freya was horrified:

"Oy Herregud! Where are we going to lodge an ex-Queen of England and her entourage."

Father Benedict said she had just one lady-in-waiting and no maids that he knew of. Olaf confirmed that when she left Ely, she was accompanied by just Fionne and Esla. He presumed Esla must have left the ship in London when the fleet stopped for supplies.

Freya sighed:

"Well, I suppose we do have two guest-rooms, but they are not nearly good enough."

Olaf continued:

"Ealdgyth endured great hardship when Sweyn's fleet was besieged at Ely, there was practically no food as the Normans had wasted the North to such an extent that all farms and livestock were destroyed. I haven't yet told you the half of my story but the last year at Ely was by far the worst. Ealdgyth and Fionne endured all of that without a murmur of complaint. Ealdgyth's own baby son, Harold, succumbed to pneumonia. I know they will accept your kind hospitality with the utmost grace."

Father Benedict added:

"Oh yes, I forgot, the young King gave me this to give to you both as his wedding gift. It is quite heavy." He placed the leather pouch on the table with a bump and a chink. Olaf knew the weight of one hundred gold coins, but this seemed twice the weight.

"Just a guess, but it feels like two hundred Hardråda-mynt," said Olaf.

Olaf III 'The Peaceful' silver penny 1070. © British Museum.

Father Benedict shook his head:

"I have taken the liberty of removing one coin for my expenses on the journey and I can tell you they are brand new 'Olaf III' gold coins, including silver pennies." Olaf and Freya peered into the pouch and the light falling upon the coins was dazzling.

"Jøss! (wow!) there's more than enough here to pay for two weddings and I've had the rings made already!" said Olaf blinking.

Just then Olafsson ran in and asked if he could go riding with Anja. When Freya asked if he needed Olaf's help with Vanir, he shook his head and laughed: "No, I've got Anja for company!"

"Well, they seem to be getting on well," said Freya, with all the suspicion a mother could have when her only son first discovers female company, "isn't she a bit old for him?"

"Give it time," said Olaf, "give it time."

The weather was fine for the week of the wedding as the whole town was buzzing with the news that an English queen was coming to Lillehammer. The ferry moved slowly up the fjørd towards the town with its precious cargo of Queen Ealdgyth, Fionne, her lady-in-waiting, Asgaut, Bishop of Oslo, Thorkel, tutor to King Olaf III and two burly huscarls sent for their protection. The whole town turned out to greet them and there was much cheering as they disembarked on foot with the carriage and horses being carefully led by the coachmen off the boat. Freya made a short curtsey to Ealdgyth who then kissed her on the cheek with the remark:

"My dear Freya, I hope you don't mind us crashing your wedding like this. It was the only way we could get the Bishop to attend. Olaf told me everything about you when we were in England. He thought never to see you again and now look! This is Lady Fionne." Freya kissed her on both cheeks in greeting:

"We are so honoured to have you here, and you, my Lord Bishop."

The bishop puffed some unintelligible greeting.

"But where is our lovely boy?" said Ealdgyth. Olaf stepped forward, almost unrecognisable in his fine clothes, his hair and beard groomed and not a trace of mud or blood anywhere.

"Ha-ha!" roared Ealdgyth, "where is my fierce warrior huscarl? Olaf, you look wonderful," and to the astonishment of Freya and half the town, she took him in a warm hug and Fionne likewise. A great cheer went up and Thorkel stepped forward pouting to either side:

"And I, who have travelled all this way to be your 'Best Man', where is my greeting?"

"Thorkel! You made it!"

"So, Olaf the Fair is finally settling down with this fine lady. Lady Freya, I am Thorkel, tutor to the King. I have known Olaf since he was seventeen, so I am honoured to act as his second."

Finally, they all piled into the two carriages and made their way to Freya's house for some food and drink before being shown their quarters. The wedding was scheduled for the next day and was to last for three days.

That evening, Freya and Olaf went up to the Viking Church with Olafsson, Anja and Thorkel to rehearse the marriage ritual in the morning. The Bishop and Father Benedict were there to go through the service and explain what they must do. Of course, it was all in

Latin, so mostly they had to watch the bishop for the cues. Soon it was all rehearsed and ready for the morrow. Olaf returned to the hotel with Anja for the last time.

The following day, the sun rose, glinting off the great fjørd called Mjøsa living up to its meaning, 'bright shiny one'. The fishermen had been out early and were returning with a good catch of trout ready to go freshly onto the wedding tables. Olaf was dressing in his wedding clothes that Freya had had made for him with a matching suit for Olafsson. Freya was being helped into her dazzling costume, holding back the silver veil until the last so that she might partake of a light breakfast. Her bridesmaids giggled and fussed around her, irritating and frustrating her maid who was trying to plait her hair. Ealdgyth was being attended to by Fionne. Thorkel had stayed at the hotel and the Bishop had stayed with Father Benedict. At around ten o'clock, a group of musicians assembled outside Freya's house. One played a Tagelharpe, another a Pan Flute, a third a Rebec and a fourth a skin drum as used by the Sami people of North Scandinavia. The town's people gathered around as they played, then gave a great cheer as Olaf and Thorkel came across from the hotel and followed the musicians in a procession up the hill to the Viking Church. Once they had all reached the church, Freya boarded her carriage along with some of her bridesmaids and Ealdgyth boarded hers with Fionne, Anja and the remaining bridesmaids. Olafsson followed behind on Vanir who had been decorated with flowers which he seemed pleased with, as he tossed his head proudly. Inside the church, Olaf waited patiently beside Thorkel and was joined by Olafsson. In what seemed an age for the bride and bridesmaids to decant, Freya appeared in the doorway with her silver veil jingling gently in the breeze. As she made her way up to Olaf's side, the Bishop in a throaty voice began to intone the nuptials:

"Olaf, Vis accipere Freya hic præsentem in tuam legitimam uxorem juxta ritum sanctæ matris Ecclesiæ?" (Olaf, do you take Freya here present, for your lawful wife according to the rite of our holy mother, the Church?)

Olaf replied: "Volo." (*I do*)

The bishop then asked Freya likewise if she will take Olaf as her lawful husband to which she replied:

"Volo."

The bishop then sprinkled the couple with holy water and asked for the rings. One was produced by Thorkel and the other by Olafsson and placed on a purple cushion held by Father Benedict. The Bishop blessed the rings and signalled for Olaf to place the ring on Freya's finger which he noticed was trembling a little. She then placed the other ring on Olaf's finger. The Bishop raised his hand with two fingers together pointing upward:

"Ego conjungo vos in matrimónium. In nomine Patris, et Filii, et Spíritus Sancti. Amen." (I ratify and bless the bond of marriage you have contracted. In the name of the Father, and of the Son, and of the Holy Spirit).

The Bishop smiled: "Olaf, you may kiss the bride." A great cheer went up in the church as Olaf gently lifted the silver veil to reveal Freya's eyes glistening with tears and planted a lingering, tender kiss upon her lips. Another great whoop went up causing Thorkel to pout to one side with disapproval. He did not care for rowdiness.

Finally, Bishop Asgaud spoke for all to understand:

"We beg you, Lord, to look on these your servants, Olaf and Freya, and graciously who vow to uphold the institution of marriage established by you for the continuation of the human race, so that they who have been joined together by your authority, may remain faithful together by your help. Through Christ, our Lord. Amen"

Olaf and Freya processed down the aisle where a crowd, who could not fit in the church, was waiting. The musicians began playing and the crowd outside threw rye and barley grains which Freya was supposed to catch. The congregation then spilt out of the church; bridesmaids first followed by Thorkel and Olafsson, then by the Bishop and Father Benedict, Queen Ealdgyth with Fionne and then the townsfolk in order of importance. Outside it was positively raining barley and rye so Olaf and Freya decided to lead the procession down the hill to the house for the marriage feast. Freya gripped Olaf's hand tightly and Olaf remembered the 'I choose you' look she had given him all those years ago in Dalby village.

The wedding lasted for three whole days with a huge tree trunk making up the centrepiece of the main hall where the feast took place. The trout was served, hot, freshly-caught, also fish which had been salted and smoked with aromatic wood chippings for at least twenty-four hours. This was Olaf's favourite and something he missed most whilst away in England. The top table consisted of Freya and Olaf with Olaffson and Anja seated on Freya's side and Thorkel, Ealdgyth and Fionne on Olaf's side. Then the clergy on Freya's side with a smattering of åldermen and councillors in order of importance. Most of the others were seated under the large marquee attached to the front of the house where two new pine trees had been planted on either side of the door to signify the union. Freya stood up and everyone thought she was going to make a speech, but it was only to remove an uncomfortable silver coin from her shoe which she had placed there to ward off evil spirits as per the old Norse custom. Øl was served to all the guests with the exception of the top table who had the added option of fine Rhenish white wine which had been chilled in the icy cold water of the fjørd.

As the delicious food and ample drink began to have a pleasing effect, various Norse traditions began to come into play. When the guests began to hit their flagons with their knives it was the signal that Olaf and Freya must stand on the stump and kiss, but if the guests stamped their feet on the floor, it meant that they had to crawl under the table and kiss there. If the groom needed to go to the bathroom all the men would try to kiss the bride and likewise if the bride left the room all the girls would try to kiss Olaf with Ealdgyth, Fionne and Anja first in the queue. Then came the toasts which were many and varied and then the dancing which had to be started by Olaf and Freya standing on the tree stump. These revels went on for three days, but the happy couple showed no signs of exhaustion and, indeed, on the second day Freya seemed to have gained a happy glow after rising late from her wedding night.

Finally, it was time for all the guests to depart and Olaf and Freya settled down to enjoy a peaceful married life.

Chapter Thirty-Two
'Beatitudo Matrimonii' (Married Bliss)

Life for Olaf was about to change radically. He and Freya were considered to be the most important people in the town. He was wealthy in his own right with his generous allowance of one hundred gold pieces a year plus the considerable wealth of Freya. Bjarke, good to his word had left her a great deal of money, fisheries, two farms and the largest house in Lillehammer. Olaf greatly enjoyed the change of lifestyle, and he loved Freya in a way he had never loved anyone. He and Olafsson were very close but his son's crush on Anja was growing steadily and, although she treated him like an affectionate puppy, they became inseparable. Olaf seldom went out riding with them anymore as they seemed to be most content with their own company.

For Olaf, as the months turned into years, he became restless. Having lived a life of great turmoil and danger, rubbing shoulders with kings and queens, and fighting epic and historic battles, the peaceful life in Lillehammer began to bore him and Freya noticed a restlessness about him which worried her. There just wasn't enough for him to do. His one distraction was his son whose voice had now broken and who starting to develop some blond fur about his face. He had grown much taller, to Olaf's relief, and was now learning archery and swordcraft from his father. At night, Olaf would regale them with stories of Harald Hardråda, of Tostig, Harold Godwinson, William of Normandy and Hereward the Wake. Olafsson's eyes would glitter in the firelight as he dreamt of taking part in such adventures.

Eight years passed and Olafsson was now a tall fully grown man of twenty. He had the combined beauty of Freya and the handsome features of his father. Anja no longer treated him as a puppy but more her soulmate. However, she was forced to spend less and less time with Olafsson as her father was very sick and she not only had to care for him but run the inn as well. Freya brought her nursing skills into play but to no avail. When he finally passed away, he was buried up on the hill in the Viking churchyard. At the wake which followed, Anja and Olafsson were very close and, unknown to either Olaf or Freya, Anja had told Olafsson that if he proposed to her now, he would be accepted. He did so immediately and was accepted on the proviso that it remain a secret to allow a respectable period of mourning. After a month, the bans of marriage were read out in the Viking church by Father Benedict, to the huge excitement of the town. People still talked about the lavish wedding of Olaf and Freya.

It was now 1080 and the whole town was brimming with excitement. Anja was to be married as a pure maiden with the silver crown of St. Mary and Olaf lent his son the sword of Edgar the Ætheling to wear as a sign of his protection for his bride. Apart from having a bishop and a queen present, the wedding was on a similar scale and all the guests brought gifts of money which they placed in a great basket for the couple. After the service the wedding feasting went on for three days as before.

As Anja was now twenty-five and Olaffson twenty, it came as no surprise when, a few months later, Anja announced that she was expecting her first baby. Freya invited Anja to stay at the house as she and her husband had been living together at the inn. In 1081, Anja gave birth to a healthy baby girl.

A steward was hired to manage the inn and Olaffson and Anja lived at the house on a permanent basis. Apart from this blessing, Olaf was very aware that not much of any excitement was happening in the backwater that was Lillehammer.

Occasionally, a traveller would pass through and stay at the inn that Anja and Olafsson had owned since the passing of her father. Each time, Olaf would hurry over there to try and glean some news of goings on in England. The news was thin and sketchy, but it seemed that King Olaf III had made peace with William. William, it seemed, was hell-bent on taxing his conquered people until the pips squeaked. Not content with decimating the North in an act of brutal and savage genocide, William had sent tax inspectors to every corner of his land to record the exact value of every town and village down to the last pig and planted field. This was being written up in a great survey by the monks and a copy was presented to William at a castle fort called Sorviodunum often called Sarum. This was the year of 1086. The great book has since been called the Domesday Book because its findings were unalterable and, like the Last Judgement, its sentence could not be quashed. Olaf listened in fascination to this appalling news and thought if Rhys had not knocked his aim at the critical moment this monstrous tyrant would be long in his grave but for that split second.

Another year passed and yet another traveller brought tidings from England. This time it was to declare that William, known as The Conqueror, had died and his massively overweight body was taken back to Rouen and thence to Caen where the body, already decomposing, was found to be too big for the tomb. When attendants attempted to force the body into the tomb, it burst, filling the cathedral with a foul aroma, and causing many present to vomit.

Olaf listened to all of this with great interest. It was also mentioned that William on his deathbed had begged for forgiveness from God for his harsh treatment of the people of the North of England and forgave many outlaws, including Olaf and ordered the release of many nobles including Ealdgyth's brother Morcar and Harold's youngest brother, Wulfnorth Godwinson.

'Now, now,' thought Olaf, 'now is the time to return to England and claim my rightful land granted to me by King Harold and stolen by the Normans.' He still retained the documents granting him this land and granting him the title of earl. None of this came to fruition because of the Norwegian and Norman invasions. But, if he was no longer an outlaw in England and, if he moved swiftly, he might prove his rightful claim on the land in Leicestershire.

Olaf discussed all this in great detail with Freya and Olafsson. The latter was more than keen to go on his first great adventure. His daughter had been baptised 'Krystyna' which was the old Norse word for 'Christian'. Father Benedict was delighted. She was growing into a beautiful child and Freya and Anja had become close so he felt confident that he might ask Anja to leave her and Krystyna safely with Freya. The plan was to regain Olaf's land and settle in England, a land that was rich and prosperous with green meadows and none of the severe winters that Norway endured. He would then move Freya, Anja and Krystyna to England. What Olaf didn't know was that William's son, also named William and known as 'Rufus', on account of his red hair, was not a gentle soul. He had Morcar and Wulfnorth immediately recaptured and returned to captivity for the rest of their lives and all outlaws who had been pardoned were once again declared outlaws. So, after a decade of peace and happiness, Olaf was unwittingly putting his head back into the wolf's mouth (*Inn i munnen til ulven*).

Chapter Thirty-three
Return to England

Olaf and his son bade farewell to Freya and Anja and headed down the fjørd to Minnesund and then rode on to Oslo. There they visited Ealdgyth and Thorkel. Olaf III was away in Nidaros overseeing the work on the Cathedral being built over the tomb of Olav II which had started in 1070. Finn Arnesson had died, and King Olaf III had long since reached his adult status, so Thorkel didn't have much to do except remain as advisor to the King. Ealdgyth was looking positively middle aged now and her beautiful black hair was turning silver, but she still retained her fine features. She and Thorkel kept Queen Ingerid company. Olaf had met her in Denmark when she had made a pass at him just before her arranged marriage to Olaf III in 1067. Their marriage never produced any children. Olaf remembered her as a pretty, vivacious young girl but she had grown up rather plain and clearly very bored being locked in a loveless marriage. Olaf and his son dined with Ealdgyth and Ingerid at Akershus fortress where Thorkel kept them up to date with matters in England. It seemed that William

II was a powerful and greedy man. Shortly into his reign, his father's advisor, Lanfranc, Archbishop of Canterbury, had died. William delayed appointing a replacement and seized the ecclesiastical revenues for himself. Thorkel suggested that trying to ask such a man to restore his land when his father, William I, had declared him an outlaw, was a chancy business even if he had been pardoned by that king on his deathbed. The manor and the land attached to it would have been recorded in the Domesday Book of which there was a copy at Peterborough and another at Sarum. That way Olaf could find out who owned the land from 1086 onwards. Olaf marvelled at Thorkel's knowledge.

Olaf paid a visit to The Mermaid Inn and discovered that the landlady who had sold him Vanir was still there. Over a beer they told the lady of the two brigands who had followed him and tried to kill and rob him. Olafsson said Vanir was still alive but very old and was in retirement and being very spoilt by his daughter, Krystyna. Olaf enquired if Ari the merchant sailor still came by. At this her face lit up:

"Oh, yes," she said, laughing, "about once a month, him and the two twins, Sigurd and Ulrik, but I can never tell which is which. They haven't been by for some time so they could be here any day now."

This was just the news Olaf had been hoping to hear.

"Are you still making soap for Akershus?" asked Olaf.

"Oh yes, more than ever. There are two queens up there now, Ingerid of Norway, Ealdgyth Godwinson and of course, Thorkel." Olaf roared with laughter:

"Making three in all! Well, we are staying there as guests, so if Ari and the twins arrive, can you get a message to us?"

"Yes, of course, I'll send one of my lads up to the fortress."

Just a few days later, a runner arrived at Akershus with a message for Olaf to say that a trading ship had docked from Bergen. Sure enough, it was Ari and the Orkneyan twins, Sigurd and Ulrik. Olaf and son said their farewells to Ealdgyth and Thorkel and made their way down to the Mermaid. When they saw each other having aged ten years, there was much mirth and hugging, and amusement that Olaf had a son of six foot in height. After that there needed some catching up of stories and drinking of beer. Ari immediately agreed to take them to York via Bergen and Orknye. Ari stressed what a dangerous country England had become but mentioned that Guillaume de Malet was no longer a problem as he had only outlived William I by a few years and had died in 1071. Astrid had become plump and middle aged but was still full of fun and laughter. She was a delightful hostess during the short stay there. After another overnight stop on the Orkneys, they finally disembarked up the Humber and made their way to York.

The Sheriff of York from 1089 was a Norman called Ralph de Paganel. He was William II's man and represented everything about the Normans that the Anglo-Saxons detested. Olaf, his son and his three travelling companions made for the inn where he had parted company with Hereward. The atmosphere in the inn was hushed and suspicious, although the locals recognised Ari and the twins, they eyed Olaf suspiciously. He was dressed in fine clothes as was Olafsson which marked him out as a Norman spy. With Olafsson a muscular six foot and the two twins of similar height, nobody took it upon themselves to start any trouble. But Olaf wanted information so struck up a conversation with some of the locals:

"Hello, this place hasn't changed much since I was last here with Hereward the Wake."

"You wos wiv 'Ereward? Cum an' listen to this, lads! 'Ee says 'ee wos wiv 'Ereward the Wake."

The locals began to crowd around to get a look at this prosperously dressed stranger.

Olaf had got his audience:

"Yes, I was at Ely with Hereward. We smuggled the Lady Torfrida into an Abbey. Whilst we were away the Normans stormed the island from both sides and killed everyone inside, sparing a very few nobles and maiming every prisoner. We were lucky to have got away. And then I came to York and met my friend Ari, that's him over there, who got me out of England and out of William's clutches. Hereward headed to Scotland with a few housecarls, and I've not heard anything from him since. I suppose the Normans have seized his lands?"

The crowd nodded and mumbled: "Aye."

"So, who is the Sheriff these days?"

"Ah," says one, "It's de Paganel, Sheriff of York. He is very free with hangings against the local people. He's a big supporter of William Rufus who gets him to steal land from the Church. He seized all the lands of William de Calais who was a Norman, but a godly Archbishop of Durham. They say he has more wealth than the King but there is no end to his greed."

Olaf downed his ale and nodded: "Nevertheless, he is the man I need to see. I have lands in Leicester given to me by King Harold that are rightfully mine."

A ripple of laughter broke out and someone shouted from the back:

"Good luck with that one! The Normans have England by the throat and no legal documents are worth anything anymore."

The night passed without incident and the following day Ari and the twins left for Orkney. Olaf and his son made their way up to the castle to see if they could speak to the Sheriff. The castle had been substantially extended and improved upon and boasted a moat fed with water from the River Fosse. Two armed guards stood on the castle side of the bridge barring the way to any intruders. Olaf asked if he might speak with the Sheriff and was told brusquely in an Anglo-Norman dialect that he was out hunting and wouldn't be back till the evening when he would be feasting and not receiving anyone. He might see them in the morning around eleven if the matter was important. Tomorrow was Saturday and that was the day he heard any petitions or complaints. As Olaf and his son were well-dressed, the guards treated them with a modicum of respect, as opposed to the short shrift they would have dished out to the local peasants.

The following day they returned and joined the throng of people trying to cross the bridge into the castle, all with their grievances and petitions. A monk acted as scribe and noted down everyone's name and case. Ralph de Paganel was clearly very bored at having to fulfill this dullest of official duties so that a hearing could last no longer than a few minutes, whereupon the Sheriff, with a weary wave of his hand and an aching head from the past evening's excesses, would come to a random and arbitrary decision much to the distress of the one making the petition. When Olaf's petition was read out, the Sheriff became a little more attentive as this was land handed down by a royal decree, albeit an Anglo-Saxon one.

"You'll have to take this one down to London as I am not authorised to deal with major land disputes which are for the King to decide. I would urge you to travel to Peterborough Cathedral and ask the monks to show you the Domesday Book regarding Wold Dalby. That will tell you how much the land is worth, the tax it must pay, and it will give you the names of the tenant and the overlord. If the lord is a Norman, then I think the chances of you regaining this property are very remote. You are a conquered people and to the victor go the spoils. Next case!"

Olaf and his son departed the castle and made their way into the town to find the local horse trader. They chose two fine-looking English horses, a chestnut, and a larger bay for Olafsson and with them two excruciatingly uncomfortable-looking Norman saddles made of wood covered with leather. The wooden frames had been painted in bright blue and red and the leather bridles were matching. It was fitting that they looked like noblemen when they rode into London.

Olaf took the good advice of Ralph de Paganel and headed down the road to Peterborough. He wasn't aware that the Abbot was still Turold de Fécamp whom he had fought against with Hereward the Wake. The ride down to Peterborough was uneventful and they covered the distance much faster than they would have on Viking amblers. The saddles were much more comfortable than they looked and they both arrived in good order. The first thing Olaf noticed that was different was that Turold had built a motte and bailey castle just outside the Cathedral, after the attack by Hereward. It was called Turold Castle. The good Abbott was clearly intent on protecting his wealth. Olaf and his son were greeted as noblemen by the monks who offered them every courtesy and hospitality. They did indeed possess a copy of The Domesday Book known as 'Little Domesday'. 'Great Domesday', the one presented to William I at Sarum in 1086, was housed at Winchester. Nevertheless, Olaf was able to discover that Wold Dalby was valued at 4 pounds and consisted of 13 villagers, 2 freemen, 8 smallholders and 1 man-at-arms. Furthermore, there were 12 ploughlands, 1 lord's plough team and 7 men's plough teams. Other resources included a meadow of 1.5 leagues and woodland of 2.1 furlongs. The name of the Tenant-in-chief was Ralph, son of Hubert. For the owner by the words 'Lord in 1086' was simply written: 'Robert'. No further information. The monks, however, were pleased to fill in the details. It appears that the Robert in question was none other than Robert of Mortain, the brother of Odo, Bishop of Bayeux, and half-brother to William I, who was illegitimate. In 1088, both Robert and Odo participated in a revolt against the new King William II who was their nephew and much disliked. Robert was very much an absent landlord and remained in Normandy most of the time.

Olaf and his son listened to all of this with great fascination. It may be that William Rufus might care to restore Harold's gift to Olaf just to spite his uncle. Olaf asked one of the monks if he would transcribe the information onto a parchment in return for a donation to the Order and the monk obliged. They both remained there for a few days during which time they were greeted by Turold who was now practically blind and he thanked them for their generous donation. He had absolutely no idea who Olaf was!

Thanking the monks for their kind hospitality, father and son Olafs set off on the journey South to London with the parchment transcription from Little Domesday and the Royal decree from Harold II. Having no knowledge of quite how ruthless William II could be, the two Norwegians trotted happily towards the capital.

What Olaf didn't know was that the third son of William I, Henry, who was about the same age as Olafsson was also making his way to London to petition his much older brother, William Rufus, about the confiscation of his lands. Henry had been in Normandy plotting with his other brother, Robert Curthose, who was very aggrieved that his father had not left both Normandy and England to him. And so it was that the fates or divine intervention brought together Prince Henry and Olaf Slagbjørn at the same time and the same place in a meeting that would ultimately change the course of history.

William II 'Rufus' 1087-1100

Chapter Thirty-four
The Justice of William Rufus

Olaf and his son arrived in London shortly before sundown and the first thing they noticed was the heavy security on all the gates. It seemed more like a garrison than a capital city. The great abbey built by Edward the Confessor stood magnificently above the dwellings around Westminster Palace. But now, over to the East, a new landmark had sprung up. Nearing its completion was a fabulous, white-stoned Norman-style keep, dominating the skyline from its raised position by the river. It stood there as a permanent reminder to Londoners that they were a conquered people. William Rufus had also commanded that it be surrounded by a moat and a circular stone wall, the work for which was just commencing. Olaf led the way to the Great Hall where two guards and a few monks were just about to call it a day.

"We've come to petition the King", said Olaf. Obligingly, the monk sat down again and dipped his quill in the ink:

"Is it a financial grievance?" asked the monk.

"Property in respect of land granted to me by the King," replied Olaf.

"Which king?"

"I have the papers here," said Olaf taking out the parchments. "This letter bears the royal seal of King Harold II granting me these lands as documented in Domesday Book."

The two guards guffawed: "Good luck with that one mate!" Olaf had heard that said before, quite recently. The monk didn't flicker.

"The King has one petition on Saturday so he may deign to hear you but, as the other petition is his own brother, Prince Henry, it may run on a little longer than usual. Be here for ten o'clock in the morning and we'll see if we can get you heard." The monk was a Saxon and was clearly sympathetic to Olaf's cause.

Olaf thanked the monk and left with his son to find a stable for the horses and somewhere to sleep. Olaf remembered the inn on the embankment which was where he and Rhys had ambushed Gospatrick of Bamburgh and his followers and that same inn was where they stayed for the next few days. On Saturday morning they rose early and rode their horses up to the Great Hall of Westminster. The horses were secured, and Olaf and his son made their way into the huge, vaulted hall. At the far end was a dais upon which was placed an elaborate throne covered with scarlet velvet and white ermine. A small throng of monks, lawyers and clerics were outnumbered by the Norman guards all wearing chainmail armour and carrying the trademark pear-shaped shields and lances. It was as if they were expecting a fight.

A large man, who Olaf guessed must be the usher, crashed his staff onto the wooden floor and called out in a commanding voice:

"Silence in court! All rise for the King!" which he then repeated in French. William II, King of England was one of four sons fathered by William the Conqueror and Queen Matilda. Robert was the eldest with Richard, the second son, being killed in a hunting accident, leaving William 'Rufus' and his much younger brother, Henry. William had been called 'Rufus' since his childhood days on account of his reddish hair which now extended to a moustache and a short goatee beard. He was short and stocky like his father with his eyes close together, but he looked kingly enough in his purple robe and golden crown.

"Prince Henry, come now into court!"

All heads were turned to the entrance where Olaf had entered. A handsome young man with an aristocratic swagger that reminded Olaf of Orre Eystein, Tora's brother, entered, and his charisma seemed to fill the room.

The monk who had taken Olaf's details spoke:

"Your Royal Highness, I have taken a statement of your grievance against the King, your brother. It is that your brothers have been granted the Crown of England and the Duchy of Normandy whereas you, as the youngest were granted a purse of five thousand pounds and modest lands around Buckinghamshire and Gloucestershire which have been sequestered by the Crown leaving you, young Prince, landless." The monk turned to William:

"As these lands were left to the Prince by Queen Matilda, his mother, these lands belong by right to her fourth son and he hereby petitions the Crown to return these lands to their rightful owner, that being Henry, son of William and Matilda. Failure to do so will clearly demonstrate that King William II only seeks to subvert the laws and justice of the kingdom to profit his own greed. Forgive me, your Majesty but I must read the grievance as it was dictated to me."

There was an intake of breath around the hall and Olafsson looked to his father thinking that this was probably not the most diplomatic way to address a king even if he was your own elder brother. Olaf remained inscrutable. From the throne and lit by the sunlight on his golden crown, it was clear that Rufus was turning puce with a rage that he was struggling to control. He stood up without consulting his legal advisors:

"How dare you! How dare you address me, the King of England in this churlish manner. You have consorted with Robert against our person; you have committed acts of treason in plotting to invade this land whilst I am its rightful king. Guards! Confine the Prince Henry in the Tower until I have consulted with our advisors, to decide what is to be done with him. If you were not my brother, your head would shortly be on a spike on London Bridge. Take him down!"

Henry's hand went instinctively to his sword as did Olafsson's. Olaf grabbed his son's sword arm before it was noticed whilst four Norman soldiers struggled to subdue and disarm the prince. Henry was removed from the hall roaring and swearing profanities, leaving Olaf to ponder on the fact that he had possibly not chosen the best day to have his case heard.

As the yells and commotion died away, the monk, somewhat nervously, proceeded to the second case on the agenda. Rufus was visibly shaking with rage as the monk read out the case as dictated to him by Olaf.

"Your Grace, this Norwegian here who goes by the name Olaf Slagbjørn has petitioned the Crown to have his land and good name restored. Having been in the service of the Godwin family, Olaf visited your father, then Duke William, where he saved the life of Earl Harold Godwin who would otherwise have drowned in a shipwreck off the coast of Normandy. When the Witan elected Earl Harold to succeed Edward, known as 'the Confessor', as King of England, Harold rewarded Olaf with a Manor House and land around the village of Wold Dalby in Leicestershire, which was in his gift, along with a title of Olaf, Earl of Dalby, which was not bestowed due to the impending invasions. The plaintiff petitions your Grace that this land for which he has the deeds and Royal Charter be restored as it is currently the property of Robert Count of Mortain, brother of Odo and therefore your uncle. Robert has been an absentee landlord for many years and resides in Normandy. Despite owning extensive lands and manors in Devon, Cornwall and Yorkshire, the Count seldom visits England, and this will become less likely given his age. Olaf further states that should you feel inclined to bestow upon him the title promised by the last Anglo-Saxon king, he would be pleased to put his services and those of his son at your Grace's disposal."

There was silence as all waited to hear the King's reply.

The King spoke in a high tenor voice:

"It seems that you must have been out of the country for some time, and you have not done your homework. The information that you gleaned from Domesday Book was correct when it was presented to my father, the King in 1086. In 1087 he died leaving me the throne of England. His two brothers Odo and Robert of Mortain decided to support my own brother Robert Curthose, Duke of Normandy in his spurious claim to my throne. They led half the country against me, and my youngest brother, who is currently on his way to the Tower, lent Duke Robert the money to raise an invading army from Normandy. Such treason! Robert never invaded due to bad weather and I captured Odo and Robert after a siege of Pevensey and Rochester castles in 1088. I banished both uncles and divested them of their lands and Henry of his. Now these lands all belong to the Crown and if you notice this thing on my head you will realise that these lands belong to me." Rufus paused as the sycophantic courtiers laughed politely.

Rufus continued in a questioning vein:

"Tell me Norwegian, when you were in the service of the Godwins, was it as an archer housecarl?" Olaf nodded.

"Speak up! We can't hear you!" screamed Rufus.

"Yes, I was." Olaf didn't like this line of questioning one bit.

"And in that capacity, did you kill the King of Norway at Stamford Bridge and break my father's nose at Senlac and then cruelly maim Guillaume de Malet during my father's coronation?

"I did."

"You have quite a penchant for regicide it seems and now you have the gross affrontery to come here, cap in hand, asking for a gift of Crown land? My father once said you were the most wanted man in England and declared you an outlaw."

"I was told your father, the King, pardoned all outlaws on his deathbed and that included Hereward the Wake and me."

"But I am the King now and I say both you and Hereward are still outlaws and are hereby sentenced to life imprisonment. Take him to join the traitor Henry in the Tower before we find some remote and uncomfortable castle to send him to. Son of Olaf, I suggest you leave England and never return. Say goodbye to your impetuous father. Take him down!"

Rufus smiled as Olaf was grabbed roughly, his sword removed and given to his son and then dragged outside to be manacled and taken by cart to Tower Hill. It had been a good day with both a traitor and an outlaw feeling the justice of William II, he thought to himself.

The usher crashed his staff onto the floor:

"The court will adjourn; all rise!"

William Rufus rose and swept out of the hall followed by courtiers and a small cohort of guards. The hall emptied, leaving Olafsson standing alone and bewildered under the great wooden beams. He felt an arm across his shoulder and turned to see the kindly monk smiling at him:

"Don't despair boy. We must decide what to do to get both of them freed. It may take six months, but I have some influential friends. Come with me to a tavern and let us talk and plot."

Embankment Tavern

Chapter Thirty-Five
New ally – Brother Cuthbeorht

As the cart carrying a dejected Olaf clattered through the cobbled streets from Westminster to Tower Hill, Olafsson led the two horses back to the inn, accompanied by the monk who had identified himself as Brother Cuthbeorht (Cuthbert) of Cranbourne Abbey. He explained to Olafsson that he was officially a Recorder or Clerk to the Court of William II. He had left his post in Dorset when the Saxon owner of the manor of Cranbourne was imprisoned by William I for an act of disrespect against his wife, Matilda. The manor including the Abbey and its lands were given over to Robert Fitzhamon, a Norman nobleman. Cuthbert decided to move up to Westminster where he worked for the Italian scholar Archbishop Lanfranc who had recently died in 1089. It was Lanfranc, a fellow Benedictine, who had appointed him to such a senior post. Lanfranc it was who secured the succession of Rufus over his wayward elder brother Robert Curthose, so was able to pull strings. Cuthbert lamented the passing of such a good man who had managed to keep Rufus in check:

"Now that he is gone Rufus has refused to appoint a new Archbishop of Canterbury and is happily funnelling all the very substantial funds from the See of Canterbury into his own treasury at Winchester."

The horses were stabled, and the young Viking and the Benedictine monk ordered some food and beer at a table inside with a view of the Tower of London. Cuthbert was keen to learn more about Olaf's history from his son and was astonished to hear what he had achieved. Olafsson listened intently to Brother Cuthbert and was becoming aware that his father had fallen into the hands of a tyrannical ruler whose greed and avarice overcame any scruples he might possess.

"I must tell you Olafsson, that from what you tell me, we will need to break Olaf out as soon as possible, as Rufus will have him moved to a remote corner of this island where you will never find him. As you are not a Saxon there is a possibility that we might be able to secure you a post as a guard at the tower. Nobody will suspect that Olaf is your father. Let's hope not. The guards at Westminster hand over prisoners to the guards at the Tower. They never go in so would not recognise you. I know they are recruiting young guards at the moment after the King complained that there were too many gaolers who had served Edward and Harold. He wants non-Saxon guards. I will make enquiries."

Olafsson realised that this was a very risky strategy akin to walking into a den of wolves, but he had to free his father quickly before he disappeared. Another consideration was that he only had a finite amount of money and it was costly to stay at an inn in London. This job would pay his board and keep.

Olafsson and Cuthbert talked long into the evening about many issues. It was clear that William Rufus was at war with the Church which he saw as a cash cow for his coffers, whereas Henry on the throne in his place would be infinitely preferable as a respecter of the Law and the Church. Cuthbert was impressed by Olafsson. A wise head on young shoulders with an almost aristocratic bearing:

"I'll visit the Tower in the morning; I know the Saxon warden there. I'll also get you some more clothes as befits a lowly guard rather than the fine clothes you are wearing."

Meanwhile, in the Tower, Eardwulf, the bad-tempered head warden had just received a visit from a Norman upstart called Ranulf Flambard, the King's financial administrator and Keeper of the Privy Seal. Ranulf was as arrogant as he was efficient. He spoke down to everyone except the King and liked to publicly humiliate Saxons. He had told Eardwulf that he was to expect a Royal Prince, second in line to the throne and was to vacate the largest chamber to accommodate him, he must also expect a Norse nobleman claiming to be an earl.

"They'll have to share the large chamber then. All the other chambers are either taken or not yet completed. I don't have enough guards as it is and the rate the King keeps sending petitioners to the Tower is more than I can keep up with."

"Just get on with it and stop your whining if you want to keep your post."

Eardwulf winced and wrung his hands, nodding obsequiously as Ranulf swept out, imperiously. He made his way to the kitchen, cursing that such a Norman dog should impose a senior royal into his charge:

"Get some decent food prepared and some beer. We've got Prince 'enry staying with us. We'd better take good care of him as he's very likely to be the next king and we don't want him taking royal revenge on us poor servants, do we?" There was a flurry of activity in the kitchen as noises and shouting outside suggested the arrival of a very angry man. Four armed guards were struggling to remove Prince Henry from the carriage and a small crowd had gathered to watch the commotion.

"Take your filthy hands off me you scum! I am the future King of England and I have a long memory." Eardwulf appeared at the entrance:

"Un'and him at once! My lord, we have lit the fire in your chamber and the kitchen is preparing a meal for you. Would you prefer wine or beer?" The guards registered astonishment and immediately unhanded Prince Henry who was as astonished as the guards.

"We 'ave never received a royal guest before, but I shall see to it that your stay with us is as pleasant and comfortable as we can make it."

The effect on Henry was instantaneous and he followed Eardwulf meekly over the drawbridge and into the Tower.

Henry's chamber was decked out with tapestries and cushions and there was a desk laid out with quill and parchment. He had half expected to be chained to the wall but there was none of that. It was more like an inn than a prison although the cries emanating from other cells were a sharp reminder that he was receiving very special treatment, but the clank of the lock confirmed his status as a prisoner. Henry was left alone for a short time and just as he was admiring the view across the Thames to Southwark the rattle of keys and a chain announced the arrival of a guard with a kitchen porter bearing hot capon, fresh bread and a flagon of wine. Henry's mood began to soften and, by the time he had finished eating, he felt the only thing he lacked was some company to talk to. Right on cue the rattle of keys outside preceded the entrance of Eardwulf:

"My lord, I am very sorry to ask this of you, but I must ask if you would consent to share your cell with a nobleman. He has been in the service of 'arold Godwinson and King Sweyen of Denmark and, like you, 'as 'ad 'is lands confiscated by King William, your brother. The cells are all full of n'er-do-wells and riff-raff and 'ee wouldn't do very well there with 'is fine clothes. There is a second bed in the ante-room."

Henry was in a generous mood after his fine supper:

"Yes, I need some company. Show him in."

Eardwulf had divested Olaf of a large purse of gold coins which he said would go towards the expense of his keep. He felt obliged to see that the Norwegian was also well looked after. Olaf entered the chamber and Henry's face lit up with a smile:

"Ah! I recognise you from this morning. Come in, there is some food left. Bring some more wine gaoler, for my new friend. Let us light the candles and amuse each with tall stories."

As the sun set over the Thames, Olaf and Henry regaled each other with sagas whilst half a mile down the Embankment, Olafsson and Brother Cuthbert plotted as to how they might spring Olaf and the Prince from the Tower.

The White Tower

Chapter Thirty-six
Olafsson joins the wardens

The following day Brother Cuthbert returned to the inn with some different clothes for Olafsson. He then headed off in the direction of the White Tower to try to arrange things with Eardwulf. Two guards blocked his passage at the main gate and asked his business. They were quite used to priests entering to say mass for those unfortunate enough to be hanged or beheaded on Tower Hill.

"I've come to speak with Eardwulf and to deliver a message to Prince Henry from the King." One of the guards gestured to Cuthbert for him to follow as he turned and walked through the gateway and into the keep. They found Eardwulf in his office counting the gold coins he had taken from Olaf, which he hastily slid back into the leather pouch from which they came:

"Ah, Brother Cuthbert, what can I do for you today?"

"Does Ranulf Flambard know about that small fortune you've got there?"

"No, he doesn't and he's not going to neither, now state your business!"

Cuthbert laughed: "Alright, I shall keep quiet about your stealing from prisoners, but I need your help. How soon is the Viking due to be moved to a more permanent prison?"

Eardwulf had heard news of this that very morning: "He's staying here for the next two weeks then he's to be moved to Hereford Castle on the Welsh border for a permanent stay."

"Eardwulf, do you know this Viking is a Saxon hero? He fought as a housecarl for Harold at Stamford Bridge and at Hastings and survived the battle of Ely with Hereward the Wake. We must get him out of here, along with Prince Henry."

Eardwulf laughed: "No-one escapes from here! In any event, Henry is to be released and sent to Normandy before Christmas. If Olaf, or especially, the Prince were to escape, my head would be on the block before sunset."

Brother Cuthbert was thinking on his feet: "How many guards would escort Olaf to Hereford?"

Eardwulf sighed:

"I could only spare two at the most, I am so short of guards here and the law now forbids me hiring any Saxons."

Brother Cuthbert's eyes had a clever sparkle:

"If I found you a Norse lad looking for a job, he could help Olaf escape once he was outside London and he would, therefore, no longer be in your jurisdiction."

"Yeah, right, and what's in it for me?"

Cuthbert nodded to the leather pouch, "I think Eardwulf, that Olaf appears to have paid you a year's wages already."

And so it came to be that Olafsson was taken on as a Tower Guard amongst the Normans. The two weeks passed quickly and Olafsson kept his father and Prince Henry up to date with the plans. Henry suggested that it was pointless for him to try to escape as he would most likely be recognised. In any event it was only a few months and he wasn't in any discomfort. Henry planned to go to Normandy and meet up with Robert and he invited Olaf and his son to join him there.

On a chilly October night, Olaf was released from the Tower and taken to a carriage containing a cage in which he was locked. Olafsson and an elderly Norman guard formed the escort. Brother Cuthbert and Eardwulf were present to see that all ran smoothly. Olafsson had brought a blanket in which was wrapped Olaf's bow and quiver and the sword given to him by Edgar the Ætheling. The cart was pulled by two cart-horses and tied to the back of the cart were the two fine horses they had bought in York with the brightly coloured saddles. The old Norman guard was curious as to the purpose of these horses, but Olafsson told him that they were to leave the cart at Hereford with the handover of the prisoner and ride back to London on the spares to shorten the journey and allow the cart-horses to rest.

They clattered through the Western Aldgate of the London Wall and soon the lights of the city were far behind them. They took the route along Watling Street and then veered off at St Albans, to

Gloucester, and thence on to Hereford. At about three in the morning the Norman guard complained that he needed to get some sleep. This was what Olafsson had planned on. The guard wrapped himself in his cloak on the grass verge and soon the night was disturbed by the sound of his snoring. He awoke on a cold autumnal morning to see the two cart-horses grazing nearby. The carriage was there but of the two other horses, the Norse guard and the prisoner, there was no sign. The Norman cursed loudly in the knowledge that his job as a guard was over and that he daren't return to London.

As the sun rose, Olaf and Olafsson rode happily, heading due South to seek shelter at an inn for the night, either in Winchester or Southampton. The two weeks spent with Henry had created a friendship, they had planned and plotted from their prison. They would make their way to Clausentum, where there was a large dwelling called Bitterne Manor belonging to the Bishop of Winchester. Brother Cuthbert had already sent word to Bishop Walkelin, a strong supporter of anyone who might depose Rufus and they were, therefore, expected and welcome until Henry was able to leave the Tower and join them for a crossing to Normandy.

Olaf and Olafsson arrived at Winchester that afternoon, cold, tired and hungry. After an inspection of the narrow streets, they found an inn with a roaring fire. It was called 'Emma's Hus' as it had been a gift from King Ethelred to his Norman bride, Princess Emma. She was crowned as the first Queen of England in 1002. When he died in 1016, she married Canute, King of both England and Denmark and was crowned a second time. She was also the mother of Edward the Confessor. Both Olaf's were fascinated by this history as told to them by a large blond lady who said that the house was left to her mother in 1052, when Queen Emma died, she having served her loyally as lady-in-waiting for many years.

The food was most welcome, as was the ale and Olaf and son turned in early, exhausted but replete and with much to do in the morning.

Emma marries King Cnut

Chapter Thirty-seven
Laying low in Winchester

Olaf and son thanked the landlady after a good breakfast of bacon and eggs and made their way to the Cathedral of Winchester. They were somewhat surprised to discover that work had only just started on the Cathedral which was situated just South of the two minsters, the Old Minster and the New Minster begun by Alfred the Great and completed in 901 by his son Edward. These two magnificent Minsters co-existed side by and it was in the New Minster that the monks showed Olaf and Olafsson to where Bishop Walkelin was poring over architectural plans with the master masons. They had started work on this huge Cathedral in 1079 and it was just starting to take shape at 558 feet in length.

Olaf knew almost nothing about his new protector, but he would be surprised to learn that Walkelin had been William the Conqueror's chaplain before the conquest and was a Canon at Rouen Cathedral. The Archbishop of Canterbury, Stigand, who was also Bishop of Winchester was deposed for pluralism by the Papal Legate at the

Council of Winchester in 1070 and Walkelin was nominated as his replacement. Despite being a Norman, Walkelin had great respect for the Saxon monks, particularly, Cuthbert. When the request arrived to shelter the two Olafs, prior to Henry being released, he agreed without question. Although he wasn't to live to see Henry on the throne, he was keen to have Rufus removed as early as possible.

Olaf approached the bishop, dropped onto one knee and kissed his ring. Olafsson, a little surprised by this, did likewise.

"Ah, you must be the Vikings sent to me for your protection? Well, as far as I know, there is no manhunt underway for any escaped prisoners. Hereford has its hands full at the moment with raiders from the Welsh borders. The last thing they would want is another prisoner to feed. You may stay at Bitterne Manor until the Prince Henry arrives. Apparently, he has plans for you."

Olaf and son were taken to Bitterne Manor. It was a comfortable enough place by the River Itchen surrounded by farmland. As it was used as a distribution centre for wine, the Olaf's wanted for nothing. The monks also baked bread and tilled the fields, herding cattle and growing vegetables of every description. Nobody came looking for them as no report was sent back to London of the disappearance of two Norman guards and a prisoner. Rufus had more things to worry about and had forgotten about Olaf. For the time being they were safe and comfortable.

As Winter set in Bishop Walkelin gave Olaf and Olafsson light chores to keep them busy, chopping wood for the fires in the manor and keeping them stocked from the dry logs in the barn, distributing wine to outlying parishes, helping the monks with the cattle, and so on. Finally, on the first Sunday in Advent, Prince Henry arrived, newly freed from his captivity. He seemed in high spirits and had regained his sword. The Bishop ordered a feast in his honour at which some monks sang carols in the great hall of the manor. Henry announced that he wanted Olaf and Olafsson to be his housecarls and travel with him to Normandy after Christmas, when a crossing might be possible.

Now that Henry was around, life became a little more exciting. He organised regular hunts in the New Forest to procure deer that, strictly speaking, belonged to the King. Rufus had other things to deal with such as the invasion from Scotland by Malcolm III. Henry had heard of Olaf's skill with a bow but was nevertheless astonished at his accuracy in dispatching a running hart from the saddle of a galloping horse and never wounding the creature but killing with the first arrow. The seed of a plan was beginning to ferment in Henry's mind and it would, of course, involve Olaf.

As Christmas approached the services continued in the New Minster where the body of Alfred the Great was interred. Work on the Cathedral, right next to the New Minster, was continuing on apace with much of the East section nearing completion. But between the Old Minster and the New Minster, a war was raging. The two Minsters were so close together that, when the choirs of each were singing at the same time, cacophony reigned with each group of monks trying to sing louder than the other. Bishop Walkelin eventually intervened and ordered the monks of the Old Minster to relocate to Hyde Abbey just outside the city wall and peace was restored just in time for Christmas.

Meanwhile, unbeknown to the two brothers, Duke Robert and Prince Henry, William Rufus was stirring up trouble in Normandy. William had sent a gift of money to a wealthy burgher in Rouen called Conan Pilatus and urged him to rise up against Robert. This he did with the support of many in Rouen and Conan appealed to all outlying garrisons to join him. In the New Year of 1091, Robert sent urgent appeals for help to his barons. Henry, sensing a week of calm weather, set sail with Olaf and son and a handful of sailors. The seas were unusually calm for that time of year and the journey was uneventful, so that they were able to disembark at a fishing village called Dieppe, which was only just beginning to realise its strategic importance as a port between England and Normandy. At an inn on the road to Rouen, Henry overheard a conversation that referred to a rebellion against his brother Robert, who was in Rouen Castle. Like a warhorse at the sound of a trumpet, Henry sprang to his feet, knocking over Olaf's beer.

"Come on you two housecarls! Allez, allez, time to earn your pay!"

"Allons-y!" replied Olaf, wiping the beer from his trousers. He had picked up a little French from the Normans and knew the expression for, 'Let's go'.

Mounting their horses, they set off at a good speed in the direction of Rouen.

Chapter Thirty-eight
Civil war in Rouen – Conan's Leap

The three riders approached Rouen at sunset where the streets seemed crowded with a lot of angry men. It was clear that a fight was due to break out between the supporters of Duke Robert and those who followed Conan, financed by William Rufus. Henry led the way up to the castle where a very nervous Robert Curthose was hoping that his letters to the barons would bring support soon.

Henry and the Olafs were the first to arrive, to the astonishment of Robert:

"Henry! How did you get here so quickly? My letter was sent to you in London only four days ago." Henry laughed:

"That turd of a brother, having stolen the English lands that Mother left me, had me lugged to the Tower where I've been for the last three months. I decided to leave England to check that my lands in Cotentin, Avranche and the Bessin are still under my control and that

William has not tried to steal them as he plans to steal Rouen from you. Who is this Conan anyway?"

"He is a traitor!" roared Robert. "Conan Pilatus, the most influential burgher in Rouen, who is far more wealthy than any burgher should be and keeps a retinue of many knights in abject defiance of me, the rightful Ducal Lord of this city."

"He is not even a nobleman! Has he sworn fealty to you?" asked Henry.

"Yes, of course he has but he is taking bribes from William to take Rouen and has considerable support in the town."

"Then he is indeed a traitor and a dead man. We are safe in the castle so we must wait until any loyal barons arrive with enough forces to sally out and destroy them. I am only sorry I have only two housecarls with me. They are Olaf and Olafsson, a crack archer and his son, a tall Viking who is able with a sword. I met Olaf in the Tower, so I know quite a lot about him. His lands were also stolen by William. You'd want him on your side, trust me, I've seen what he can do with a hunting bow."

Robert turned to the two Norseman and smiled:

"You are very welcome here to fight on our side." Then, turning back to his younger brother:

"I have summoned William, Count of Evreux, his nephew, William of Breteuil, and Gilbert de L'Aigle, of whom the first two served me previously as military commanders. They answered my summons quickly, prompted not only by loyalty to their lord, but also, perhaps, by outright shock at the effrontery of the ignoble citizens of Rouen and by the hope of extracting immense ransoms from them. I even had the temerity to seek help from two recent victims of mine, including Robert of Bellême, and both of them, impelled perhaps by similar motives of outrage and greed, will bring their contingents to Rouen to fight on our behalf. Your willingness, Henry, to come to my rescue and your leadership in the forthcoming mêlée, may well save the city, for without Rouen my prospects might be considered fragile indeed."

The castle was situated at the far end of the city walls which meant that any reinforcements could enter from the South gate directly into the castle without going through the town. The first signs of violence began when Gilbert of L'Aigle crossed the Seine with his knights and entered through the South gate to support Duke Robert. At the same time Reginald of Warenne, a Rufus ally, entered the city through the Cauchoise gate (West) to reinforce Conan. Conan's supporters greeted Reginald and his knights with cheers whereas they harassed the knights of Gilbert de L'Aigle who had to fight their way in. Fighting broke out in the streets between the majority of citizens who supported Conan and the minority who supported Robert. At this juncture, from the vantage point of the castle tower, Henry declared that they must burst out of the castle to even the odds. Robert didn't look much like he fancied going down there to brawl with the common people, but he followed his brother down the stone steps to the courtyard where the knights had dismounted and whose horses were being held by their pages. Much better to fight on foot rather than be unhorsed in the mêlée of the narrow streets of Rouen. Henry had Olaf and Olafsson either side of him whereas Robert was surrounded by friends and courtiers who looked nervously around at the dismounted knights.

The gates suddenly opened, and they were at once hit by the deafening noise of screaming men and clashing steel echoing around the narrow streets. Henry led the phalanx of knights at a jog into the violent throng. Three men ran at Henry, recognising his princely coat of arms over his chain mail. Olafsson strode forward to protect the prince and, using his height, brought his long sword down and through the left collar bone of the astonished assailant. The short man was dead before he hit the ground. Olaf had his bow well-nocked, and his arrow flew straight into the chest of a second attacker, throwing him backwards onto the cobbles with a yelp. The third ran at Henry with a wild off-balance lunge, which the Prince deftly side-stepped before swinging around with his heavy sword and crashing it into the stumbling man's vertebrae. He fell straight on his face unable to move as his life trickled into the gutter.

With a roar, the knights behind rushed forward and joined in the savage hand-to-hand fighting. Meanwhile, Gilbert de L'Aigle had taken a group of his knights around the city wall and, with the help of some citizens loyal to Robert, had managed to take the West gate, which was now open, with his mounted knights pouring into the city to hook up with Henry's force. Conan's men were now fighting on two fronts as many of the knights in the pay of Rufus, sensing defeat, decided to break and run into the nearby woods.

It appears that Robert had fled the scene early on as there was no sign of him nor his courtier friends. Henry's forces, however, were growing all the time as the knights of William of Evreux and Robert of Bellême arrived belatedly to ensure that Conan's forces, sponsored by William Rufus, were forced to surrender as they had nowhere to run. The knights were all searching for wealthy prisoners to take and ransom. There in a blood-soaked side street, hiding among the dead and wounded, they found the wealthiest prize of all. Conan Pilatus was dragged to the castle to be given as captive to Prince Henry. Conan, covered in other people's blood where he had been hiding, was pale and shaking as he was dragged before the young prince. Henry was incandescent with rage and ordered his captors to bring Conan to the high tower of the castle. On reaching the top of the tower Conan's fears began to manifest themselves in panic. He screamed for mercy, offering Henry all the considerable wealth and ill-gotten gains he possessed, if Henry would spare his life. Henry's rage was palpable, and his face was red:

"By my mother's soul, there shall be no ransom for a traitor, only swifter infliction of the death he deserves."

Conan screamed:

"For the love of God at least allow me to confess my sins!"

Whereupon Henry bent forward and grasped Conan around the thighs before lifting him up and thrusting him, headfirst over the parapet to his death below. Olaf peered down at the bleeding corpse on the cobbles, somewhat shocked at young Henry's barbarous execution of a prisoner. There was some activity around the body as a few citizens in an act of revenge against Conan, were tying his wrists to a horse, prior to having his body dragged around the streets of Rouen, as became Hector at Troy, to show the citizens what happens when a traitor turns against his feudal lord.

Prince Henry's Justice

'Conan's Leap'

Chapter Thirty-nine
Return Home

The aftermath of the Battle of Rouen established two things; Henry's reputation as a warrior was proven and he was given heroic status as a man not to be trifled with. The tower, that he had hurled the unfortunate leader of the uprising from, was hereafter to be known as 'Conan's Leap'. Robert's reputation, by contrast, was in tatters as it became known that he and a small band of courtiers had fled the battle and crossed the Seine in a ferryboat, where they were met by a monk named William of Arques who escorted them to the sanctuary of a Bec priory church, Notre-Dame-du-Pré. This had clearly been pre-arranged. Robert Curthose emerged with a severely damaged knightly reputation. In the face of grave danger to his principal city, the Duke of Normandy had retired to the safety of a suburban church while a younger brother, some fifteen years his junior, had fought energetically to save his duchy. The spectacular execution of Conan and the renaming of the tower doubtless added salt to the wounded ducal psyche. His own principal residence, looking down on his capital city, would henceforth bear the nickname that rekindled embarrassing memories. Seen in this light, it is comprehensible that the Duke's gratitude toward Henry was both grudging and short-lived. Within a year Robert was plotting with Rufus to drive Henry out of Normandy.

Olaf and his son were now highly regarded by both Henry and Robert. Robert even attempted to negotiate for them to join his forces at Rouen. Olaf politely declined and, having heard word from some traders that the King of Norway was gravely ill, Olaf asked Henry's permission to return home as both he and Olafsson had left their wives abandoned in Lillehammer, albeit in the comfort of Freya's home. Henry reluctantly agreed on the proviso that should their services ever be needed again, he would send word via Oslo and they were to return as his housecarls. Olaf agreed and Henry sent them off with a very generous gift of £1000 between them. They rode down to the coast with their horses and a mule to carry the gold, which had been taken from Conan's treasury!

At Dieppe they sold their fine Yorkshire horses and the mule and took a boat along the coast to Calais. There they rested at an inn and enjoyed some fine food and wine from Monsieur le Patron, as Olaf addressed him. Olafsson had changed since the battle. He was far more confident and his polite shyness had been replaced by a soldier's swagger, as of one who had hewn down many foes in a recent battle, which he had, and had barely received a scratch but for a small scar on his cheek. The inn was a large one as befitted a busy port and Olaf was amused to see that it was now his son who was on the receiving end of fluttered eyelashes and winning smiles from the serving girls with their enticing low-cut smocks and curvaceous bosoms. Olafsson was enjoying this attention until Olaf made an announcement in broken French:

"Mes belles Dames, je suis desolé d'anoncer, mais cette gentilhomme est mon fils et il est déja marie!" Some of the ladies made pretence of weeping with cries of "quelle domage!". One of the ladies remarked:

"Ah, mais vous êtes des voyageurs et ce qui part en tournée reste en tournée!" followed by much raucous laughter.

(Translation: *"My beautiful ladies, I am very sad to announce, but this gentleman is my son, and he is already married!"*

"What a shame"

"Ah, but you are travellers and what goes on on-tour stays on tour!")

Olaf and son were not led into temptation, on this occasion, and enjoyed several days rest in this comfortable and convivial inn before finding a ship that would be sailing to Denmark or even Norway. Some ships were sailing for Gothenburg and some for the new fishing port of Copenhagen until finally a ship docked that announced it was accepting travellers for a return trip to Oslo. The ship was new and a good size. It would travel along the coast of Flanders, then up to the Northernmost tip of Denmark before crossing the Strait of water called Skagerrak, between the North Sea and Kattegat before arriving in Oslo.

After an uncomfortable journey, Olaf was reminded of his return many years previously with Hardråda's fleet and the relief of sailing up the long and narrow Oslofjørd with its calm waters to the final destination of the fortress and trading port of Akershus. Olaf and his son thanked the crew for the long but uneventful voyage and made their way to a favourite watering hole known as the 'Havfrue' (Mermaid). Not much had changed although Olaf was disappointed not to see Ari and the twins drinking in a corner. They were able to book two rooms and had a boy send a letter up to the castle. The gossip in the inn was centred around the fact that the King was ill and that, as he and Ingerid had had no children, who was to inherit the throne of Norway? A violent Viking, in the mold of Hardråda was claiming to be King Olaf's illegitimate son but anyone less like his father would be hard to imagine. He was called Magnus Barefoot and was very much not an heir to the peaceful reign of Olaf Kyrre whose young life was being threatened by an undefined illness. After a day a letter was received from the castle. It was from Thorkel asking what they were doing in an inn and to make their way up to the fortress at once.

Thorkel greeted them with tears and embraces and the servants saw them to their comfortable quarters. Olaf handed over the soap the landlady from the Havfrue had asked him to take to the fortress and Thorkel laughed:

"Ah yes, cleanliness is next to godliness! Now you two go and bathe and we shall meet in the dining hall as I want to hear everything about your adventures. You have come back alive, which is something."

Olaf was keen to hear about his son, the King, but all Thorkel would say was that it was probably consumption and it came and went with increasing frequency and that, at present, the King was not in a fit state to meet visitors other than his physicians who seemed to be useless.

Olaf and Olafsson presented themselves in the great hall for dinner. The King's chair was empty and Thorkel sat to one side at the table. He was now the senior councillor and advisor to the King but, as the King was mostly bed-ridden, he was effectively the ruler of Norway. Two bishops were present, Torov and Aslak as Asgaut had died shortly after he had presided over the wedding of Olaf and Freya. There were a few faces he did recognise though. Queen Consort Ingerid sat at the top of the table opposite Thorkel and a little further down he was delighted to see the Queen Dowager of England, Ealdgyth, her beautiful black hair now an elegant silver. There was an empty chair next to her and Thorkel signaled for Olaf to sit there and his son to sit next to Queen Ingerid. The topic of conversation first centred around the saga of Olaf and son in England and Normandy, but soon moved on to the crisis facing Norway. With the King terminally ill, the crown was going to be contested by Magnus 'Berrføtt', Olaf III's alleged illegitimate son, and Haakon Magnusson, the legitimate grandson of Harald Hardråda and son of Olaf III's elder brother Magnus. Both were highly volatile and warlike Vikings, so civil war seemed imminent after such a stretch of peace in Norway. Olaf glanced across at his son and knew what he was thinking. Norwegian politics could wait. He was just anxious to get back to Lillehammer and be reunited with his mother, wife and daughter. Olaf concurred with this thought.

Akershus 1091

Chapter forty
Lillehammer to Oslo

After a few days rest in Oslo, father and son felt up to making the two-day journey to the great fjørd and thence by ferry to Lillehammer. Thorkel had had a one-to-one discussion with Olaf regarding the political situation:

"Olaf, you know I am not military minded, but I have grave concerns about the security of the King and indeed the realm of Norway. The guards here are mostly old retainers of Tora's and are past retirement age. What would I need to offer you and your son to form a robust Palace Guard of strong young warriors or huscarls as they used to be known in Hardråda's time?"

Olaf's eyes widened: "We would need to be based here at Akershus and that would mean leaving our wives again. I don't think Freya or Anja would be very happy about that."

Thorkel pouted: "Don't think I haven't thought of that. Tora had commissioned a beautiful house on the hill overlooking the Oslofjørd. She never lived in it as she married the Danish King Sweyn, and it now stands empty. You could live together there when you are not on duty here and the Crown owns a number of properties on the waterfront, any one of which would suit Anja and Krystyna, and Olafsson would not be charged any rent. Your position would be Captain of the Guard and your son would be your lieutenant. The Treasury is in a very good state as Norway has not had the expense of any wars with Denmark under the rule of Olaf the Peaceful, so we have money to spend on our defence. What say you?" Olaf privately thought it was a wonderful idea as he knew about the lack of excitement in Lillehammer, but he proceeded with caution:

"I am very flattered that you would place such trust in me and were I younger and single I would have no hesitation in accepting. However, as it concerns all of my family, I will discuss it with them and send a message back to you by the end of the week. What sort of remuneration are we talking about?" Thorkel wrote on a piece of parchment. Olaf's eyes widened further.

"That is just for Olafsson. You will receive double and here is the hundred gold Olaf-mynt you are owed for the previous year. I have ordered two horses and a mule for you to ride home. They are from the royal stables so please bring them back when you come."

The journey to Mjørsa fjørd took them by the hamlet of Bjørnholt and there they stopped for the night as the elderly blacksmith and his wife Jorunna insisted they stay with them to try her new fermentation of mjørd. It was very fine but very strong and both Olaf and Olafsson woke at sunrise with heavy heads for the journey to the ferry at Minnesund that could take the horses. They bade farewell to the hospitable couple and reached Minnesund by midday. The sun was gleaming off the still water of the fjørd, reflecting the mountains to the Northeast. On the boat, Olaf shared Thorkel's offer with Olafsson who received the news with great excitement. Like his father, he was not relishing a long stay in Lillehammer after the great adventures he had had, and this seemed to be the answer to solve all their problems. By late afternoon they reached their destination and were discussing what a great surprise it would be for Freya, Anja and Krystyna when they arrived. It was, therefore, something of a surprise to themselves to see a crowd gathered on the jetty and a large flag flapping in the breeze with the words embroidered on it:

'VELKOMMEN HJEM OLAF OCH OLAFSSON!'

In the centre of the cheering crowd were the unmistakeable silhouettes of Freya, Anja and Krystyna with old Vanir by her side.

The reunion was an emotional one for all concerned and they walked back to the house followed by a great procession of townsfolk. Freya had arranged for the marquee they had used for the two weddings to be re-erected outside and Anja had arranged for the staff of the hotel to bring down all the barrels of øl to the tent for a huge street party with free beer for all.

"But how on earth did you know?" asked Olaf laughing.

"Ah," replied Freya, "we are civilised now. Since you left, King Olaf has set up a postal service of riders carrying letters across the land and even to Denmark by ship! I had my very first letter from Thorkel yesterday telling me that the poor King was very ill and that you would be arriving here today and also that you had something very important to discuss with me. I'm intrigued. What is it?" Olaf laughed:

"Oh yes? That Thorkel doesn't waste any time, does he? We can discuss it as a family when all this hiatus has calmed down and we can sit quietly around a table so you won't be rushed into anything."

"I'm even more intrigued now!" laughed Freya with a winning smile that compelled Olaf to give her a loving hug.

The street party finally subsided, when the beer ran out, and both Freya and Anja made it clear to everyone that it was bedtime and that the separation from their menfolk had been a long and lonely one. The townsfolk nodded knowingly and thanked their hosts before heading off into the dimly lit town chattering and laughing.

The sun rose brightly on another beautiful day and the servants were busy in the kitchen baking bread, preparing milk for the grøt and keeping the smoked trout warm for breakfast.

After breakfast, Krystyna left the table to tend to Vanir and Olaf gently put Thorkel's proposal to the ladies. As Olaf concluded there was silence and Freya looked down.

"I have lived happily here most of my life," she said, "but I have always dreamt of going to Oslo."

"Anywhere to get out of Lillehammer even if just for a while," added Anja. "Krystyna's only friend here is Vanir and we can bring him with us as that is where he came from originally."

Olaf and Olafsson looked at each other in astonishment. They never thought it would be an easy thing to sell the idea to their wives, but it seemed that all were in favour. It was too good an opportunity to miss. A letter was dispatched to Thorkel and preparations were made for moving. Anja's hotel was already being run by tenants and Freya's house could be sold to one of the wealthy farmers in the district. She already had tenants running the fishing and cloth businesses so that could continue. Oslo was just a twelve-hour journey so they could return to keep an eye on things if any problems arose. Within the month they had made all the preparations for the move and Thorkel sent two large wagons with two guards to help. The carriages would be too large for the ferry so they would go overland, and the ladies could sleep in Freya's coach.

And so it was that as the long Summer drew to a close, Olaf's entire family including the elderly ambler, Vanir II, trundled their way out of Lillehammer. The whole town and many of the people from the outlying villages including those of Olaf and Freya's home of Dalby, lined the main street to wave off the town's First Lady, loved and respected by all. With Thorkel's two guards leading, with pennants fluttering from their lances, and the two Olaf's as the vanguard beside the carriage and the carts to the rear, it looked like a royal procession with the ladies waving regally from inside.

They left at nine o'clock in the morning and rolled into Oslo at nine o'clock at night to be greeted at Akershus by Thorkel and most of the fortress' household, who held lighted torches to guide their way into the main courtyard. Freya, Anja and Krystyna could barely contain their excitement. In the main hall a light meal had been prepared and their guards were invited into the kitchen. The day had been pleasant, but the evening was chilly and the great fire had been lit to give the hall a cosy ambiance, enhanced by an Irish Wolfhound, who had been given as a gift to Olaf III by Ua Briain, Muirchertach, Lord of Munster and regarded as the first King of Ireland, upon signing a peace agreement with Norway. The hound had been banished from the King's chambers by the physicians and was now sulking and hogging the heat from the fire. Krystyna's love of dogs and horses caused her to immediately head for the fireplace to make a fuss of the dog who apparently was called Séamus. It was the beginning of a beautiful friendship.

The following day Olaf and Freya made their way up the slope from the fortress to the house that Queen Tora had commissioned to be built. Thorkel went with them and, ceremoniously, handed Freya the keys. The smell that greeted them was of burning logs and pine branches. Thorkel had employed two servants to prepare the house by lighting the long fire in the central hall and also in the sauna. Olaf couldn't believe he now had his own sauna. The house was furnished in good taste although Freya had brought some of her own furniture from Lillehammer. Both were similarly overwhelmed. The house in Lillehammer was by far the smartest in the district but this was in another league. The two servants made a little bow and retired to the kitchen. Olaf and Freya took Thorkel's good advice to have a sauna and then return to Akershus to collect Olafsson, Anja and Krystyna, who had slept in after the tiring journey.

They returned to Akershus to find Thorkel waiting for them. Krystyna seemed very excited as she appeared to have found a new friend. A handsome lad of about fifteen stood next to Séamus the wolfhound, with Krystyna, now a pretty and precocious teenager, holding the lead of the dog. Thorkel managed to pout and smile at the same time:

"I have found a job for your granddaughter Olaf, and her father and mother approve. She is to take on the duties and responsibilities as Keeper of the King's Dogs along with Eric here. There is a small stipend. As the King disliked hunting, the royal hounds have been disbanded and the post vacated. But now we have a dog once more he must be looked after and exercised."

Olaf and Freya agreed that it was a wonderful idea, so long as she didn't neglect Vanir. Séamus seemed to sense the joy in the room and wagged his tail vigorously. Olaf addressed the lad:

"My father's name was Eric, he was a mighty huscarl who held a bridge against the whole Anglo-Saxon army outside Yorvik, buying time for the Norwegian army to form up. But he paid with his life as he was inevitably overwhelmed."

The lad gulped in awe at this revelation. Freya changed the mood.

"Come on Olaf no time for your sagas now. Let them enjoy some time together by walking the royal wolfhound on the green slopes outside the castle."

"All right but be careful, he's a very powerful animal and could easily pull you over if he saw a rabbit or a deer. Make sure you both hold the lead."

"Yes, morfar," said Krystyna.

"I will, sir," said Eric and they both left the hall with Thorkel inwardly satisfied with his matchmaking skills:

"They make a pleasing couple, don't you think?" said Thorkel.

"Not yet," said Anja and Freya, almost in unison. "She is just fourteen and still a girl. We will see how things pan out. They have only just met!" Anja remembered the long courtship with Olafsson when he was just a boy.

"Now we have to choose you a house," said Thorkel, come, let us head down to the harbour wall. The five of them walked down the edge of the great Oslofjørd and were shown a few houses standing empty. Anja and Olafsson opted for an attractive house painted blue and just big enough for the three of them. The gulls called overhead, the water lapped gently, and the boats bobbed at their moorings. Away to the left or Eastern side of the house the sound of Viking travellers partaking of a lunchtime øl was just audible from the Havfrue inn.

"This is perfect for us, thank you so much!" said Anja with some emotion. "And just a short walk to the inn," laughed Olafsson.

Freya frowned at her son: "Pick up Anja, carry her across the threshold, give her a kiss and then you and your father may go for a beer at that mermaid place that seems to attract you. Both Olafs laughed heartily and once Anja, objecting somewhat at having been being bundled across the threshold, the ladies were able to make plans for the furnishings, whilst their menfolk headed off in the direction of a strange sign.

Havfrue

Olaf and his son entered the dimly lit inn whereupon there was a great shout from the corner containing three very familiar faces. The chances of meeting Ari and the twins at the Mermaid were reasonable as they stopped there once a month for trade with Orkney, Bergen and Oslo. Olaf let out a great cheer of excitement as he was keen to introduce his son to these old friends:

"Ari, Sigurd and Ulrik, may I introduce my son Olafsson. Olafsson these are old friends of mine from Orkney."

"Not that old," said the twins in unison and there was much handshaking and man-hugging. Beer was called for and stories were swapped. The travellers were particularly impressed with the battle of Rouen and the story of a future King of England tipping a rebel leader over the castle parapet. Ari had some good news:

"Olaf I must tell you my wonderful news, Solvej and I now have a beautiful eleven-month-old baby girl called 'Astra' who is just now learning to walk. Her name in old Norse means 'as beautiful as a goddess.' Of course, we named her after Astrid, who has been so kind to us."

"That is wonderful news indeed, Ari. Congratulations to you both."

Olafsson suggested that more beer was required to celebrate, and it arrived promptly and was swiftly consumed, with a rowdy toast, and much cheering and clapping from all in the inn.

Olaf and Olafsson returned to the house on the seafront in a far less stable condition than they had been in when they left and sustained suitable rebukes from their wives.

During the following months, having moved into their new homes, their lives settled into a new normality. Olaf and son set about their task of building up a force of huscarls in preparation for the impending turbulence. Olaf visited the King on occasions as it was clear that he was slipping away. He wished to reveal to the King that he was, in all probability, his father. But he was never allowed to get close enough to impart this to him as the coughing caused by the tuberculosis was considered to be the carrier of the bacteria and, if breathed in in sufficient quantities over a period of time, could be infectious. Olaf gave up and decided that it may come as a shock strong enough to finish off the very ill King. 'Best let sleeping dogs lie', he thought to himself.

After just over a year, King Olaf III, known as 'The Peaceful', died. He was to everyone in Norway, Olaf Haraldsson and no one ever questioned that he neither resembled nor had any of the characteristics of his warlike father. In accordance with the dying King's wishes, Thorkel organised for a ship to take the King's coffin up to Nidaros to be buried in the cathedral there. A great procession carried the cask from Akershus fortress to the seafront. Krystyna and Erik followed, leading Séamus the wolfhound, followed by Ingerid, his widow. Olaf, his son and ten huscarls flanked the casket which was covered with flowers. Thorkel, Ealdgyth and the people of Oslo followed in respect to their much-loved King. Thorkel and Ingerid boarded the boat with Olaf and Olafsson and ten huscarls of equal height to carry the coffin to the cathedral when it arrived in Nidaros.

After the service, Thorkel was faced with the problem of who to name as the successor. With great diplomacy he announced that Haakon Magnusson should rule in Nidaros and the North and the warlike and illegitimate Magnus 'Berrføtt' be recognised as Olaf III's only son to rule from Oslo in the South. Olaf and his huscarls escorted

Thorkel and Ingerid by ship back to Oslo to inform Magnus of the situation. Ingerid announced that, as King Olaf had only shared a bed with her on three occasions (despite her obvious beauty), it was highly unlikely that he had fathered Magnus, an aggressive thug, so very unlike him in every possible way. But Thorkel remained with his decision which, he hoped, would prevent a civil war. She also announced that as soon as a respectable time of mourning had elapsed, she would marry the rich landowner, Svein Brynjulsson, and would take no further part in life at court as she intended to have children before it was too late. Thorkel pouted at this but made no comment.

Chapter forty-one
Olaf Retires

The next few years were not as Olaf and Freya might have hoped. Magnus, almost immediately after being declared joint ruler of Norway, decided to raise an army to campaign in Orkney and take advantage of local disputes. Olaf and Olafsson with their small professional army of huscarls played a major part in deposing the two sons of Thorfin the Mighty, Paul and Erland who had on many occasions snubbed Olaf and referred to him as an upstart. This was sweet revenge for Olaf as the sneering brothers were exiled to Norway and their sons Magnus and Erlandson were retained as hostages. As Paul and Erland were being led down to the harbour wall in chains, Olaf sat astride his horse and noticed the confused look of recognition on their faces as they were bundled past him. Olaf did not show any expression but stared at them resolutely, reminded of the insults they had piled upon him. 'Thorkel would also be pleased' Olaf thought.

On returning to Norway, Magnus Berrføtt decided to Winter 1094/1095 at the new royal estate of Nidaros, established by Olaf III. This was far more comfortable than the old royal estate of Harald Hardråda where Olaf had had his early training as a huscarl with the Byzantine master archer, Urbicus Acropolites. He remembered too the friendship with Eystein Orre and the disastrous dalliance with the beautiful Queen Tora which had been the start of all his troubles. It was so long ago it seemed like another age. Hardråda, Tora, Urbicus and Eystein were all now long gone and even the son he had fathered with Tora was now gone. What was he doing campaigning at his age when he should be with Freya in their lovely home in Oslo? 'But', he thought, 'this is what I am being paid to do'.

In January 1095, Haakon arrived at the city of Nidaros with a small army and, finding the new royal estate occupied, took up residence in Hardråda's old estate. Haakon had taken control of all the lands held by his father, Magnus, son of Tora and Hardråda. This included the city of Nidaros although technically the royal estates belonged to both joint rulers. The tension though was palpable. Magnus decided that, as Haakon was on home turf, he would be able to summon considerable forces far greater than the small army commanded by Olaf. Therefore, in February, he embarked his force and sailed out of Nidaros with the intention of raising a much larger force to attack Haakon from the South. Haakon, on observing the fleet depart decided to march South overland and attack Magnus when he stopped at Bergen to resupply. Magnus and Olaf had anticipated this and had come up with a plan. Olaf would take his son and six huscarls and track the army of Haakon and await a moment to take him out.

Haakon wasted no time in summoning the Øyrating (assembly) to ratify the recruitment and, with so many new faces, it was easy for Olaf and Olafsson to infiltrate this body of soldiers. Within a week he, his son and the six huscarls, whom he trusted, were battling their way over the still frozen Dovrefjell, a mountain range running down the centre of Norway. Olaf observed how poorly organised this expedition was. All the men were on foot with a few carts carrying spears and spare shields. Nobody seemed in command, and nobody knew when they were going to get fed. Finally, word was passed down that they were to forage for food from the rich habitation of animal life along the way. Olaf waited for the order to pitch camp and moved out away from the main body with his small entourage. Haakon also left with four spearmen and began to head up the lower slopes of the Snøhette, the highest of the mountains, in search of reindeer, boar or even a snow-rabbit. There was not a bow between them. Both Olaf and his son were doubly armed with hunting bows and swords whereas the huscarls had swords and shields but also throwing axes. Haaken was shouting that he had spotted a small herd of deer higher up but with the wind blowing in that direction, the heads of the deer all came up to the alert position. Haaken's men began stumbling up the slope through the fresh snow. Olaf worked his way around by a copse of pine trees, so they were now on the flank of the group. Haaken ordered two of his men to try to encircle the deer if they stampeded. Unfortunately, this involved passing through the same tree line and they were quickly and silently dispatched by throwing axes. Olaf and his group were now behind the deer who would not pick up any scent due to the wind direction. Haakon and his two spearmen were lying on the snow and crawling forward. Olaf fired an arrow into the nearest deer who fell causing the others to run in the direction of Haakon. Of course, they stood up with their spears poised as Olaf ran towards them. Two axes apiece felled the spearmen whilst Olaf and his son shared the third target of Haakon Magnusson, who fell back silently into the snow. Arrows and axes were retrieved, and the bodies were left for the wolves.

Olaf and his team returned to the camp carrying the hart which was greeted with a great cheer. When asked if they had seen Haakon they replied:

"Only at some distance trying to climb the Snøhette looking for reindeer when there were deer on the lower levels."

Night fell, fires were lit, and venison was cooked. In the morning when Haakon hadn't returned, the army broke up and headed home. Nobody volunteered to go and look for the grandson of Hardråda, so Olaf and his team headed South to Bergen.

Following a forced march of several days, Olaf and his team arrived at Bergen. By good fortune, the fleet of Magnus Berrføtt was visible on the horizon. There would be just enough time for a visit to Andershus to say hello to Astrid and Solvej. Olaf asked the six huscarls to wait on the jetty whilst he and Olafsson headed off to the traveller's lodge. The door was opened by Solvej who recognised Olaf but not his son. She called to Astrid:

"Astrid, your prodigal lover has returned and this time he has brought a friend!" She laughed like a proper fishwife, and it was clear that Olaf was somewhat offended by her lack of greeting. Olaf hoped that she wasn't turning into her mother.

Astrid came to the door, wiping her hands on her apron:

"Olaf! My god man but you've aged some since I last saw you! And who is this handsome young man. He looks like you when we first met, only he's quite a bit taller."

"Astrid, Solvej, this is my son Olafsson. His mother is Freya of Lillehammer to whom I am now married."

Olafsson smiled as the two women studied the likeness of father and son.

"Oh, by the gods!" squealed Astrid. "Solvej, now we have two Olaf's!" Olaf gave Astrid a hug. "I wanted you to meet my son, but where is yours, little Anders?"

"Not so little, he is twenty-five now and over six foot tall. These past years he has been away with Ari and the twins, so we don't see much of him."

Olafsson spoke: "Were those the sailors we met in Oslo last year in the Havfrue Inn?"

"Yes, they were," said Olaf, "but no sign of Anders. They did not mention that he had been working with them."

"That's very odd," said Astrid, frowning. At that moment there was a cry from within.

"That must be baby Astra that Ari was so proud to tell us about. May we go and see her?" asked Olaf.

"Of course," said Solvej, "she has just had her nap so she probably wants a drink of milk."

They all went into the house to goggle at the pretty little girl. Olaf picked her up and gave her a kiss on the forehead:

"That's from your Daddy who I met in Oslo." Astra chuckled prettily.

"Right, let's get you boys something to eat and drink before King Magnus gets here," said Astrid, ever the hostess. They all huddled around the fire and ate and drank. As ever, the quality of her cooking was appreciated, and Olaf watched his son devour his plate with relish. Olaf retold the tale of Astrid, noticing an archbishop ogling her bosom asking him if he liked dumplings. They all roared with laughter and little Astra clapped her hands by way of joining the jolly commotion. At that point, there was a knock at the door. Olaf answered it:

"Fleet's just docking now sir." Olaf thanked the huscarl who departed.

"Sir, is it?" laughed Astrid.

"Well, he is Captain of the Kings Guard," said Olafsson proudly. "We have formed them together to protect Norway and keep the peace, but Magnus seems to use us as his private army for marauding our neighbours and settling his quarrels."

"Just as Hardråda had done back in the 60's." added Olaf.

"Right, lovely ladies, we must away. Thank you for your kind hospitality."

Olaf and son gave them both an embrace as though they were family and made their way through the chill air to the dockside, where a large number of longboats were jostling to get ashore.

Magnus was among the first to disembark and was delighted to see Olaf, Olafsson, and six burly huscarls standing on the jetty with not a scratch on them.

"Tell me your news!" he yelled, rushing towards them with his arms in the air. "What has happened? Tell me!"

Olaf stood at the front of his men but waited until Magnus approached out of earshot to all others.

"Sire, Haakon's army is disbanded. The grandson of Hardråda is dead. My arrow only winged him in the shoulder but my son here, his arrow flew true and straight into his heart. Haakon is no more. You are the sole ruler of Norway."

Magnus began to tremble. He grabbed Olaf's arm and with a moist eye and with a quivering voice he pledged exactly what Olaf wanted to hear:

"How can I ever repay you? I am now the undisputed King of Norway." But in his thoughts, he was thinking that this man has control and loyalty of the huscarls who he has trained and raised. He must be got rid of.

"I have done your bidding Sire, but now I must ask your leave to stand down. My son will continue in your service and I will remain as an advisor only. There should be peace in Norway now and I ask only to retire in Oslo with my ever-patient wife, Freya. I am too old at my time of life for continued active service, the fact that my arrow did not strike where it should have only goes to prove that the keen eye of Olafsson is what is needed and he should take my position as Captain of the King's Guard."

Magnus was immediately attracted to this proposition. With Olaf gone the huscarls could concentrate their loyalty on their King and he believed that the young Olafsson would be far easier to control and manipulate than his father who had grown far too popular and powerful with the army. He need only ensure that Olafsson knew who his rightful King and commander was and to show due loyalty.

Although Haakon was dead there was still the problem of his foster-father, Tore Tordsson, a powerful nobleman who would never accept Magnus as king.

"I will grant you your request, Olaf and accept Olafsson as your very capable replacement as Captain of my Guard. You have served the Norwegian Royal family well. We may call upon your great experience in an advisory capacity but, for now, you may stand down and spend some time with your family. Olafsson and I will build up the army in Oslo and then we shall march North to stamp my authority on Nidaros and have that upstart Tore Tordsson dangling from a tree."

And so it was that Olaf returned to Freya and Olafsson returned to Anya and Krystyna. Thorkel was pleased about the incarceration of Paul and Erland and, as he put it, *'it couldn't have happened to two nicer brothers'*. The Winter melted into Spring and Magnus and Olafsson worked hard at building and training a sizeable army for the campaign North in the early Summer. By mid-May the army was ready with archers, axemen, and spearmen. Olaf had helped to organise the logistical side with carts of food plus four doctors with medical supplies to tend the wounded. Olaf, Freya, Anja and Krystyna all waved Olafsson off at the head of a great column and the only one other than Magnus to be on horseback. Erik held Séamus by his lead who barked with excitement at the noise of eight thousand men going off to war. Olaf felt terribly about not being there to watch his son's back, but he knew his son could more than take care of himself. In the event, the march to Nidaros was stoutly opposed by the men of the North and there was fierce fighting for nearly three weeks. Finally, Olafsson led a breaching attack on Nidaros and surrounded Tore Tordsson and another nobleman Egli Aslaksson. The city of Nidaros surrendered and Magnus, leaving half his army as a garrison, hooked up with his fleet on the West coast and sailed to a small island called Vambarholm just by Hamnøya. There Magnus gave the order for all the prisoners, of whom most were Norwegian nobility, to be hanged from the trees. These included Tore Tordsson and Egli Aslaksson.

The hanging of Egli Aslaksson

Olafsson was appalled that these noblemen should be executed but, having witnessed Prince Henry throw a rebel from a castle parapet, it came as no great surprise.

For the next few years Olaf saw very little of his son as Magnus embarked on seemingly endless campaigns around the islands of the North and Irish Seas. He even fought a battle with the Normans in Anglesey to the delight of the Welsh. Olafsson wondered if he would ever be allowed to return to Norway.

One morning, back in Oslo, a ship arrived and delivered some letters from England. One contained the royal seal of Prince Henry and was addressed to Olaf. It was the letter Olaf had been waiting for.

Chapter forty-two
Return to England

The contents of the letter may not have surprised Olaf but the political news between William Rufus, Robert and Henry was unexpected. In 1095 Pope Urban II summoned Christian knights to The First Crusade against the Seljuk Turks to take Jerusalem. Robert mortgaged the Duchy of Normandy to William Rufus for 10,000 marks to raise an army, and, in 1096, he arrived in Constantinople with his army alongside his neighbour, Stephen of Blois. Since his pitiful and unchivalric behaviour at Rouen his reputation was in dire need of some heroic deeds. Henry had heard that his brother Robert had acquitted himself well at the battle of Antioch and had helped in the capture of Jerusalem in July 1099.

Robert Curthose at the siege of Antioch

Robert had turned down a lucrative position working for the Byzantine Emperor Alexios in Constantinople. Instead, he travelled to Naples where, on his outward journey, he had stayed for the winter. Here he met and fell in love with Sybil of Conservano, daughter of a wealthy Norman count. He again wintered in Naples and during this time he married Sybil. The dowry attached to this marriage was huge and allowed Robert the opportunity of paying off his debt to Rufus and regaining Normandy.

All this Olaf read with great interest. Why did Henry want Olaf to come at once? It was clear that with Robert away for only a few months longer, Henry was planning a coup against Rufus and the throne of England. Henry had asked for Olafsson as well, but this was not possible as he was somewhere in the North Sea with Magnus. Olaf wrote a letter and sealed it. It was for Henry's eyes only. He would leave Norway in the New Year when the weather was calmer and head towards Calais where he would await Henry's contact. The letter was sent on a trading ship to London where Henry was attending Rufus' court. It seemed that Rufus now trusted his younger brother despite having stolen from him and clapped him in prison. Henry had been biding his time, but he sensed that the hour of retribution was fast approaching.

Early in the New Year a ship arrived in Oslo that Olaf recognised. It was Ari and the twins carrying furs from Sweden. He had a good view of the harbour from his residence on the hill and could see clearly that there were only three men on board. No Anders. Olaf waited patiently for them to unload their cargo into the cart of the waiting agent before making his way down to the waterfront and thence to the Havfrue Inn. There was the usual boisterous greeting from the trio. Olaf was keen to find out what had happened to Anders whereupon they all laughed heartily.

"We heard that you and your son had been working for Magnus III and that you had deposed Paul and Erland in Orkneyjar. I'll bet that felt good!" said Ari. "I loathed those two arrogant, entitled prigs."

"Yes, yes, but what of Anders? Astrid said he was working for you."

"Well, he was but he got into a terrible fight in an inn with some huge dockside scrapper who objected to his fiancé flirting with Anders. What can I say but our boy came second. It was a fair fight so no third party could get involved. We returned the battered and bruised lad to Bergen to be nursed by his mother. She wasn't happy and blamed us for not taking more care of him!"

They chatted for some time until Olaf brought up the subject of Prince Henry's letter. Olaf explained that he had informed Freya and had obtained permission from Thorkel to leave his post and travel to England, as Olafsson was now the appointed leader of the huscarls and the King had accepted his request to stand down. Ari jumped at the chance. Trade had been difficult with Magnus waging war in the North Sea and a trip to Calais under royal patronage seemed like an adventure not to be missed.

"Olaf, my ship is at your disposal. When do we leave?" The twins were equally pleased to be going on another adventure with Olaf.

Farewells were said to the ladies, Freya, Anja, Krystyna, Ealdgyth and of course, Thorkel.

On a bright February morning in the year 1100, Olaf and his friends set sail for the coast of Denmark and then followed the coastline South and then West until finally reaching the port of Calais. Olaf had written to Henry to inform him that he would take lodgings at *L'enseigne de l'Ange* (The Angel Tavern). Olaf explained that the inn probably got its title for possessing the least angelic serving girls he had ever encountered. The twins brightened up noticeably after the long journey. Olaf led his team into the inn and was greeted by the 'madame la patronesse':

"Olaf, tu es de retour. Où est ton beau garçon et qui sont ces voyous?"

(Olaf, you have returned. Where is your beautiful boy and who are these ruffians?)

Olaf replied with vigour: "I'll sont des bons amis des Orcades. Il sont des amis de confiance."

(These are my good friends from Orkney. These are my trusted friends).

"Ah, oui? D'accord, il sont les bienvenus."

(Oh yes? Alright then, they are welcome.)

Ari and the twins understood a little French from their travels and raised a great cheer. Soon they were seated and drinking French wine with several of the 'angels' draped over them and whispering offers and advancements to the shy twins. Ari was respected as he wore a wedding ring but the twins were fair game.

After a few days a messenger arrived at the Angel Tavern, sent by Prince Henry. It transpired that the very hospitable Bishop Walkelin had died in 1098 and William Rufus, as was his habit, had failed to appoint a replacement and, instead, was taking the revenues for himself, just as he had done with Durham and Canterbury. Olaf and his three companions sat and listened to the impassioned rant of the Anglo-Saxon yeoman who spoke in a strange dialect quite different to that spoken in York or London and he clearly hated Rufus with every fibre:

"He, Rufus, is in the thirteenth year after he assumed the throne. The King is very harsh and severe over his land and his men, and with all his neighbours; and very formidable and through the counsels of evil men, that to him were always agreeable, and through his own avarice, he was ever tiring this nation with an army, and with unjust contributions. For during his rule all rights fall to the ground, and every wrong rises up before God and before the world. God's church he has humbled; and all the bishoprics and abbacies, whose elders died in his reign, he either sold for a fee, or held in his own hands, and let for a certain sum; because he would be the heir of every man, both of the clergy and laity; so that on the day that he dies he will have in his own hand the archbishopric of Canterbury, with the bishopric of Winchester, and that of Salisbury, and eleven abbacies, all let for a sum; and (though I may be tedious) all that is loathsome to

God and righteous men, all that was customary in England during his reign. And for this he is loathed by nearly all his people, and odious to God, as his end testifies for he will depart in the midst of his unrighteousness, without any power of repentance."

Olaf and his friends listened with incredulity. The twins understood very little of what was said but to Olaf it seemed quite clear, Henry was planning to kill his brother just as Caine killed Abel so, apart from fratricide, he was also committing regicide. The alarming part of it was that Henry was proposing that the assassination of the King of England should be carried out by Olaf himself. Henry had nurtured this idea since he had seen Olaf shoot a running stag from a galloping horse and, now that he was back in England, he must seize the throne and ensure that Rufus met with a tragic accident whilst hunting in the New Forest, just a short ride from the treasury in Winchester.

"I have a boat with a crew", said the yeoman.

"I also have a ship," said Ari and I have no wish to leave it here.

"So be it", said the yeoman, "then we shall be two ships. Do you know where Southampton is? If we are separated, we will meet you there. Here is gold from Prince Henry to pay for this inn and the one in Winchester."

The bag was heavy. It was more than enough.

"I suspect that Ari's trading ship will travel much faster than your 'boat' so I suggest we head to Winchester where we will get some supper at a fine inn I know called 'Emma's Hus.' We will meet you there when you arrive."

The yeoman nodded to Olaf and headed back to his vessel. Olaf paid the bill for his group and they also headed down to the quay to embark on their crossing of what the French called 'La Manche' but in England it was called the 'English Channel'. It looked overcast and the water was choppy but they headed due North, nonetheless.

Olaf was very pensive during the journey and considered the great danger he was facing when he arrived in England. Fortune was with them as there was a brisk South Westerly breeze and neap tides so that Ari was skilfully able to average about six knots. After four and a half hours the coast of England appeared in the form of the White Cliffs of Dover. Ari headed the ship Westwards for another hour or so until they sighted the Isle of Wight whereupon he expertly navigated his ship up the Solent into the calm Southampton Water and thence up the Itchen River to a shallow where a small settlement had sprung up around a priory being built by a group of Augustinian monks. This was later to be the Priory of St Denys. Here they disembarked and enquired from the locals as to where they may hire a cart. A youngish monk offered to take them to Winchester for a small donation to their priory. After a rickety journey to Winchester, it was a relief to see the great tower of the latest cathedral construction and the monk knew exactly where Emma's Hus was situated. Olaf gave the monk a gold coin for the priory and invited him to join their party in a fine meal with ale. Ari and the twins brightened up and soon there was much cheering and laughter with the young monk showing that he could drink with the best of them. Once the alcohol had begun to work its magic, Brother Martin, as he was called, began to open up on the subject of the King and his shameful treatment of the Church. It wasn't far from the opinions held by the yeoman but much clearer to understand.

Night fell and there was no sign of the yeoman. Brother Martin made his way back to the priory as he had missed Compline at eight o'clock and had to be up at half past five for Vigils, the first service of the day. Olaf and his boisterous party turned in just before midnight, having consumed a good portion of the inn's stores of beer and mead. He was awakened early with a thumping headache by a knocking on his door. It was the landlady (named Emma by her mother in respect of her Queen), who said there were some armed men downstairs asking for him. Olaf buckled his sword and woke the others. There was, however, no cause for alarm. It was none other than Prince Henry himself accompanied by the yeoman and several men at arms. Olaf was delighted and took the proffered hand of the Prince. They had shared a prison cell in the Tower and had fought against a rebellion shoulder to shoulder, they were indeed brothers-in-arms. When Emma realised who it was, she made a deep curtsey and asked permission to bring them some breakfast victuals.

Emma kept a fine table and a good breakfast of bacon and eggs was not long in coming, including fresh bread and milk from the dairy. Henry complimented the landlady, who blushed prettily and curtsied once again before leaving them to talk. Henry would not be drawn into discussing the reason for his summoning of Olaf and chatted happily about things of no consequence. As the meal was completed, Henry arose and asked Olaf to accompany him as he wished to have a stroll around the building works of the cathedral. He signalled for the others to remain seated. Once outside, his carefree demeanour changed, and he appeared serious and earnest. When they had walked away from the houses and into open space the prince divulged his purpose:

"Olaf, thank you for coming all this way. We have some very serious business to attend to. What we shall discuss is for your ears only. You may tell no-one, not even your closest friends. Your three companions are working for me now and if they know nothing they can say nothing if they are taken. The King employs many spies who are controlled by Ranulf Flambard. I trust no-one, with the possible exception of yourself and that simpleton, the yeoman.

The King, my brother, is ruling this land in an appalling manner. He steals from the Church at the highest level and it appears that nothing can satiate his greed and avarice. He has stolen my lands in England and Normandy which he had stolen from our brother Robert who was obliged to mortgage the Duchy in order to restore his reputation after that shameful business in Rouen. Robert is now returning from Naples with a new wife and a dowry large enough to buy back Normandy. If Rufus should have an accident, then Robert would be next in line unless I claim the throne before he reaches England. The plan is that we lay low in Winchester until Rufus arranges a hunt in the New Forest. It may take a few months as he hates the cold weather but come the Summer he surely will. That will be our time, Olaf. I will be with the hunt and will lure them to a place when our men will release a stag near to where you will be hiding. The King will pursue and that is when you repeat the shot I saw you make when we were hunting, only this time it will be through the heart of the most godless and undeserving King of England. I will blame one of the Royal Party and say it was a hunting accident and then we will ride swiftly to the Royal Mint in Winchester where I will declare myself the rightful King of England. The eldest of my brothers, Richard, was killed in just such a way.

Chapter forty-three
The New Forest plot

Henry and Olaf returned to Emma's Hus where Ari and the twins were waiting. Henry asked who had brought them from Southampton and when it was explained that Brother Martin had joined them for a rowdy supper Henry said:

"Right, we are heading to Bitterne Manor where you will be staying for the next few months. We'll go via the priory and collect Brother Martin as he will be staying with you as well. William Gifford, the King's Chancellor will pay you a visit and give you instructions and ensure you have everything you need including money. Once we arrive at Bitterne, you may not travel back to Winchester.

"As you wish, my lord," said the twins in absolute unison.

"I like these two," said Henry, laughing.

The stay in Bitterne Manor was comfortable but dull. The months dragged and occasionally Henry would arrive with William Gifford and take Olaf riding in the New Forest. The others were not invited. It was a damp and cold Spring and, as the weather warmed up it seemed perfect for a Royal hunt in June or July, but Rufus had taken an army up North to quell an uprising. Finally, as the month of July came to a warm close, news was that Rufus was at Sarum and had asked Henry and Sir Walter Tyrell to arrange a Royal Hunt on the afternoon of 2nd August .

At last, Henry found something for Ari and the twins to do. They were four including the yeoman and their job was to take a cart to an appointed place in the forest where the gamekeeper would deliver to them a stag bound by ropes. When the hunting party approached, they were to release the stag into the direction of the on-coming horses and then conceal themselves. It all seemed very strange to them, but they obeyed the Prince's instructions to the letter.

The night of August 1st/August 2nd saw a huge electric storm pass over Hampshire and Wiltshire after many hot and airless days. As it reached Sarum, Rufus awoke at around one in the morning with a scream that echoed around the small stone castle. Servants came rushing into his chamber to find his hair matted with sweat and as the lightening lit up his room, his face was pale and his eyes wide with fear. He had suffered a terrible nightmare in which he saw blood spurting out of his chest and hiding the sun; this he babbled to his attendants and commanded them not to leave him alone for the remainder of the night.

The following morning the sun rose brightly to reveal a countryside that appeared relieved that it had had such a deluge. The grass was green and the flowers gave off a powerful scent whilst droplets of water fell from the green and red apples. The sky was clear, a perfect day for a hunt. Henry had heard of Rufus' nightmare and was concerned that the hunt might be cancelled. He need not have worried. The King had slept for the remainder of the night and was now at breakfast, shouting orders at attendants. Also in the hall when Henry arrived were Gilbert and Roger de Clare, William of Breteuil, Sir Walter Tyrell, Robert Fitzhamon and a few others.

William Rufus took a sheaf of arrows with the Royal crest and gave them to Tyrell with the words:

"To my finest marksman go my finest arrows."

The air was clean and clear as the party made their way down the steep slope of Sarum to Five Rivers and thence an hour's ride to Bramshaw (Bramble Wood) and the Royal hunting lodge known as 'Studley Castle' where they would water the horses and enjoy a splendid lunch that had been organised by Henry and Tyrell.

It was mid-afternoon when the actual hunt began. At first, they didn't have much luck as the deer were perhaps sleeping in the warm afternoon sun. Henry encouraged Tyrell to accompany the King further Southward, claiming he had seen some stags in the area of Stoney Cross. Meanwhile Ari, the twins and the yeoman had taken charge of a stag from the gamekeeper which had a sack over its head and its hooves bound. Olaf was mounted on a slope with his bow ready. Henry suggested that all other riders, including himself, continue straight on and that Tyrell and the King veer off to the right in a Westerly direction. Looking over his shoulder as he rode South, Henry gave a loud blast of his hunting horn. At this signal the stag was untied, kicking and struggling and the sack removed. It was the stag's dearest wish to get as far from these people as possible and he rushed up the slope only to see Olaf on horseback straight ahead. Charging down the slope brought him directly into the path of Tyrell and Rufus. With a yell of glee Rufus charged forward into the low sunlight of a Summer's afternoon. For a second the stag froze to consider his options. Rufus fired directly into the sunlight and missed his static target. Tyrell, not far behind, released his arrow but again missed his mark just as Olaf loosed his bolt, with the high ground and the light behind him. His aim was unerring and there was a thud and a scream as Rufus instinctively tried to wrench out the arrow whilst falling from the saddle. This almost certainly sped up his end as he had had his lung pierced. Sir Walter arrived at the scene as blood spurted from the wound and from the King's mouth. Kneeling by the King during his last moments, he noticed with horror that the arrow showed the King's cypher, just like the ones he had been given at Sarum. Olaf had moved his horse gently backward and was concealed by a large tree. Sir Walter Tyrell felt the sweat on his back turn cold. He let out a cry of despair, mounted his horse and rode as hard for Southampton as his horse could bare. He could not have known that Henry had furbished Olaf with a sheaf of arrows from the Royal fletcher which he as a prince had every right to.

Meanwhile, Henry had brought his party around in an arc to where the ambush of Rufus had taken place. There they found the body of William II of England; his tunic heavily stained with blood and the protruding broken arrow clearly showing the silver royal cypher stamped into the shaft. Robert Fitzhamon was the first one to speak:

"That's one of Tyrell's arrows! The King gave him a quiver of those at breakfast in Sarum. Where is Tyrell?"

Medieval depiction of death of William Rufus

Nobody in the party had noticed Henry drop back. Everyone was staring in horror at the dead body of the King. Henry had gone around to the rear of the slope to meet with Olaf who then walked their horses quietly away to where Ari and the others were standing by the cart, not daring to move. William Rufus' horse was grazing near the body, oblivious to the murder of his rider. The hunting party began looking at each other nervously. Nobody dismounted. Gilbert de Clare murmured to his brother:

"We need to be somewhere else, come on Roger, we don't want to get caught up in this." The two brothers spurred their horses and galloped off in the direction of Bramshaw. This precipitated a general panic and exit from the scene, leaving the body of William Rufus alone and unattended. Fifty yards away, Henry and his party, including Olaf, abandoned the cart, saddled up, and headed off East to cover the twenty-mile journey to Winchester.

Some thirty minutes later, a charcoal maker named Purkis, who lived in a thatched cottage in nearby Thorougham was making his rounds to collect wood when he came across an abandoned cart with no horse. He then heard a soft sighing noise from a horse through the glade. Purkis assumed it must be the horse from the abandoned cart. Approaching gently, he took the reins and stroked the nose of the horse. It was definitely not a cart-horse but a beautiful chestnut hunter whose saddle bore the royal cypher.

"Oh! dear God!" Purkis' heart missed a beat as he gazed past the horse and cried out loud. Could it be that he had come upon a murdered King of England? Securing the horse, he went back for the cart and loaded the blood-soaked body onto it. He then attached the yoke to the horse and walked him back to his cottage where he covered the body with his winter cloak. The light was fading into a beautiful sunset. He would wake early at sunrise and walk the twenty miles to Winchester Cathedral where the monks could give the body a Christian burial.

Henry had ridden hard to Winchester and his party arrived with the setting sun. Olaf had noticed a lone rider behind them who was not only keeping up with their forced pace but appeared to be gaining on them. After a while, with Olaf squinting into the sunset, the rider disappeared. Riding into the Treasury building in Winchester, Henry declared to the guards and the monks, who kept the Treasury secure, that William II was dead, and that he, Henry was now the rightful heir to the throne, and as such, demanded access to the Crown Jewels. The captain of the guard explained that William de Breteuil had entered the place where the jewels were kept five minutes earlier and had vowed to protect them on behalf of Robert, Duke of Normandy who he insists is the rightful heir to the throne of England. Henry's face turned puce with rage:

"Give me the key to the Crown Jewels!" roared Henry.

"I cannot do that, Sire, as the only key to the door has been taken by William de Breteuil." Henry stormed past the guard and into the chamber followed by his men. William stood alone, sword in one hand and a large iron key in the other.

William of Breteuil covered the doorway with his body.

"Lord William!" roared Henry, "do you have any knowledge of the Law of Porphyrogeniture?"

"I do not sire, but as a nobleman of Normandy my duty is to my overlord the Duke of Normandy and eldest surviving son of William the Conqueror."

"Well, let me explain, William. It is a theory of inheritance from Constantinople that is now set in English law. It means 'born to the purple', or, in other words, born the son of a king or emperor. It means that my brother Robert was not born of a king but merely a duke. When I was born much later our father and mother had become crowned king and queen and therefore, I was born to the purple. My claim takes precedence over the son of a duke. I am the son of a king. I also outnumber you substantially and would not hesitate to have you hurled from the cathedral tower. Do you remember Conan of Rouen?"

William de Breteuil's eyes shifted around the assembled armed men and realised it was surrender or die. He had done his best for Robert. Standing to one side he handed the key to Henry and offered him his sword.

"Put up your sword in the scabbard. You are a good, loyal man and I shall need good loyal men if I am to bring peace to this realm. I am your lord now."

Henry turned the heavy key and the Crown Jewels were brought out by several monks. Henry lifted the Coronation Crown from its cushion and placed it on his head. Everyone in the chamber dropped to one knee, including William de Breteuil, as Henry remarked:

"Good, I seem to have the same size head as my father. This was always too big for Rufus."

On 5th August ,1100, Henry was crowned King Henry I of England in Westminster Abbey by Maurice, Bishop of London, as Anselm, Archbishop of Canterbury, was in exile in France. Among his first acts as King of England, Henry appointed William Giffard as Bishop of Winchester and wrote to Anselm apologising for being crowned in his absence but inviting him to return as Archbishop of Canterbury. Ranulf Flambard was escorted to the Tower. Eardwulf, the gaoler of the Tower could not have been happier.

Chapter Forty-four
To the victor go the spoils

Olaf and his colleagues travelled up to London with Henry, being met along the way by many notable barons keen to affirm their allegiance to the new king-to-be. Olaf was housed at Westminster and was granted his request of the very chamber he had occupied whilst wounded. Henry had barely spoken to him since he had seized the treasury as most of his dealings were now with the Church. Although Olaf was invited to attend the Coronation, Ari and the twins were obliged to stand outside with the common people. Olaf remembered the chaos he had helped to cause at William the Conqueror's coronation all those years ago on Christmas Day, 1066. Robert Fitzhamon had informed him that the King was very busy securing his position and filling many empty clerical posts but had assured him that his service would not go unrewarded. Olaf was somewhat concerned, knowing the utter ruthlessness of Henry's character that it might be expedient for the witnesses of Rufus' demise to 'disappear'. A large body of mounted soldiers now stood guard outside the Abbey, so the chances of any disruption were minimal, and the coronation service went off without incident.

Several weeks later an official letter arrived from the King informing Olaf that he was to take charge of the two hundred horsemen who were to be Henry's personal bodyguard and were to accompany him around the country at all times. Olaf was delighted to learn that the lands around Wold Dalby were to be granted to him as promised by Harold Godwin. Robert of Mortain had died in 1095 and, as usual under Rufus, the revenues had reverted to the Crown. This was now Henry's gift to bestow. Olaf was to be knighted with a coat of arms and given the Saxon title of 'Olaf of Dalby'. Ari and the twins were rewarded with gold and returned to the ship in Southampton to take the news back to Freya in Oslo.

Olaf was summoned to the College of Heraldry to have his Coat of Arms designed. Because of his violent history, red was chosen as the colour of fire and blood. In heraldry yellow is the colour of honour and loyalty therefore this was chosen by King Henry for Olaf. The armour top emblem was a dedicated Griffin which in heraldic terms is called 'a demi-griffin sergeant proper'.

(The motto was added many centuries later).

The Dalby Griffin

In order for Olaf to maintain his Manor, all revenues and levies from the fiefs, which had been collected by the Crown over the previous five years, were to be paid to Olaf from the Treasury, enabling him to rebuild the Manor House which had been neglected by the absent landlord, Robert of Mortain. Olaf was now a knight and landed gentry.

Henry had got his reign off to a good start, considering there was great antagonism from the Church, many Barons who still supported Robert, and mistrust from the Anglo-Saxon people. He issued a Coronation Charter or a Charter of Liberties which sought to address the abuses that William Rufus had perpetrated upon his people, high or lowly born and particularly the Church. Copies of this were sent out to all the shires in both English and French. One declaration:

'I impose a strict peace on the land and command it be maintained' resulted in Henry being known as 'The Lion of Justice'.

The Coronation Charter was later considered to be the precedent for Magna Carter in 1215. Henry made a popular marriage in November 1100 when he married Matilda, the Saxon niece of Edgar the Ætheling, and daughter of Malcolm III of Scotland and Margaret of Wessex. The Anglo-Saxons were pleased to have a queen descended from Alfred the Great and it cemented a peace between England and Scotland.

For over a year Olaf waited for news from Oslo until finally word arrived that Freya, Anja, Krystyna, her new husband Eric and a certain Irish Wolfhound had landed and were resting in Winchester before travelling up to London to try and find Olaf. By chance, Olaf was in London helping King Henry prepare to take out an extremely troublesome Norman noble called Robert de Bellême. Robert had played a leading part, wholly unscrupulously, in almost every trouble that had arisen in the previous reign. Furthermore, he had recently acquired the estates of the House of Montgomery and was therefore the most powerful and dangerous of the King's enemies in England. Henry refused Olaf's request to head down to Winchester but sent a messenger with a command for Olaf's family to be housed at Bitterne Manor and afforded every comfort and that Brother Martin was to bring them to London only when the troubles with Bellême had subsided. The King had summoned Bellême to answer charges that his spies had been judiciously collecting against him. Realising such a trial would be a forgone conclusion, Bellême put all his castles and strongholds in a state of defence. Olaf had prepared a powerful army which included flat packed trebuchets that could be easily transported and assembled. The King took to the field in person as a large force of some five thousand men headed West. One by one, the castles being besieged by the King of England, submitted – first Arundel then Tickhill followed by Bridgenorth and finally to the castle where Robert of Bellême felt he might be safest, Shrewsbury. It took only two launches of the great rocks from the six trebuchets to induce the garrison to open the gates and Olaf rode forward with his two hundred horsemen, all wearing the King's Royal crest except Olaf, who proudly wore his own for the first time.

Bellême was speechless with rage and humiliation as Olaf accepted his sword on behalf of the King. Olaf wasn't sure if Henry was going to fling him from the castle wall, but he escaped with only a banishment from the Kingdom. Bellême returned to Normandy where he wreaked havoc on the Duchy, perpetrating unspeakable atrocities on the unhappy and unoffending people irrespective if they were peasant, women, or clergy. Normandy was in a state of chaotic anarchy.

Henry returned in triumph and there was much rejoicing and relief of the news that Bellême had been banished from the land. A carriage was sent down to Bitterne Manor with an extra cart for the luggage and the wolfhound. Olaf met them at London Bridge and escorted them to Westminster. That evening the King held a great feast in Westminster Hall in their honour. Olaf was at last reunited with Freya who explained that things in Norway had taken a turn for the worse. Thorkel had finally passed away whilst Magnus Berrføtt was fighting wars with the Swedes. For a short time, the army returned home and they were able to see Olafsson again. But it was short-lived as Magnus now decided he wished to take Dublin under Norwegian rule and had set off with a huge fleet in the direction of Ireland.

Olaf's family stayed in London for a few days. Brother Martin offered to go with them up to Leicestershire, he had become quite attached to the family. Olaf had a better idea:

"Brother Martin, how would you like a Parish Church of your own? Come with us and we can build you one. King Henry can appoint you and now he has got Archbishop Anselm under control, he can bless your appointment as priest."

Brother Martin was thrilled:

"May I dedicate it to John the Baptist?"

"You may dedicate it to any Saint you wish except perhaps St Olaf.

He was the father of Harald Hardråda, and I shouldn't like to be reminded of him every time I went to church!"

They all left Westminster early in the morning and with a few stops they completed the journey in twelve hours over two days. As they approached the village, the Manor came into view. Carpenters, stone masons, thatchers, and plasterers were all busy toiling in the warm sunshine and the village looked an absolute picture.

Freya sighed:

"Oh Olaf, this is just beautiful. No wonder they call it Eng-land – land of meadows. Everything is so green and lush."

Olaf smiled:

"I hope we can be at peace here. There is an inn where we will stay for a short time until the manor is ready but, as you can see, they have almost completed it. Then they can start on the church!"

Brother Martin clapped his hands with glee and even Séamus seemed to be smiling – this was much more like his home back in Ireland.

Meanwhile Magnus III's fleet was approaching the Irish Sea and his army were preparing for their invasion of Ireland. There was a power struggle going on there and Magnus had hoped to extend his sphere of influence by exploiting the fierce rivalry between Muirchertach and Domnal who both claimed to be the High King of Ireland. Magnus had forged an alliance with the highly untrustworthy Muirchertach and together they had made some gains. Magnus wintered just outside Dublin 1102/1103. The Norwegian army campaigned throughout the Spring and Summer but without any real success. Olafsson was constantly trying to keep up the moral of his men who all wanted to go home. There was nothing to be gained here. Finally, Magnus agreed and Muirchertach was supposed to bring cattle and provisions on 23rd August for their journey home. The Norwegians moved inland to collect the cattle but were ambushed by a large force of the men of Ulaid who fell upon the totally surprised

Norwegian army who were not drawn up in battle order. Olafsson desperately tried to steady the disorderly mêlée but, when the contingent commanded by an Uplands nobleman, Torgrim Skinluve, broke and fled to the ships, the battle was lost. King Magnus was badly wounded in the legs by a spear and then rushed by an Irish axe man who all but removed his head. Olafsson made a fighting retreat to the boats and the Irish, on seeing the Norwegian King dead, broke off the attack. Olafsson was furious. If Torgrim had held, the battle might have gone the other way as there were more Irish dead than Norse.

The fleet sailed away without provisions and was forced to seek supplies in England. Arriving at Chester the locals were highly suspicious, fearing it another Norwegian invasion and fired arrows at the ships from the castle. Olafsson ordered the fleet to sail down to Anglesey where Magnus himself had killed the Norman Earl, Hugh of Shrewsbury, in 1098 and the Normans had pulled out of Anglesey leaving Gruffud to return from Ireland to reclaim his lands. The Norsemen were greeted as friends by the Welsh who were obliging in providing provisions for the journey home. Part of Gruffud's forces contained the formidable longbowmen. One such, an elderly warrior, approached Olafsson and, with a pronounced Welsh accent called out:

"Hey boyo, yes, you there. You remind me of someone long ago. Who are you?"

Olafsson replied:

"I am Olafsson, son of Olaf Slagbjørn and I was Captain of the King's guard until the King got himself killed."

"Olafsson, is it? Well now, there's a fine thing. I was at Hastings with your father. I saved his life so many times I lost count. I'm Rhys, see, Rhys of Prestatyn."

Chapter Forty-five
The Last Battle

Back in London Henry was busy plotting how to rid himself of an accumulation of enemies in Normandy. Ranulf Flambard had, incredibly, escaped from the Tower and was now set up as Duke Robert's principle advisor. William de Warenne, Earl of Surrey had been accused of various crimes and banished from England, likewise Robert de Bellême after Henry had destroyed his powerbase in England. In addition, there was the 'incorrigibly turbulent' William of Mortain, the second Earl of Cornwall, whom Henry had banished, and who had also joined forces with Duke Robert. It was a formidable coalition.

In Wales, Olafsson had decided that his contract with Magnus III had been completed on the death of the King. He also felt strongly that he would not serve with Torgrim Skinluve whom he considered a coward and a traitor. He was astonished to have met Rhys about whom his father had spoken so often. Olafsson resigned from the

Norwegian army and decided to head for London in search of Olaf. Rhys had a better idea. Why didn't he and his fifty longbowmen head for London to offer their services to Henry I as he had heard there was a fight brewing with his brother Robert. Of the fifty archers, five still remained who had fought at Hastings with Olaf: Arwyn, Osian, Griffith, Gethin and Rodri. They were now in their early sixties but hardened warriors and still deadly with the longbow. Henry could use such men who scoffed at the idea of the long march to London.

Olaf and his family remained throughout the long Summer of 1103 at the Manor, which the locals now called Dalby Hall. It was a splendid building restored with great skill which Freya and Anja had furnished tastefully. Olaf was now sixty-three, his blond hair grey, and who looked forward to a peaceful retirement with his family. Krystyna and Eric lived in the annex with Séamus who continued to hog the fire, as he had in Oslo. Christmas arrived at the Manor which proved warm and homely as Olaf and Freya introduced the locals to some traditional Viking Yuletide customs. Father Martin celebrated his first Christmas Midnight Mass in his nearly completed stone church dedicated to St. John the Baptist. A Nativity crib scene was created, and a local farmer brought a real donkey into the church for authenticity. Everyone sang 'Orientis Partibus' (Song of the Donkey) telling of how the donkey brought Mary to Bethlehem. At this point the West door was opened and a cold snowy breeze revealed two weather-beaten travellers. Closing the door and turning to face the altar the blond hair and demeanour of the tall one was immediately recognised in the candlelight by Freya and Anja and then by Olaf. It was Olaf, son of Olaf. A great cry went up and there was much hugging and some tears from the family. The second traveller removed his hood and was only then recognised by Olaf:

"Happy Christmas boyo! You've aged since I last saw you!"

"Rhys! You've brought my son back to me! How are you?"

There was a cough from Father Martin:

"Ahem! If we may continue? The mass is ended go in peace. And a Merry Christmas to you all."

There was a second of silence as they crossed themselves and then much jabbering and laughter. Freya said it was the best Christmas present she could have wished for and Anja nodded hugging her husband but not speaking as she was prevented by emotional tears of happiness. They all went back to the Manor for a traditional meal of spiced ham, ale and mead in which Father Martin was invited to bless the supper.

The next few years were marked by Henry's forays into Normandy. Olaf had to return to duty as the army was being prepared on a professional level for one major decisive battle such as happened at Hastings. Henry had been working on the tactic of a predominantly dismounted defensive force in three parts with a cavalry strike force to the rear with infantry reserves to follow up any successful flanking manoeuvre. All the while he was working on diplomacy to weaken Robert's force. Normandy was in a state of chaos and anarchy, well out of Robert's control. In 1104, Henry took a force into Normandy which did not include Olaf or Olafsson nor the Welsh archers as they were needed to continue the training of the main force. He took possession of the county of Évreux before returning home. In 1105 he was at it again, this time taking Olaf and son plus the Welsh archers. He burnt Bayeux and received the surrender of Caen. He left Olaf to interact with Elias of Maine. Henry had agreed to drop his claim on the region and in response, Elias had agreed to support Henry with troops. He had been very effective during the siege of Bayeux. It was also agreed that Elias' contingent should make up the reserve force of cavalry and infantry which would deal the hammer blow once Robert's frontal charge had been stopped. Meanwhile, Henry had patched up relations with William de Warenne and had restored his lands to him. It also seemed that he had courted the support of Ranulf Flambard who may well have been acting as a double agent. Olaf had expanded the cavalry from two hundred to two thousand and these were to make up most of the reserves for the counter-measures.

Henry returned to Normandy in the Spring of 1106 only this time he brought his entire force of seven and a half thousand men. He laid siege to the castle at Tinchbrai held by William, Count of Mortain. In August, Robert arrived with a force to break the siege. He had with him Robert of Bellême and, of all people, Edgar Ætheling with whom he had fought in the First Crusade. Including the garrison, he could muster an army of a size to match Henry. Henry's army was divided into three sections. The main two were commanded by William de Warenne and the reserves, including the cavalry were commanded by Olaf and Elias of Maine. After some unsuccessful negotiations, Robert decided that a pitch battle was the only solution as Henry was not in a mood to bargain but desired a once and for all battle for which he had been preparing for years. Furthermore, the date was 28th September 1106, forty years to the day when William the Conqueror set foot on English soil. The Anglo-Saxons in the army were baying for revenge for Hastings.

Henry ordered all his knights to dismount and join the infantry on foot in two lines and prepare to receive a cavalry charge as they had been training to do for the last two years. Olaf with his cavalry was in a dip with Elias and his infantry from Maine. William de Mortain led the charge which smashed into Henry's front line who then gave some ground before being reinforced by the second line. At this point Olaf led his 2,000 horsemen out of the dip and crashed into the flank of de

Mortain's infantry. The Welsh archers prevented Robert of Bellême from bringing up the seven hundred reserve cavalry. As Olaf's riders ploughed through the startled Ducal army, Elias and his infantry closed the gap so that de Warenne could order a general advance. It was a rout. After just an hour, most of Robert's army had been killed or captured, with the exception of Robert of Bellême and his horsemen who retreated promptly and in good order without striking a single blow. Olaf and his son followed up hard on the retreat, capturing Robert, Duke of Normandy, William de Mortain and, most surprisingly, Edgar the Ætheling. Olaf was still carrying his sword.

The Battle of Tinchbrai 28th September 1106

Medieval depiction 14th century

Chapter Forty-six
Aftermath

Olaf returned to Henry's lines bringing with him the Duke of Normandy, William de Mortain, Edgar Ætheling (who was released) and a handful of lesser nobles. Henry retained the nobility, including his brother, as captives to be ransomed, except for Robert, who he held a prisoner in England for the rest of his long life. The remainder of the captured soldiers had but to swear fealty to Henry and they would all be released. All of them did so. Robert's future was to be a grim one. He was first imprisoned in Castrum ad Divisas (Devizes Castle) for twenty years and then removed to Cardiff Castle where he escaped. Henry ordered his eyes be burnt out when he was recaptured. Robert died in captivity at the age of eighty-three. He had one child with Sybil de Conversano, William Clito, who was three at the time of Tinchbrai. He remained a thorn in the side of Henry's claim on Normandy but died aged just twenty-five from a gangrenous wound in his arm in 1128.

Henry was delighted with Olaf and his son and extended their lands South across Leicestershire. Many settlements sprang up around the crossroads of Melton Mowbray which became a flourishing market town. Olaf returned to Wold Dalby which, with the relatively new villages of Great Dalby and Little Dalby, was now called Old Dalby. Olafsson built a hall for himself and Anja and Krystyna and Eric at Little Dalby. This became known as Dalby Hall and a large stately home, built on that site in 1830 still bears that name.

Dalby Hall 1830

Olaf had fought his last battle. He and Freya finally settled down to a peaceful retirement. Olafsson and King Henry became close friends, being the same age, and he continued in the service of the King, spending half of the year at court. Henry still had many battles to fight and rebellions to put down and lived on for another thirty years before succumbing to a 'surfeit of lampreys' on 1st December 1135, leaving no male heir and a future of anarchy for England.

On a warm afternoon in July 1123, Olaf, now in his eightieth year, was resting outside in his garden when Olafsson and Anja came to visit. Freya greeted them and showed them where Olaf had fallen asleep in the afternoon sunshine. At his feet was an Irish Wolfhound. Séamus had long since passed so Olaf had sent to Ireland for a puppy to replace him. He was now almost fully grown and was called Séamusson. He was sitting with his head resting on Olaf's lap. Freya gently placed her hand on Olaf's shoulder to wake him.

"Olaf, we have visitors."

Olaf's arm fell from the armrest. The wolfhound gave a quiet whine. The great man was gone, the saga over.

Olaf Slagbjørn, Earl of Dalby 1043 – 1123.

THE END